Façade

Façade

Nyrae Dawn

FOREVER

NEW YORK   BOSTON

Forever
Hachette Book Group
237 Park Avenue, New York, NY 10017
www.hachettebookgroup.com
www.twitter.com/foreverromance

Printed in the United States of America

RRD-C

Originally published as an ebook
First Trade Paperback Edition: September 2013
10 9 8 7 6 5 4 3 2 1

Forever is an imprint of Grand Central Publishing. The Forever name and logo are trademarks of Hachette Book Group, Inc.

The Hachette Speakers Bureau provides a wide range of authors for speaking events. To find out more, go to www.hachettespeakersbureau.com or call (866) 376-6591.

Library of Congress Control Number: 2013940346

ISBN 978-1-4555-7631-9

To Steph Campbell.
For always listening.
For never judging.
May our friendship be infinite.

Acknowledgments

I have so many people to thank for this that I'm not sure where to begin. First, to my husband. Your support is invaluable. I couldn't do this without your love, faith, and sacrifices. To my two beautiful little girls for asking about my writing and showing me how proud you are of me. I wish I had been as cool as you are at your age! My mom because you've always had faith in me. Thanks for giving me wings and teaching me not to be afraid to fly. Wendy Higgins, I couldn't do what I do without you. You're my confidante, my best friend, and the most wonderful critique partner a girl could have. To my other beta readers, Jolene Perry for all your help and Morgan Shamy for brainstorming with me. Big thanks to Allie Brennan for dealing with my obsessiveness over covers. HUGE thanks to the readers of *Charade*, who were so supportive and wonderful. Jane Dystel and all the folks at Dystel and Goderich, I am honored to have you in my corner. You are the definition of hard work and dedication. And to my editor, Latoya Smith. There are not enough words to thank you. Thanks for seeing something in my work, for believing in my writing, and for helping make my dreams come true. Last but not least, to everyone at Grand Central Publishing. I still can't believe I am able to say I write for Grand Central. Thank you for taking a chance on me. I hope to do you proud. There are so many other people who made this possible. Know that I didn't forget you. I thank you all.

Façade

Chapter One

~Adrian~

I didn't sleep for shit last night. Not that I ever really sleep that well, but last night was particularly bad. About 1:00 a.m., I was sick to death of all the drunk, high, loud-ass people in my house. Jesus, I wanted them gone. Wanted quiet, normal, but instead I'd smoked another bowl, lied and said I was going to bed before locking myself in my room.

The party went on without me because that's what people do. It's not that they really need me to have fun. I just have the house, shitty as it is, and everyone thinks I'm always down to have a good time. Scratch that. I *am* always down to have a good time. One look at me shows I'm stoned half the time. Weed? It clouds out the past. Parties drown out the stuff in my head I don't want to hear. But last night of all nights? I deserved to hear that shit, since I'm the one who caused it. So that's what I did. All night. Got blazed out of my head but kept myself awake so I could think about today.

Around six this morning, I jumped in my car like I have every January 12 for the past four years and drove my ass here. Rockville, Virginia. Home sweet fucking home, except I hate this place with a burning passion. When you spend your childhood getting beat by your dad, all you want to do is escape where you came from. I wouldn't have come if I didn't have to, but after everything, I figure it's the least I can do.

Not that my sister, Angel, will ever know I came.

After all this time, I wonder if she'd want me here. If I were her, I wouldn't.

Shaking my thermos, I realize I don't have any more coffee. I toss it onto the passenger side floor and lean back in the seat. Four hours is a long-ass time to sit in my car, but I don't want to risk getting out and her seeing me. Probably a good thing I ran out of coffee; otherwise I'd have to piss again.

Looking across the street, I see all the headstones. Most of them are laid flat, so I can't see them from a distance, but I still know exactly which one belongs to Ashton. It's under the big tree. He would have liked that. I bet he would have wanted me to lift him up and put him in that tree if he'd ever had the chance to see it. He thought it was cool to ride on my shoulders. I'd carry him all around the house and he'd laugh like it was fucking Disneyland or something.

Pain grabs hold of me, threatens to pull me under, and for the millionth time I wonder why I don't let it. It would be so much easier than walking around in the masks I do now.

"Fuck." I drop my head back. Run a hand through my dark hair. Feel my pocket for the pipe there and wish like hell I could light up. Seems kind of wrong to smoke weed at a cemetery, especially under the circumstances.

I hate the drugs anyway. You wouldn't know it, though. No one does. *Adrian's always down to smoke. Adrian's always good for it.* That's what everyone thinks, but really I just want to be swept away. To ride a tide or the wind or whatever the fuck will take me far from here. Weed is the only thing I can find. Sometimes it works; most of the time it doesn't.

I'm itching to shove the key into the ignition, to push down on the gas pedal and get the hell out of here. Not that I ever went real far. I only live four hours away in Brenton because I couldn't make myself leave the state. But I can't live in Rockville anymore. I don't want to see this. Don't want to be here. I wish I could wake up and find out this has all been some fucked-up nightmare. Even if it meant going back in time before Ash and having to deal with shit from my parents.

Leaning forward, I push the useless thermos out of the way and reach for *The Count of Monte Cristo*, which is shoved under the seat. The cover's all old and ripped. The spine's cracked from how many times I've read it. It'll probably fall apart any day now.

The thing is, I've always respected Edmond. He went through hell and back but fought despite it. He didn't fold. He pushed through and worked his ass off to become so much more than he was. He was strong. Not me. I just can't seem to make myself overcome the past.

There's nothing to do but deal with it. And maybe lose myself behind a cloud of smoke or a girl.

I need to turn off my thoughts.

Even though I can't stand hats, I grab the one beside me, push it low on my head, open my book, and read. Maybe Edmond can help me clear my head.

Hours later, when I see my sister, Angel, walk over to Ash's grave, I don't get out of the car. When some guy walks up and grabs her hand, I don't know who he is and yet, I don't bother finding out. They hug, and I don't walk over and do the same thing to her. It's not our thing to stand around having some group mourning session over the two-year-old boy who died too soon.

Nope. This is real life. Not like all the stupid fucking books I read or the movies people watch or the reality shows that couldn't be further away from reality.

Without moving an inch, I watch her. Watch as she sets flowers on Ashton's grave. As the guy pulls her into a hug. As they kneel on the ground, probably talking to him in a way I'll never have the balls to do.

The guy says something to her and then gets up and walks away. I duck lower in my seat, but no one is paying attention to me. He heads back to a little car and waits.

Angel's hands go to her face and I know she's crying in them. Know she's mourning the loss of Ash, the boy she loved so much. The boy she took care of better than any mom could. I know she sent the guy away because she's like me and needs to handle shit on her own. Only unlike me, she'll never run.

She cries out there for probably thirty minutes. The whole time my chest is tight. Aching. It's hard to breathe and I want to turn away, but I don't. I deserve to feel this way and deserve to see this.

A fist squeezes tighter and tighter around my heart. My face is wet, but I don't bother to wipe away the tears, either. Real men don't fucking cry. That's what Dad always said before he hit me in a series of body shots, until I couldn't stop myself from doing just what he said I shouldn't do.

Then he'd beat me harder for being weak.

Angel's shoulders are shaking. I can tell from this far away.

I'm not an idiot. Never have been. I know it wouldn't make me weak to walk over there and hug her. To hold her and tell her it'll be okay, but I still won't do it. What right do I have to try and console her when I'm the one who destroyed everything?

When I'm the one who let Ash die?

So I sit here and watch her, just so I'll never forget the pain I caused.

Chapter Two

~Delaney~

I'm yanked out of a deep sleep by the sound of my cell. My room is still pitch-black, which means it's the middle of the night. My heart immediately starts setting off rounds to the speed of a machine gun.

"Hello?" my voice squeaks out.

"Is this Delaney Cross?"

The official-sounding female does nothing to slow the rapid-fire beating in my chest. If anything, it makes it worse. "Yes. This is she."

"I'm Doctor Marsh over at Three Valley's Hospital. Your mother was brought in a little while ago. She's okay, but—"

"What happened?" Now I pray for my heart to pick up again. It's silent, almost as if it's gone, and I miss the pounding in my ears. Miss it because as ridiculous as it sounds, it takes the loneliness away.

"We'd really like you to come down. It's not—"

"It's not something I haven't dealt with before," I cut

her off again. I don't need her to try and make this easier on me. The fact is nothing would make me deal with it better. Saying it on the phone won't make it any less real than in person.

"We're assuming it was a suicide attempt. She took pills. We don't know if she changed her mind or if she wasn't lucid enough to make decisions, but sometime after, she must have tried to leave her apartment. A neighbor found her collapsed in her doorway and called nine-one-one."

The tears that I didn't realize had formed in my eyes are brimming over and starting their slow descent down my face. This is her third suicide attempt in the last four years.

"I'm sorry," the doctor tells me.

"Me too," I whisper. I'm sorry about all of it.

I push out of bed and race to my closet. "We'll be there soon," I tell the doctor before dropping my cell to the dresser. Yanking a sweatshirt over my head, I'm already shoving my feet into my tennis shoes. My heart seems to have found its beat now and as I finish shoving my other foot into my shoe, I try and concentrate on it. It's a crazy thing to do, but it keeps me from cracking apart.

"Maddox!" I yell as I run into our small hallway. "Get up!" My fists come down on my brother's door hard. "Come on! We have to go." I try for the doorknob, but like I knew he would, he'd locked his room. Before I can knock again, he's jerking the door open, his eyes wide and frantic with worry.

"What the fuck happened? Are you okay?"

"It's Mom. She..."

Anger washes over the worry on Maddox's face. His jaw tenses. Veins pulse in his hand; he's gripping the doorknob so tightly I think it could break. Quite the pair, aren't we? While I worry, he gets pissed.

"What did she do?" It's almost as though he blanks out in times like this. Goes numb. All I have to do is bring up either of our parents and I can see the emotion drain from him and I hate it. He and Dad used to be so close... and then something switched and I was the one who got his attention, yet Mom was all about Maddox. Now he can't stand to talk about either of them.

"Pills. We need to go, Maddy."

"Don't call me that. I hate it when you call me that."

I reach for my older brother's hand, but he jerks it away. "Yeah, because that's what's important right now. We need to go see her."

He's shaking his head and I know what he's going to say before he speaks. That he doesn't want to go. That he doesn't care if she needs us. Before he can, I say the one thing that I know he can't say no to. "I can't do this without you. I need you."

"Fuck," he mumbles under his breath. "Gimme two minutes." The door slams, guilt tingeing the edges of my pain. I shouldn't manipulate him like that, but he's my brother. Her son. Mom and I both need him. She can't help that she fell apart after what Dad did.

Realizing I forgot my phone, I grab it and the car keys, and I'm pacing the living room when Maddox comes out, his dark hair all disheveled. He doesn't look me in the eyes. He's pissed and I know he knows what I did.

We head out to the car and I drive us to the hospital because I don't trust him to do it when he's mad. He likes to go too fast, and the last thing we need is to get into an accident on the way.

I'm shivering by the time we walk through the hospital doors and only part of it is from the cold. Maddox isn't wearing a jacket, even though it's a frigid, cold January in Virginia.

"We're here to see Jennifer Cross," I tell the desk clerk. Maddox doesn't step up beside me. He has his arms crossed about five feet away from me.

"Are you family?" the clerk asks.

"Yes. We're her children."

She puts bands on each of our wrists and directs us where to go, as if we don't know where the ER is. We could find anywhere in this place.

I'm not surprised when my eyes pool over again. No matter how many times this happens or how many times she slips back into her depression, it doesn't get easier.

Right before we leave the sterile white hallway and head for the emergency room, Maddox grabs my wrist.

"Don't cry for her, Laney. Don't cry for either of them."

Maddox is so much older than his twenty-one years. He's always been the strong one and both of us know it. It's not that simple for me. My mom just tried to take her own life. My dad is in prison and my brother—my best friend—hates the world.

"Why did this happen to us?" I ask. He grabs me and pulls me into his arms, letting me cry into his chest.

I can feel his awkwardness as he holds me. He's not real big on affection and it makes me feel like crap that he has to console me again. But that's what he does. He hates it, but he tries to make everything better. Mom couldn't take care of stuff, so Maddox did. He's still doing it.

"I don't know" is all he says. Honestly, I'm a little surprised I got that much out of him.

"We need to go see her." I wipe my eyes with my sweatshirt.

Maddox nods at me, but before we can go in, a nurse stops us. As soon as I tell her who we are, she gets that small smile on her face that says she feels bad for us, but she's trying not to let it show.

"Let me get the doctor first, okay? She wants to speak to you." She disappears behind the sliding doors, the sound echoing through the halls. The emergency room is quiet tonight and I almost wish for more people around to distract us.

Right away, the door slides open again. A woman with graying hair, wearing the same smile as the nurse, comes out. "You're Ms. Cross's children?"

"Yes." Of course it's only me who answers.

She leads us over to a small room with a couch. Goose bumps blanket my skin the second we walk in. It reminds me of the place they take family members to let them know when someone has passed away.

She's okay...she's okay. They would have told me if she wasn't.

"As I told you on the phone, your mom overdosed on pills. Some of them seem to be medications that have been prescribed to her, but we're not sure if that's all she took."

Oh God. Has she been buying pills illegally? How did this happen? How did we go from a normal family—with a mom and dad who used to laugh together, a mom who used to love cooking dinner for her family, a brother who could have gotten a football scholarship, and me, who was just happy to have the people I loved close—to this? "Okay..."

"She's sleeping right now, but she's been in and out of it. You need to know that she's still a threat to herself. She..." The doctor pauses for a second before sighing. "She's continued to say she wants to die, and she attacked one of the nurses. I just want you to be prepared when you go in. We had to strap her down for everyone's safety."

A cry climbs up my throat and I clamp my mouth closed, hoping it won't be able to escape. Why aren't we good enough to make her want to stay? I don't under-stand her not wanting to be with me. With Maddox.

My brother's hand comes down on my shoulder and he gives it a comforting squeeze. No matter how angry he is, he's always here for me. I hate how all of this has scarred his soul.

"Where do we go from here?" Maddox asks her, but I want to be the one who's angry now. I want to yell that we've been through enough. That I'm eighteen fuck-ing years old and Maddox only twenty-one. We're not supposed to be dealing with this. We're supposed to be in college and going home for long weekends instead of being alone.

"We did a psych consult and we think it's best that she be admitted to our inpatient ward. It's a thirty-day stay. They'll be able to help her better there. I would hate for her to be in a situation where she's able to hurt herself further or, God forbid, someone else."

It feels like a fist squeezing my chest so tight it shatters my ribs, shatters everything inside me, but I just want to be whole. Why can't we all be whole again?

I look at Maddox and he's emotionally gone again. His hand is still on me, but the rest of him looks as though he's checked out, leaving me alone.

"Okay...I agree. Can we see her now?" Is it bad that part of me doesn't want to? That I'm scared to death to walk in there and see her? To risk that her anger will come out at me like it always does?

"Of course. Follow me."

I know before he stops me that Maddox isn't going. His eyes that look so much like mine soften as though he's trying to tell me he's sorry—words he'll never say out loud.

"It's okay," I tell him, but really it's not. I need him and he knows it. Mom needs him. We both know she'd rather it be Maddox with her than me.

My legs tremble slightly as I walk into the room. She looks so small in the bed. Her blond hair, so different from my dark brown, is stringy and matted. I just saw her two days ago. Two days, and she didn't look like this.

"Hey, Mom," I say. The doctor is gone, leaving me

alone in the room with her. Gray cloth shackles keep her hands tied to the metal on her bed, almost covering the scars on her wrists from the first time. The time I held her while she bled.

Of course, she doesn't answer.

I stand next to her bed and touch her hair, but then pull back, afraid to wake her. Instead, I stand there wishing I would wake up and we'd be the family we were four years ago before everything changed. Before my dad got drunk and, while his girlfriend went down on him, drove into a yard and killed a little boy. Before we found out about his gambling and the other women. I guess we were never the typical family I thought we were. That isn't true either. I knew that even then, when Mom would get pissed at me for spending time with Dad, and Maddox stopped playing ball with him.

Tears roll down my cheeks in synchronized wave after wave, like a crowd at a football game. Maybe one of Maddox's old games.

I think of the woman, Angel, who I visited a few weeks ago.

The pain in her eyes when I told her who I was. But also the forgiveness she showed even though my father took away her little boy.

Maddox hates the idea bogging down my brain, but I don't know what else to do. Maybe the only way to end our family's suffering is to continue to make amends, the same way I did with Angel.

Chapter Three

~Adrian~

Party at my house. Are you in this time or does Cheyenne have that collar too tight around your neck?" I ask my best friend, Colt, when I sit on the chair in his studio apartment. He hooked up with his girl Cheyenne not too long back. She's good people. Loves his ass something fierce. She didn't leave his side while he watched his mom die or when we almost lost Colt the same night.

A little flash of Colt on the ground jumps into my head, so I pull a pipe out of my pocket and fill my lungs with smoke, hoping the high will cloud it away. Too close to home, except unlike with Colt, when it was Ashton there was blood. So much fucking blood.

Colt falls onto the bed, on the other side of his place. "Don't talk shit about her, fucker, or I'll kick your ass."

I smile at him because I expected him to say something like that. The cool thing about them is he loves her just as much as she loves him. She's changed him, and I don't think he even realizes how much. I might give him hell, but I'm happy. One of us deserves that bullshit storybook ending.

"Don't look at me like that. I hate it when you give me that dissecting look like you're trying to pull out all my fucking secrets."

I tap my head and play that stupid psychic game that he likes to give me hell about.

I don't see the future; I just notice shit. When you're seven years old and scared of your own fucking shadow, too scared to get close to anyone like I used to be, you learn to pay attention. To study people's lives because it's the only way to feel like you're living and to think about how differently you'd be doing it if you had the balls to man up. Or, hell, if you hadn't been given such a shitty hand to begin with.

"You know I'm just playin' about Cheyenne. And I'd be more afraid of her than you," I tease, putting the pipe to my mouth before taking another pull. I hold it out to Colt, knowing he'll say no. He found his solace in Cheyenne, and I have as close to it as I'll ever get right here.

Colt shakes his head. "I have shit to do. I'll talk to Chey about tonight. You act like having a party is something new. It's just like every other night, right?"

Yeah, except for tonight I'm trying to forget watching my sister cry over Ash's grave. Trying to forget I didn't have the balls to go to her. That I watched him die.

"Just another night." Inhale. Exhale. Then I stand, hardly feeling the tickle of my high, and follow him out the door. When we hit the bottom of the stairs, which lead to the parking lot, his girl shows up all dark skin and dark hair. She's half Native American and has an exotic look about her.

"Hey, baby." I wink at her, teasing both her and Colt. Cheyenne gives me a smile before Colt wraps his arms around her and kisses her.

"How are you?" She runs her hand through his hair, a dark look washing over her face that tells me she's probably thinking about that night a couple months ago when he got his head injury.

"Better now," he says before glancing at me. "So, Adrian's having a party tonight that he wants us to go to."

"*No!* Adrian having a party? I never would have guessed," Cheyenne replies.

She steps away from Colt, so I grab her and throw an arm around her shoulders. "Don't give me shit. I thought we were a team now?" When two people watch someone who means something to both of them almost die, it creates a bond. I know how fast someone can be taken from you, and I don't take that shit lightly. People come in and out of my house all the time. They party with me and use me for whatever the hell they want, but Colt's real. Cheyenne too. They're the only people besides Angel I let myself give a shit about.

"Quit hitting on my girl." Colt shakes his head, but he knows nothing's going on. He might have turned over a new leaf by trying not to be such a bastard all the time, but he would have tried to take my ass out a long time ago if he thought I really wanted Cheyenne.

I think he likes that we're cool.

"I wouldn't have to try—" My words are cut off

when I see a dark-haired girl get out of a car. She's tall, wearing some kind of yoga pants or some shit with a big-ass sweater. I don't even have to use my imagination to see how nice her legs are. She's got these long curls in her hair that I want to weave my hands through and gently tug.

And I talk about people using me? It's no secret I do the same fucking thing. I don't know who this girl is, never saw her before in my life, but I know I want her. Want to use her to forget.

"Oh my God," Cheyenne says, and I know she sees the girl too.

"Your boyfriend used to be just as bad," I say without taking my eyes off the girl.

"What the fuck?" Colt says, but then Cheyenne starts talking.

"No, he wasn't. I know he wasn't an angel, but he didn't go out looking for girls the way you do, Adrian. You're like a lion or something, stalking your prey."

Glancing at Cheyenne, I wink at her. She huffs and Colt starts laughing.

The brunette walks to the trunk of her car and starts to pull out a box. "Hold that thought. I'm about to go be a gentleman and help the lady out. We'll argue later tonight." I wink at her again. "If I'm not busy."

Colt shakes his head and Cheyenne looks like she wants to punch me, but I'm already walking away. Looking at this girl—hell, any girl—I see a distraction. When I'm concentrating on a girl's body, there's not much room for the stuff from my past creeping in, like the way Ash used to try and sneak up on me. I'd pretend to jump and he'd laugh and laugh before covering his face and sitting on the couch, thinking I couldn't see him.

She's still fumbling with the box when I get to her. There are a few more of them in her trunk. "That looks like a lot of work. It'd go much quicker if you let me help you and then we'll go somewhere and celebrate a job well done together."

She jumps, obviously startled, and hits her head on the trunk. "Ouch!"

Shit. That wasn't part of the plan.

"You okay? I'd offer to kiss it and make it better, but I'm guessing it's too soon for that."

She takes a step back, her cheeks this sweet pink that I'm not used to seeing so much on girls anymore. I hold my hands up and smile at her. "Don't be scared. Other than my shitty lines, I'm not so bad." Pointing to Colt and Cheyenne, I continue, "My friend's girl is over there. She'll tell you I'm nothing but a huggable teddy bear." I almost throw in a "Wanna cuddle?" but I think it's too much.

She smiles and I know I just got a point back after making her hit her head. Maybe two.

"Well, then, I think we're going to have a problem." Her voice is as sweet as her blush. Her eyes dart around a little and her fists clench, telling me she's trying to sound a lot braver than she feels.

"And what's that?" I ask her before taking a step back. Not a big one, but enough to give her a little more comfort.

"I've always had a thing against teddy bears."

Her answer comes out of nowhere, but I have to admit it's kind of fun. It's been a while since a girl made me give any kind of chase. "How do you have a thing against teddy bears?"

"Because they're frauds. I used to have one and thought it would protect me when I slept, but it didn't. I think that's their plan. They lure you in with a false sense of security."

I hold in my laugh. She's good. Really good. She managed to insult me and shoot down my game in one swoop. It makes me want her more. Want some kind of challenge. Maybe that's what I need to take my mind off all the things that I don't deserve to forget. "Now, that wasn't very nice. We don't even know each other's names, but here you are calling me a fraud. All I wanted was to be a gentleman and help you with these boxes and then welcome you to the neighborhood by inviting you to a party tonight."

I lean against her car, watching her. Wanting to see what's going on in her gray eyes. She's thinking about what I said, trying to come up with a reply.

"I can't," she finally says. She seems a little sad when she says it. She looks at the ground and bites her bottom lip. I really want to tell her I'll do that for her, but I don't. She's gorgeous as hell. Even more so up close than she was from farther away. Plump lips. A little mole under her nose and damned if she doesn't look both sexy and innocent at the same time.

"You won't."

She sighs. "I don't even know you. Even if I did, that's not what I'm here for."

Her response is a little strange. I'm about to ask her about it when a motorcycle rumbles up next to us. The girl's eyes shoot over to the bike, and fuck if I don't know this is some guy for her. I look over and he's pulling off his helmet and looking at me like he wants to take a shot at me because he knows exactly what's going through my head.

"Maddox, you're late." She looks at him and I look at her. She could have saved me a whole lot of trouble by telling me she was taken from the beginning.

"Who's this?" he says.

"My bad," I reply. "Have fun with those boxes."

I'm not in the mood to fight for some girl I don't know, so I turn and start to walk away. Not like I won't have more to choose from tonight anyway.

Sometimes you can't stop the past from seeping into the present. It's like an infection festering inside you. No matter what you do, you can't keep it from spreading. Taking hold of your blood so it can rip through you quickly.

And once it does, it's got you.

My house is packed with a shit ton of people just how I like it. Since I live in the old part of town, neighbors don't care. Don't complain about the music or the people because most of my neighbors are probably here. My landlord is an old lady who doesn't give a shit about what happens as long as it doesn't come down on her.

I'm on the couch and have a girl on my arm. I don't know how she got there, but I don't care either. Her hand's creeping toward my crotch and I'm begging for her to hurry up and make her destination.

Colt and Cheyenne didn't show up. I was pissed earlier, but the longer I'm here, the more none of it matters. Sometimes I think I want it to matter. I mean, it should. It's life and as much as mine's been filled with darkness, I've seen the beauty. When Angel looked at Ash or when Ash looked at me like he thought I was the king of the fucking world or something. I was amazing to him. Like a superhero who he trusted from his teeny toes to the tips of his curly black hair.

That was fucking beautiful, until it shattered.

Damn, why did that creep in tonight?

I look at the redhead who's now kissing my neck. She smells like beer, all tangy, mixed with some kind of perfume. "What's your name, baby?" I ask her. When a girl has her hand slipping down your pants, you should at least know her name. I guess if she doesn't care, I shouldn't. I'm not even sure if I really do.

"Ashley, but my friends call me Ash," she says against my skin, her breath freezing me. It's like it starts in that one spot and then slowly spreads over my body, cracking my skin and my chest and my heart as it goes. My past is infecting me again. The disease sucking the breath from my lungs. I can't fuck a girl with the same nickname as Ash—the little boy who thought I held the world in my hands.

"I can't do this," I tell her. She looks at me, confused,

the corners of her eyes squinting, but I can't stay or say anything else. Pushing to my feet, I maneuver my way through the maze of people in my house. I want them all to get the fuck out, but I won't make them. The silence is so much louder than the pulse of music and people beating through me right now.

The door to Colt's old room is open. There's a couple on the old futon I shoved in there when he left. I ignore them and go straight to my room and lock the door behind me. I fall onto my bed, thinking that maybe it would be easier if I was like Colt used to be. If I could just ball my fist and beat the hell out of something, even if it was a wall, until I felt better, until the physical pain eclipsed the emotional.

I see Ash's big brown eyes. Hear Angel's cries. Smell the fucking beer on the bastard who hit him as I shoved my fist into his face over and over before they arrested me at the same time as him. He ran over and killed someone I loved, yet they treated me just as they did him.

Which, yeah, means I heard Angel's cries after. I wasn't even there when she got home that day. She came back to find me and Ash gone. I had to tell her later that I let him get killed. She told me, fucking *told me* that day not to let him play out front, but I didn't listen and now he's gone.

I pick up *The Count*, wishing I could focus on the words. Wishing I were Edmond or anyone but me. I reach for my weed but then shove it back into the drawer. Why can't I lose myself in my own head like I used to? Get lost in my own world to block out the shit at home instead of sucking that crap into my lungs like I do now?

I wonder who that guy was with Angel at the cemetery. If he's good to her because I'm not there to protect her the same way I didn't protect Ash. The way Angel always protected me.

Suddenly the music is too loud. People stumbling into my door feels like they're doing it on my head instead. If I don't get out of this house right now, I'm going to lose it.

I shove the window open and grab my keys. It's freezing balls outside, but I don't care. It's good to feel something besides the memories. It only takes me a few seconds to walk around the side of my house and get to my car. No one will miss me here. They'll party till they pass out and tomorrow I'll talk shit about how fun it was. Right now, I need to be free.

I drive around for hours until the car's going on fumes and I know I'll run out of gas at any second. I've circled Brenton about ten times and for the millionth wonder why I still live in this state. Maybe it would be easier if I left. Instead I drive by the college that Cheyenne goes to and wonder what it would have been like to go there. College was something I always wanted, planned for, but after Ash, I figured if he didn't get to have what he wanted, I shouldn't either. I remember how Angel used to tell me how lucky I was because I was so fucking smart. It pissed her off when I left high school, but we needed money. It wasn't that long since she'd taken me from Dad and let me live with her. Plus, Ash was coming soon and I needed to help her prepare.

By this point, it's gotta be almost 3:00 a.m. My eyes are burning as much as my insides. When I see a little all-night diner, I pull in. Shove my copy of *The Count* and my little spiral notebook in my hoodie pockets before going inside.

I sit in the ugly aqua-green booth and wonder who in the hell would pick something like this.

Pulling the book out, I toss it onto the table. Grab my notebook and the pen I keep in my pocket, but I'm not sure I can make myself do anything right now. Can't write. Can't read. I need some fucking coffee and a time machine, so I put my elbows on the table and bury my head in my hands.

I try to focus on the big brown eyes in my mind and the huge smile that was definitely a Westfall trait.

"Can I help you?" someone says from beside the table.

I wish like hell I didn't have to pry my head out of my hands, but I do. I look over and see the same brown hair and beautiful gray eyes from earlier.

Chapter Four

~Delaney~

Just my luck that I have to run into the flirty guy from this afternoon. He is *super* sexy with his dark hair and intense eyes, though. He has brown stubble on his face, but I can't help but look at his eyes again. They look dimmer than they did earlier. No laughing in them. I almost feel like they could transfer me away. Like you can drift forever in those midnight pools because there's so much space between what he wants to show and what's really buried deep inside.

I wonder what my eyes look like to him.

I have no excuse to think that. I didn't come all the way to Brenton to hook up with some random guy.

I can practically see the façade slip into place as he gives me a half-smile.

"If it isn't the box girl. Your boyfriend's not going to show up again, is he?"

I shake my head. Almost don't tell him the truth, but I do. "He's not my boyfriend. He's my brother."

The smile grows slightly. "Why didn't you say that earlier?"

"Because I didn't feel like being hit on." I try not to bite my lip. It feels good to have a guy try and pick me up. Any girl who doesn't admit that is lying. Whether you want him or not, it's a boost to the ego. I didn't date much when I was younger. I was focused on school and was just *young*. Too busy riding my bike and trying to follow my big brother around. Then Dad got locked up and Mom lost it and boys never had a chance to be important.

"All girls like being hit on," he says.

"Are you going to order anything or not?"

"In a rush to get back to all those other customers?" He smiles.

Yeah, I didn't really think about that. I look around and remember there's only one other person in the place. My eyes wander over the table and I notice the book sitting there. *The Count of Monte Cristo*. I don't know why, but it surprises me. He doesn't look like the read-for-fun type. "Your book?" I ask, even though I know it's his.

It's almost like he forgot it was there. He puts a hand on it and slides it closer to him, as though he's trying to protect it. "I'll take a coffee." There's a slight edge to his voice that wasn't there before. I'm not sure if its anger, annoyance, or if the tiredness in his features is now spreading to his vocal cords.

"Anything to eat?" Then I realize I have the menu in my hand and haven't given it to him. I never claimed to be the best waitress. I'm lucky I got the job so quickly when I told Maddox I was going to Brenton whether he came or not. I didn't know what else to do.

"Mind if I look at that?" He nods his head toward the menu and I give it to him.

"I'll be right back with your coffee." Without a word, I turn and walk away. I fill a coffee cup for him, a little annoyed at myself that I'm all fluttery over this guy I don't know. I came here to make things right. Not to fall for someone who has *player* written all over him.

I set the coffee cup down in front of Mystery Guy. He looks at my chest and I'm about to cover it and tell him to look away before I blind him, but when he says, "Thanks, Delaney," I realize he was looking at my nametag and not my breasts.

"You're welcome."

"Can I get some pancakes?"

"Um... sure. I'll put the order in." I'm about to walk to the kitchen when he speaks again. "Don't you want to know my name?"

"No." I came here looking for one guy and one guy only. I'm not here to flirt.

"I'll tell you anyway. I'm Adrian. Adrian Westfall."

My knees go weak and I have to fight not to fall. Blurry dots swim behind my eyes. *Focus, focus, focus.* When I open my mouth, I'm not sure what's going to come out. "Nice to meet you" is what I land on.

My legs shake as I walk away, but it has nothing on the tremble in my chest. I'm scared he's going to see through me. Take one look and know who I am. Know that I'm the daughter of the guy who killed his nephew. And that I came here for him. Hoping that with his forgiveness, my family can find some peace. I'm not ready for him to know that yet. I've never been the best liar. What made me think I could do this?

I risk a glance at Adrian as he sits at the table. He doesn't look at me and he's immediately lost in thought. It's so strange seeing the difference in him. Like the second I walked away, he transformed from the guy who was talking to me to the guy he really is. He's not smiling. His shoulders are slumped. I think about his eyes when I first saw them. How they looked like endless space. Smoke and mirrors.

And I can't help but wonder if that look is there because of what my father did to his family.

I don't know a lot of details but I know his sister was at work. Know the toddler was in the yard and he was with him. I know my father hit the little boy with his car. And Adrian spent a little time in jail for an assault on my dad. I was only fourteen and it wasn't like Mom gave me a lot of details.

"Delaney? You going to put that order in or what?" the cook, Donna, says through the order window.

"Yeah. Sorry. He wants pancakes." My voice suddenly sounds like a high tenor, only not as beautiful. Or as steady.

I grab a washcloth and pretend to actually care if the countertop is clean as I try to watch him and pry my eyes away at the same time. He's holding his book, his long fingers flipping through the pages. I wonder about him and that book. The cover was worn like only a loved book can get, so either he's read it over and over, or it isn't his. A library copy. Maybe he's in school and he has to read it.

A little pang hits my chest. I always figured I would go to college. It was the route I was supposed to take, only things got rough and I haven't made it there yet.

The bell dings and my heart jumps. "Order up," Donna says.

In. Out. In. Out. I take a couple deep breaths as my shaky hand grabs the plate. *I can do this. I have to do this.*

Taking slow steps, I make it to Adrian's table. "Here—" I have to clear my throat for my voice to work. "Here's your food. Do you need anything else?" I set the plate in front of him.

Adrian closes his book and raises his eyebrows. "Are you offering?"

I want to say something to him, to tell him that's disgusting, but when your dad kills a member of someone else's family, it's a little hard to be mean to them.

"Water?" I ask.

"Space," he replies, and I wonder if that might be the most honest thing he's said to me. There's no malice in his voice. No flirtation either, only truth.

"Sure…anything. Just get my attention if you need me." It's not the best thing to say. I know I should be going to his table to make sure everything is okay, but I won't. Not unless he calls me over. It's the least I can do, really.

For the next two hours I go about my business. Pretend it matters that I'm sweeping the floor, filling the sugar containers. Adrian eats, pushes his plate away, and then alternates between *The Count* and scribbling in his notebook. I wonder what he's writing but know I don't have a right.

I came here for him, but I don't have a plan. For some reason, I don't think it would work to sit down and tell him I'm sorry. That I hate what my father did and I hate what Adrian's family lost and that I would do anything, *anything*, to make it go away.

I did it before with his sister, but that was different. One look at me and she'd known. She'd known who I was, and we sat down and cried as I told her I was sorry.

She said she didn't hate me, that it wasn't my fault. I told her she lost more than I ever did, so she asked what I lost too. We talked about my mom and the gambling debts, which led to depression and suicide attempts.

And that's when she told me about her brother. That she hadn't just lost Ashton, this beautiful little boy, but two members of her family. Adrian too. He'd never been able to handle things well, and he'd disappeared right after Ashton died.

The private investigator found him only a couple hours away in Brenton, she'd said offhandedly. The pain in her eyes when she told me she couldn't go to him ripped me apart. But she knew him and said you couldn't push Adrian; otherwise he'd run again. At least this way she knew he was safe.

And here I am, trying to push him. Trying to dig up

his past just so I can try and give myself a better future. I've never felt so selfish in my life. I want to vomit. Tears sting my eyes and I remember how Mom used to tell me a good cry could be cathartic. Now she just takes pills or puts a razor to her wrists.

Suddenly, I don't know if I can do this. Don't know if I can do any of it. What was I thinking, coming here? Trying to dredge up his past the way I want to. It's not okay. Not fair. Maddox was right.

I think about how small Mom looked in that hospital bed. Maybe we deserve it. Maddox seems to think he does. Maybe it's all our faults for trusting in Dad or sticking by his side before we knew how bad things were. For not looking into his lies and treasuring the time he was home.

Maybe we're supposed to continue living with it.

Adrian stands but doesn't look at me. I never gave him his bill, but right now, I don't care. I'll cover it and pretend he paid. Whatever I have to do to make this right.

He stuffs his book in the pocket of his black hoodie. The other pocket belongs to his spiral notebook. Without a glance in my direction, he walks out. I wait until the headlights swing across the wall before I walk to his table.

There's a twenty-dollar bill and a single piece of paper. The paper trembles, an extension of my hand.

Space
I asked.

She agreed.
It wasn't what caught my attention.
Her eyes.
Me too,
They seemed to say,
I need space too

Thank you

I fall into his seat. Clutch the paper to my chest. And cry.

I get off work at 6:00 a.m. and head to the little apartment my brother and I are sharing. I guess that's the good thing about not having many ties anymore. We can pack up and move at any second. Maddox hates that part because it made it easier for me to come here. He'll be glad when he finds out I don't think I should go through with it.

Maddox is passed out on the couch when I get home. We could only afford a one-bedroom place and it's just like him to give the room to me. I guess it's just like me to take it too.

After the fastest shower in history, I throw on my sweats and a sweatshirt. I climb into bed, my body tired. Even my mind is, but it's not shutting off enough to get any downtime.

I read Adrian's poem what feels like five million times. It's so strange how you get it in your head who someone is before you meet them. Or even after you meet them, you get that one look and know who they are. It's bullshit ninety-nine percent of the time, but that doesn't stop people from doing it.

The words on this paper aren't who I saw when I thought of the boy who's tied into my life so much, yet doesn't know it. Questions rain down on me in a powerful thunderstorm: Does he write often? Does it help him deal? Is this something he shares with everyone?

Curiosity swims inside me, filling up every nook and cranny it can find. I shouldn't be curious about him. It almost feels morbid in a way, but I can't help but wish that maybe knowing each other would be a step toward healing us all.

"Stupid."

I look over at the clock. It's one of the only things unpacked in my room. Bringing in money is much more important than making the place homey.

It's 10:00 a.m. and I haven't slept a wink yet. I roll out of bed. My brother's out on the tiny balcony smoking a cigarette. It takes two tries to get the glass door to slide open right. "Hey," I say, tucking my hands into the sleeves of my sweatshirt and leaning against the wall.

"You're up early." I can tell by the scratchiness in Maddox's voice that he just woke up too.

"Couldn't sleep...Have you called to check on Mom today?" I know the answer to that question before I asked it.

"Did she worry about us when things got bad?"

"Mad—"

"Laney."

"Stop it."

"You stop it."

I swat him on the back of the head. "I'm not twelve. It's not going to help to mimic me."

He takes a drag from his cigarette and lets the smoke out slowly. "Think we'll be here long enough for you to register for a class or something? You should."

"So should you. I don't have the money or the time right now."

"I'd make it happen."

I sigh, hating the fact that my brother feels the weight of our family on his shoulders. That he would do anything for me but nothing for himself. That he blames himself so much for everything falling apart that it's the real reason he struggles with Mom. It hurts too much to see her. And...well, I think it's the way she treats me, too, and that makes me feel like crap. He shouldn't lose his only parent because she can't stand the sight of me. "I know you would...I met Adrian last night."

At that he whips around to face me. "That fast? What happened?" His voice is a mixture of concern and annoyance.

I shrug. "He was the guy who tried to...help me with the boxes yesterday. I didn't know it, though. Then he happened to show up at the diner last night and I figured out who he was."

"Fuck," Maddox groans.

I'm pretty sure there's a small tint of curiosity in his gray eyes. He'll never ask, though. Not Maddox.

"He of course doesn't know who I am." I pause for a

second, trying to build a coherent thought from all the bits and pieces and fragments in my mind. "He's broken, Maddy. I don't know how I know it, but I do." I kneel next to him. Drop my head on his shoulder. I hear the deep breath he inhales and exhales, knowing I'm hurting and hating it.

"Do you think it's our fault, somehow? I know that sounds stupid, but did we do something? Wrong someone? Should we have known what Dad was doing earlier? Are we being punished because we were blind?"

Another curse. Maddox doesn't move, doesn't wrap an arm around me. "None of it's your fault, Laney. You were just a kid."

"You too," I point out, but he chooses to ignore that.

After a pause, he asks, "Did meeting him make you realize this is a shitty idea? That it's not going to change anything?"

"I don't know...maybe...probably...I don't know."

He chuckles. "Typical woman. Doesn't know what she wants."

That makes me hit him again before I stand up. "Who knows? I don't know what I want, remember? I don't want to hurt him. I don't want to hurt anyone, but... we're all tied in this together. Maybe there's a way we can help each other. I keep thinking of his sister. How much she misses him. What if there's a way we can help? What if we can bring them back together?" The truth is, I couldn't imagine being in this without Maddox. Adrian and Angel need each other like we do.

"You can help, Laney. Not me. My only concern is my

family." His cigarette has almost burned to the end now, but he takes a drag anyway before stubbing it out.

I want to tell him Mom's family also, not just me, but I don't. I'm not in the mood to fight with him today. "I'm not sure what to do, but I'm not ready to leave." And then I add, "I just want everything to be okay."

Maddox stands and shakes his head at me. "You're too much of an optimistic, little sister. We've gone too far for everything to be okay." He walks into the apartment, leaving me to stand there alone.

Chapter Five

~Adrian~

I have no idea what the hell I was thinking when I left my poem at the table. It feels like a slipup. No, more like I took a razor to my skin, like I cut myself open and left a small piece of myself behind for her. I don't do shit like that, but seeing Angel at Ashton's grave not long before that, plus the girl at the party with his nickname— maybe I hadn't needed to cut myself open at all. Maybe they'd already done it for me and I was open and raw when I went in.

Maybe I had no choice but to leave that piece of me there.

Or it might be the ghosts in her eyes. The dark shadows that lurk there and make me wonder what's chasing her when the lights go out.

Hell, I might just need to let laid. No matter how I look at it, she's gorgeous and I want her.

Whatever the reason is, I don't like it. Don't like giving people a glimpse inside me to see what lives there.

Even when it was Angel who found some of my shit and read it, I felt under the microscope. Like a rat that people study. When I was young, I was the quiet kid who didn't talk but left his heart on paper. Now she'll see me as the flirtatious, fucked-up guy with a hidden depth that's not really there. It's nothing but an optical illusion.

Smoke curls around my living room like a dense fog. I haven't done anything but sit on the couch since I kicked everyone out of my place today.

The blinds and windows are all closed, so it's almost like it's nighttime, even though the sun has been up for hours.

My head hurts, but I haven't taken anything. Don't like all that unnatural shit in my body, which some people think is ironic since I medicate in a completely different way every day.

Pushing to my feet, I see the paper on the table this morning. My hand itches to grab it like I'm still back in that sea-colored diner and still have a chance to keep that one smoke screen in place. I think of her curves and her eyes and that little black mark painted on her face.

I have to fix this. Pull that mask on tight to make up for the glimpse I left behind. It's not like it won't be fun. Even through all the fucked-up feelings that swam through my head when I saw her this morning, I still felt the burn of her beneath my skin. The part of me who sees a challenge and wants to overcome it. I want to turn her into a girl at a party who wants to pass the time with me as much as I want to pass it with her. A flicker of a moment when we're nothing but hands, and lips, and tongues, together and nothing else matters, before we go our separate ways.

I need a distraction and the girl with ghosts in her eyes is as good as anything. And while I play the game, maybe, just maybe I'll be able to forget the rest of it.

When I can't rub the sandpaper out of my eyes, I go to my room, unlock my closet, and look at the picture of the little boy with the big brown eyes. "I'm sorry, Ash," I tell him, like I do every day. I might not be able to say it to Angel and I know I'll never repent enough, but I need to do this.

Closing the door, I kick off my shoes and fall into bed. My hand latches on to the tiny shirt under my pillow. I hold it tight and close my eyes.

Tonight, I'll again lock away the demons that have showed their faces too much since the morning at the cemetery.

Oscar, one of the guys I hang out with, is always down for a good time. He's different from Colt. Colt might not have known it, but he hated the way we lived our lives. There was this sort of sadness inside him that wanted more for himself. He didn't always act like it, but he knew right from wrong. Knew what he wanted for himself but had to pull his head out and go for it.

I don't have that problem with Oscar. I tell him I want a girl, he goes with me to find one, no questions asked.

I tell him I'm having a party, he makes sure people are there. Hell, half the time, he doesn't even wait for my invitation and I usually don't care either.

So, when I need someone to chill with tonight, someone I know will go along with whatever I want, he's the guy I go to.

"What's up, man?" he asks when he shows up at my place.

First thing he does is take the bong from my table and fill his lungs with smoke. I don't tell him what's up and he doesn't ask again. He takes a few shots and I laugh and talk shit and it's like every other night of the week except I keep running over poetry lines in my head. *Thank you. I shouldn't have ended it with thank you since she wanted the same thing as me.*

But then, who the hell am I to pretend to know what she wants?

I kick Oscar's ass on the PlayStation and the whole time he doesn't shut up.

"Where's Colt been lately?"

"Happy."

"Did you see that chick in the red dress last night?"

"Yeah." What I don't say is I didn't give a shit.

"You disappear with some girl?"

"You know it." *My memories, is more like it.*

I wait until about eleven before telling Oscar I'm hungry and that we should go out. He's too blazed out of his mind to drive. Since I didn't drink, it's a no-brainer that I'll be the one behind the wheel.

I don't even know if she'll be there or not, but the

closer to the diner we get, the more the competitor in me amps up. With the ghosts in her eyes, she got me to show a part of myself that no one else sees. The next score will go to me.

The second I walk inside, my eyes find her. Her dark hair is pulled back and she's speed walking through the place. There are more people in here than there were last night, so I know it's going to be a little harder to do what I want to do.

The hostess gives me a shy smile when I walk in. "What's up?" I wink at her, playing the game that's engraved in my memory.

"Um...hi. Just two?" Another smile.

"Depends. What time do you get off?" I ask her. "My buddy here wants to know." I slap Oscar on the shoulder and know he's not going to argue. He'll get her a whole lot easier if I help him than he would on his own.

"An hour." The blonde looks at Oscar, me, then back at Oscar again.

Which means that's probably when the diner slows down, leaving only Delaney and the cook. It's a Thursday night and I know they're busier and staff heavier on the weekends.

"We'll be here," I tell her.

"Okay." She leads us to our seat.

"Fuck yeah," Oscar whispers in my ear, and I fight the part of me that wants to tell him it's ridiculous. That all of it's fake and not important and that he'll forget her name in a week, but since I'm an illusion, too, I have no room to talk to him.

"Have a good meal," she says before walking away.

I turn and catch her looking at Delaney, fanning herself and then nodding toward us. Delaney's eyes follow hers. When she sees me, her feet plant to the floor, grow roots like an old tree, growing for all of eternity.

I nod. Smile. *Game on*, I want my look to tell her.

We sit in the booth and Oscar mumbles about the blonde and it being his lucky night, but I keep my eyes on Delaney. Watch her as she fills glasses of water. See her shiver and wonder if she knows my eyes are on her. Then as she comes toward me, there's this confused look on her face. Maybe it's not her who's confused, but me. All I know is that I can't read her, but she keeps coming and I know whatever it is, she's going to play through it.

Good for her.

"Coffee?" Her voice cracks slightly. It's still that sweet, girl-next-door tenor that tells the story that she's always been good. That she's fresh and innocent. If it weren't for the ghosts in her eyes, I might believe it.

"Hot chocolate," I reply.

The corners of her mouth tilt down slightly and her face tenses. She knows I'm trying to keep her on her toes. This might not be as easy as I thought.

"Whip cream?" she tosses back.

"Obviously."

She turns to Oscar and he blurts out, "You are really fucking beautiful. Like unreal beautiful." His tongue is practically hanging out of his mouth and I bite back a groan. Idiot.

"Simmer down, Romeo," I tell him, and then look at

Delaney. "You'll have to excuse my friend. He loses his head in front of beautiful girls."

This is the part where I wait for her to smile at me like the hostess did. Maybe watch as her cheeks turn pink or she shyly looks toward the ground. When none of that happens, I wait for the anger. For her to give me hell for being a sexist pig, but she doesn't do either of those things.

She laughs.

It takes her a few seconds to settle down. Annoyance slowly rumbles through me while I wait to see what she's going to say next.

"Really? Did you guys plan that before you came in?"

I shrug. "Maybe we did, maybe we didn't. Doesn't hurt for you to know the score up front, though. I came back here for you."

She gasps and I'm not even sure if she realizes she did it. She pulls that bottom lip into her mouth and I know she didn't plan on my words.

I don't turn away, waiting to see how she's going to reply next, and when I see her face pale slightly, I wonder if I screwed up. If I overstepped some invisible walls this girl has built for some reason.

Surprising me, she recovers quickly. "I'm sorry you wasted a trip." She points to the menus in front of us. "While you look that over, I'll go grab your drinks."

"You know her?" Oscar's playing with the sugar container.

"Maybe."

"I hate it when you answer with that cryptic shit."

And then he laughs. "Though I guess I'd want to keep
her to myself too."

I don't pretend to laugh. I'm running over our conversation in my head and trying to figure out how I'm going
to swing it to my favor, when she comes back. I take the
hot chocolate and order the pancakes again. Oscar gets
a burger and soon we're eating and some of the crowd is
starting to thin out.

Questions I have no business wondering climb the
wall surrounding me before plunging over the other side,
echoing as they go: *Did, did, did, did, she, she, she, she,
read, read, read, read, it, it, it, it?* Before they smash to
the concrete below.

The hostess gets off work, and Oscar tells her to sit
with us. Her name's Jamie and he tosses game at her that
she gobbles up.

The whole time I'm watching Delaney, trying to
ignore my question as it goes for the wall again. "I'll be
right back," I tell them. She's at the counter by herself.
Only two other customers are in the place and the cook's
safely in the kitchen.

"You owe me a night out," I tell her as I lean against
the counter.

"How do you figure that?" She doesn't look at me
when she talks.

Because I want you out of my system. "You were
going to say yes to the party. I could see it, but your
brother came chomping at my ankles."

At that she whips around. "How is it my fault you got

scared away? And you're not going to get me to go *any-where* by insulting my brother."

I shake my head. "Not scared. I was showing respect. That should earn me some points, right? As should honesty. I told you up front I came back for you. Come on. You're obviously new to town. Let me show you a good time."

Her shoulders slump, like my words sucked the air out of her. "Believe me, it's not a good idea."

I step closer, lean over the counter so my mouth is next to her ear. "It's a very good idea. What time do you get off? I'll come back for you." I'm always up front with a girl. She'll know exactly what this is about.

I feel the blast of ice shooting from her. See it in the set of her shoulders and the anger in her jaw. She's fighting for composure before she talks—working through what she wants to say or maybe trying to fight the words back, swinging at them with a bat and hoping to hit a home run so they can't get to her again.

"I'm not sure why I'm surprised that you're like every other guy in the world. I thought..." She shakes her head. "I don't know why I thought you might be different. If you'll excuse me, I need to get to work."

Shame takes root in my bones, breaking some as it travels through my body. I don't know what I'm ashamed about either. Why it matters what this girl thinks. If it's her that's making me feel this way or because I know if Ash can look down on me, he wouldn't think I have the power to hold the world up anymore. If anything, I'm crushing it. I have been for the past four years.

My feet carry me back to the table. The whole time I'm telling myself it doesn't matter. None of it does. It's not like I've never pissed off a girl before. It's not like I haven't pissed off a lot of people or they haven't done the same to me.

"Let's get out of here," I tell Oscar. He looks surprised but follows Jamie out of the booth when she stands up.

"What are you guys doing tonight?" she asks.

"What do you want to do?" Oscar replies.

"My friends are having a party over by the campus, if you guys want to go."

"You know it," he says.

I don't tell him I'm not going and wait while Jamie gives him the address. We don't talk as he gets in the car, but then he starts going off about how lucky we got and though the waitress didn't come through, it's not like there won't be girls at the party.

I pull up in front of the house and already hear the music pulsing and pumping on wind as it hits the car. I should go in there. Part of me wants to go in there, but it feels just like last night. And the night before and the night before.

Tonight, I can't do it.

"I have something to do," I tell Oscar.

He couldn't care less. "More for me," he says before laughing and nudging my arm. He's out of the car and heads toward Jamie, who's already there waiting for him.

The whole time I'm driving home I tell myself to go back to the party. What's the point in going home? In trying to quiet the voices in my head when nothing ever really does that?

Reaching for my cell, I'm about to text Oscar. I try one pocket and then the other, but it's not there.

I know I had it when I left home, so it has to be at the restaurant. I sigh and let my head fall back in frustration. The last thing I want is anyone going through my shit, so I head back to the diner.

I'm about to pull into the parking lot when I notice a car parked off slightly to the side. I scan it, then the restaurant. I see two guys at the register with Delaney and someone who I assume is the cook, both guys in masks with guns in their hands.

Fear spikes through me.

"Motherfucker." I feel for my phone before remembering I don't have it. I hit the brakes, throw the car in park right in the middle of the road, hoping it gets someone to stop. The guys have their backs to me. My heart's rapping an angry beat because I don't know what the fuck to do. I walk in there and they'll shoot me, but there's not a chance I'll sit here and do nothing.

I jog around the side of the building. There's a little alley back there and the door to the kitchen, which of course is locked. There's a window and I look around for something to break it. No time, so I make a fist and slam it into the glass. It cracks but doesn't go through, so I take my fist to it again, hoping it will at least set off an alarm or some shit. If not, maybe I can get in the back without them seeing.

One more time my fist hits the glass. Blood pours down my hand, coloring the broken pieces as they shatter a mixture of crystal blue and red glass.

The second the alarm vibrates through the night, I take off toward the front of the building. It doesn't fucking matter if they have guns or not. What matters is that girl inside.

Blood colors my vision as I move. Little flashes of Ash in all that fucking blood.

Save them, save them, save them is all I can think. I don't know if I'm thinking of Delaney or Ash. All I know is I'm not watching someone else die.

As I make it around the building, the glass door slams into the window. The guys run out. One of them looks at me, knowledge staring at me through the holes in his mask. His hand raises, the gun pointed right at me, and for a brief second, two words play in my head: *Thank you.*

My feet pull me to a stop and I wonder if he's about to do it when Delaney screams in the background, "Noooo!"

At the same time, the other guy says, "Come the fuck on!"

My eyes shift to her, and they're gone. Running across the parking lot and jumping into the car. They hit the street and peel away.

"Oh my God! Are you okay?" Delaney runs out to me, makeup running down her face. *They look like little roads.* A path leading her tears down her face and I think I might want to take the journey with them. Maybe they'll have the power to wash me away.

"Call the cops," I tell her. "I need to get out of here."

I'm already trying to walk back to the car, but she's right behind me. "Donna's calling the cops. You can't leave. You're a witness."

I shake my head. "A witness who doesn't want to be involved with the cops. I have shit on me that will get my ass hauled in too."

She sounds frantic. I hear her breathing and the shake in her voice when she says, "They won't search you."

I'm still walking and she's still following. "They'll take one look at me and search me." I've seen it before, especially if they run my name and see I have a record.

She reaches me by then and grabs my arm. About the same time, I already hear the sirens going off in the background.

"Shit—what the fuck?" I say as she shoves her hands into the pocket of my baggy jeans.

Her hand latches on to my pipe and the baggie in my pocket. "They won't search me." She pulls it out and before I realize what she's doing, she's running to a car, popping open the truck, and throwing my weed inside.

My feet don't move as I watch her. I feel the blood still running down my hand, but it doesn't matter. *Thank you.* The words swim in the rapids of my mind but keep getting pulled under. Running into rocks and getting hung up on the river floor. "You shouldn't have done that. What if—"

"I had no choice but to do that. I owe you."

"You—"

"I do." And then she's wiping her face. The sirens are so close I know they'll be here at any second.

"Shit," I mumble. "If anything happens, I put it in there and you didn't know."

As the two cop cars screech into the parking lot, she's grabbing my hand. "You're bleeding," she says.

It's just another wound to go with all the rest. "I've been bleeding for four years."

She crystalizes. Freezes. Her eyes, big gaping holes at the end of the roads on her face.

"Freeze! Put your hands in the air!" the cops yell.

I pull away, doing exactly what they say.

Chapter Six

~Delaney~

The police run at Adrian and me. I can't think about the sound of their feet hitting the ground or even the guns that were pointed at my head. I just hear his words. See his lips as he says them: *"I've been bleeding for four years."*

I want to tell him *Me too* but don't know if I have the right.

Want to hold him, but I'm pretty sure I don't have that right either.

And then there's the selfish part of me who wants to say, *Maybe we can bleed together.* Because it's different with Maddox. He'll listen, but he doesn't talk and I can't talk to Mom. As horrible as it makes me sound, it feels good to not be alone in the pain.

"Get down on your knees," one of the policemen says to Adrian.

"It wasn't him. The guys, they took off."

"Black Chevy Malibu." Adrian's kneeling as he speaks

and then rattles off a license plate number. Still, he links his hands together behind his head. I can't believe he thought to look at the plate. It didn't even cross my mind.

To my surprise, the cops continue to search him. One of them goes back to their cruiser, putting an APB out on the car. It's not two seconds later that more cop cars go speeding past.

"His hand. He's bleeding." The cop searching Adrian looks at his hand, but Adrian's eyes are on me. I wonder what he's thinking. Wishing I could crawl around inside his brain.

Donna comes out about then and they finally let Adrian off the ground.

"Hey, Bert. Can you call an ambulance?" a cop asks.

"I don't need it. I'm fine," he grits out.

I step toward him, wanting to help but not sure how to go about it. What to say or if he'll turn me away, so I do nothing. I've always been a coward.

We spend the next couple of hours answering questions, giving descriptions. Someone gives Adrian a cloth to wrap his hand in. The police investigate and gather evidence, while Adrian, Donna, and I stay with another cop. The owners of the restaurant are called down. The police ask Adrian a million times about the window, why he stopped, why he didn't call the cops and other questions that annoy me.

"I came back to see Delaney," he says, but I know that's not true. He came back for his phone. I found it and put it in my purse, hoping to find him to give it to him later. Or not. Maybe I'm a thief and I just wanted to hold on to a part of him. I don't know, but I also don't mention it since he didn't.

I know he has to be in pain, but he doesn't say anything. His car's parked by mine now, someone having moved it a while ago.

Finally, what feels like an eternity later, they tell us we can go. They'll be in touch if they have any more questions.

"Let me bring you to the hospital." Maybe I should have asked instead, but I don't. "You need to get your hand checked out."

"Nah." He shakes his head. "My medication is in your trunk."

I sigh. I wonder if all boys are like this or if it's just the scarred ones. "How is not taking care of your hand going to make anything better?"

We're standing by the cars now. My keys are tight in my hand. He's not getting in my trunk.

He shakes his head. His facial expressions haven't changed. I can't read him and again I think about sifting my way through his brain. "You won't change your mind, will you?"

At that, his personality shifts. Like he goes into a different mode and he's not the guy who I've been with for the past few hours. He's the one who was here with his friend earlier. "What will you give me if I do?" He steps toward me and I fight to keep myself from pulling back. He's trying to intimidate me. Or to shift my concern to anger and I'm not going to let that happen.

"How about your phone and your drugs? I found your

cell earlier and still have it." I cross my arms. I'm not this girl. Not tough and strong or the one who always has a good comeback, but I'm determined to make him believe I am.

At that, he smiles. Totally not what I expected. Adrian takes another step toward me. I beg myself not to move away before he's dipping his head so his mouth is next to my ear. "Trying to play hardball, are you? If you want to play doctor with me, you're going to have to come home with me to do it."

"How..." Oh my God. My voice will hardly work. He's so very close to me and he feels warm and strong. I want to be wrapped up in that warmth. It's not him. I know that. It's just the fact that I want to be held— wrapped up in someone's arms until it feels like everything else goes away.

"Are you going to come home with me, Delaney?" he asks, and I shiver.

Get yourself together! "I'm not sure how much help I'll be. I must have left my X-ray machine at home." I step back. "Your hand is swollen. It might be broken. Don't be an idiot."

At that he looks down at his hand and I know he knows I'm probably right.

"You write...I mean, I assume you do because of the poem. You don't want to mess around with your hands."

"That was a mistake," he says.

"I thought it was beautiful."

His head turns and he's looking me in the eyes. It's almost as though he's trying to dissect me. My insides want to find a dark corner to hide in. I'm not sure anyone has looked at me this intensely in my whole life. I want to ask him what he sees. My eyes close, afraid of what he'll find there. Afraid I'll show him who I am. Who my dad is, even though that's what I'm supposed to want.

Adrian's voice is tight when he speaks. "It's not broken. I've had enough broken bones to know that. If you're feeling like a martyr and want to take care of it, come with me. If not, I'll see you later."

When I open my eyes, he's already backing away and heading to his car.

The easiest thing to do would be to walk away. It's the smartest, but I can't. Even though he doesn't know it, we're tied together. Like there's this thin thread connecting us that Adrian can't see. He's been bleeding for years because of something my father did and I can't let that go.

Even though I know I should. I've never really had to stand up for anything in my life. Things were so easy before, and ever since, we've just been going through the motions. This small thing feels like my one shot to take a stand. God, do I want that.

"Do...do you have a first-aid kit?"

"I think it's with your X-ray machine."

I roll my eyes. "Is there a pharmacy on the way to your house?"

Adrian sighs. "Just follow me."

As soon as I get into my car, I pull out my cell phone. It's 5:00 a.m. I'm supposed to be off work in an hour, which means Maddox will be expecting me. There's no way in hell I can tell him where I'm going—he'll lose it—so I pray the whole time I'm calling that he'll sleep through it.

I cock my head so my phone rests between my ear and shoulder, allowing me to drive.

My brother's voice comes through the speaker. "Leave a message" is all his voice mail says.

"Hey, Maddy. I'm going to be a little late today. My relief is having car trouble and she won't be in on time. I'll be home later."

I click OFF and toss the cell on the passenger seat. We make a quick stop at a twenty-four-hour pharmacy before I follow Adrian to a tiny house in a run-down neighborhood. Not that mine's all that, but his is definitely worse.

I can hardly hear anything over the pulse in my ears. *Please let me be doing the right thing. Please let me be doing the right thing.*

I watch Adrian as he unlocks the door. His eyes are puffy, little dark rings beneath them that look as though he hasn't really slept in a while. It's on the tip of my tongue to ask him, but when I think about our situation, I stop myself. I'm not sure if I should intertwine my life any more with his. If it turns out as bad as Maddox thinks it will, I'll only be making things worse.

But then I'm there too. Already pulling that invisible thread tighter. Thinking about his poem and the hurt that showed through his words.

He opens the door. Without saying a word, Adrian nods for me to go inside. I step into the lonely house.

It somehow feels darker than it should. He hits the first light.

A few beer bottles litter a table. An old couch, love seat, and chair sit around a TV. No pictures are on the walls and I suddenly feel a little sadder than I did before I came inside.

Adrian walks down the hall, turning on more lights as he goes, and I wonder if I'm supposed to follow him. If I should turn around and walk back out, but I do neither. My feet are lead, welded to the floor until he peeks his head out of a room and asks, "Aren't we playing doctor now?" He raises one of his eyebrows.

I try and shake off the nerves setting my bones in concrete and head his way. He has the first-aid kit in his hand, which he sets on the counter of the small bathroom.

My eyes search the room for something personal, anything, but the only thing I see is a single toothbrush in a cup. It's blue and looks lonely.

"There should be gloves in there," he says, before leaning against the counter. I'm surprised he's letting me do this so easily, but at the look of concentration in his eyes, I wonder if it's calculated. If there is some motive behind it that I don't know. Or maybe I do know and don't want to acknowledge it.

After opening the first-aid kit and putting on the rubber gloves, I reach for Adrian's hand and start to unwind the cloth. There's always been something sexy to me about a guy's hands. I remember my first crush, a boy named Patrick. He was so cute and all the girls liked him. We had to hold hands in gym class, but his were all sweaty and warm. They stuck to mine, and somehow those sticky hands wiped away any crush I had.

Adrian's hands aren't like that. Not that I should be paying attention, but they're strong, with veins traveling across them. He has a little callus on his middle finger, where a pen or pencil would sit, and I wonder if he writes a lot. I have a feeling he does and a brief wish to read more of it flashes through my head.

Little open wounds spring to life again as I free his hand. Blood drips down a couple of his fingers. I've never done real well with blood, so I look at Adrian to see if he notices. His eyes aren't on his hand, though. They're on me. On my face, almost like he can't take them away. Like he's locked there, and I wonder what he's seeing. If the truth is in my eyes or if maybe it makes him feel close to someone in a way he won't let himself otherwise.

"What?" I finally pry my mouth open to ask.

"Nothing."

But he doesn't look away. Doesn't open his mouth to speak and I know that's all I'm going to get from him— this X-ray vision that I'm not sure what to do with.

"There might be glass in it." I look down at his hand, setting the cloth aside. I don't let him go as I use the other hand to turn on the water. Adrian's fingers begin to tremble and I'm about to ask him why he's shaking when I realize it's because of me. That I'm shaking and vibrating through him and I wonder if he'll call me on it, but he doesn't.

"Maybe," he replies, and without looking, I know he's still staring at me.

"Over the sink," I say, pulling his hand slightly. The cuts don't look too deep, but there are quite a few of them. His knuckles are swollen and I have the urge to kiss them after they're clean. An urge I have no business having. Is it him, I wonder, or who he is to me? Because I know what my father took from him.

"Pour the peroxide on."

I open the bottle and then, holding his hand, I tilt it until clear liquid is mixing with red. Each little wound bubbles and sizzles and I wonder if it hurts, if heat burns in his hand, so I risk a glance in the mirror to see he's looking at me there. I can't read the expression on his face. I never really can, but I don't turn away. We watch each other and a wrinkle forms over his eyes and he studies me like there will be a test on me later and I wonder if I passed.

If he'll pass on whatever he learns.

It's too much, and I have to look away. *He's bleeding because of me. Been bleeding because of my family and he doesn't know it.*

I suddenly wonder if my dad hadn't driven into that yard if there would be another toothbrush in the cup. A girlfriend, or maybe he'd still be with his sister and there would be a little Batman toothbrush there for his nephew.

Tears beg for release, but I don't let them come. Instead I set the bottle back down, wet a cloth from the kit, and gently wash the blood from his hand. Adrian doesn't flinch or speak and soon he's all clean and wrapped up. For the first time in what feels like forever, I let go of his hand.

"All done," I say, and I know it's a silly thing to let come out of my mouth.

Still there are no words, so I look up at him and he's close, so very close, and I notice the depth of his eyes and the stubble on his face and earring holes in his ears.

Finally his gaze leaves my eyes and they land on my lips. "I think I'll call you Casper," he whispers, and then his mouth comes down on mine. It's gentle at first. My instinct is to pull away. I don't know him and there are too many secrets and too much history between us for me to let him do this, but I like the way he tastes and can't help but moan when his tongue slides along the seam of my lips.

And then my mouth is opening and now he's tasting me and I'm tasting him more deeply. I have never, ever been kissed like this in my life. A slow tingle forms in my stomach and shoots through me and then he's twisting me and pinning me against the counter. I feel his erection against my stomach, his good hand in my hair.

My body is screaming *YES*, because it feels good to be worshipped like this, but then my mind cuts in. I see the lonely toothbrush and think about his poem, space, and know that his life is darker because of something that's connected to me.

I pull my mouth away. "Wait."

Adrian does. His lips don't move toward mine again, but he also doesn't move away. I still feel each muscled contour of his body and wish I could wrap up inside it. Just to feel protected, even if it's only make-believe.

"I can't...We shouldn't..." *If you knew, you wouldn't want to. You'd throw me out.*

"I think we can and maybe it doesn't matter if we should." His voice is low, sexy. I shiver.

"It does." He doesn't make it easy for me to squeeze around him, but he doesn't stop me either. "It does," I say again. "I should go. Make sure you clean that again and change your bandage."

"I know how to take care of wounds," he replies.

"Okay...good." Or not good because that means he's had a lot of them. My heart is beating so loudly I wonder if he can hear it. I hope he can't.

I'm walking down the hallway so fast I'm scared I'll trip. I can't stop myself from going, though. I need out of here before I change my mind. Before I decide to be a normal eighteen-year-old and pretend he's a normal... however old he is...guy and that nothing matters but hooking up and having fun.

So much more matters than that, and I can't afford to pretend it doesn't.

"I'm sorry for your hand," I say when I get to the door. "And thank you...for helping. For maybe saving my life."

It feels like a fist slams into my chest at that. Did he save my life? After my family took one away from him?

But then I pause, my hand on the doorknob. Now I can't seem to leave without asking. I turn, looking over my shoulder. Adrian's standing in the hallway, like he came partially out to get me but changed his mind.

"Why Casper?" I ask.

"Because you're the girl with ghosts in her eyes." That

simply, Adrian turns away and walks down the hallway. I'm stumbling out the door, slamming it behind me.

"Because you're the girl with ghosts in her eyes..." I don't know why that hits me so hard, but it does. And he's right.

It's not until I'm halfway home that I remember I have Adrian's phone in my purse and his drugs in my trunk.

Chapter Seven

~Adrian~

My hand hurts like hell when I wake up about one in the afternoon. I never sleep this late, even when I'm up half the night, but since I didn't have my phone, I didn't have people calling all day waking me up. I realize she gave me space for a second time, only this time I didn't have to ask for it. This time it was just because she accidentally took my connection to the world.

For a second I let myself remember what it felt like to kiss her. I would have taken her then and there if she hadn't stopped me. I need to get her ghosts out of my head, but the second she stopped feelin' it, I did.

When I was eight, I saw my dad force himself on my mom for the first time. It's the first memory I have of vomiting. Seeing her tears as she couldn't look me straight in the eye and hearing her say, *"It's okay, baby. Close the door."* But it wasn't fucking okay. I puked right there in the hallway, pizza from lunch all over my shirt and the floor.

Then I cleaned it up. Scrubbed the carpet while I fought like hell to block out their sounds because I knew if he saw my lunch on the floor, he'd beat my ass. Maybe I should have let him see it. Maybe I deserved an ass-kicking for not making him leave her alone.

Before the memories become too much, I open the drawer beside my bed and pull out the pipe inside. I fill my lungs with smoke before setting it down and wrapping my hand around Ash's shirt under my pillow.

That's all I give myself. That one little touch before I'm out of bed, grabbing clothes and heading to the shower. It stings when the hot water hits all the openings in my skin. I close my eyes, imagining the water somehow makes them spread and get deeper until they swallow me whole and all the pain is gone.

But no. I'd never take the easy way out like that.

I turn the water off, wrap my hand, and get dressed. There's not much time until people probably start showing up at my house, wondering why they can't get ahold of me and itching to party. The water did nothing to make me feel better. I wish it could absolve me, cleanse me and make it so I never brought Ash in the front yard that day. So that maybe it was me instead of him.

I head over to the little house only a few streets from me. My good hand comes down on the door three separate times before it finally opens to show a little Italian lady named Lettie who's probably not even five feet tall.

"You're late," she says. "Screwing around with some girl when you're supposed to be workin'?" The old woman winks at me. She has to be at least eighty, but you'd never know it. Her mouth is worse than Colt's and I'm not sure she isn't up to something shady, but we help each other out, so it works. She owns my house and about ten other ones in our neighborhood. She has to have money. It's obvious, yet she lives in a house almost as shitty as mine and she pays me more than I deserve for helping her take care of them.

"Nope. That was last night." I return her wink and she thumps me on the head.

"Asshole," Lettie grumbles.

"How are you?" I ask her, noticing her limp. She's tough as hell, but I see her body betraying her. That's how I ended up helping her. Came over to pay my rent and heard her cursing inside. She'd fallen and fought me like hell when I offered to help her. I did it anyway and since she wouldn't let me take her to the hospital, I sat with her for three hours and she offered me a job.

"My hip hurts like hell. I'm old. How do you think I am?" She almost trips and I reach out to grab her. She tries to shake me off, but I don't let go and walk her back to her favorite chair. "What are you doing here? If you're not going to be on time, what's the point in coming?"

"Checking on you before I go take care of some shit."

"I'm good. Don't need your help today."

At the same time her little yappy dog comes out barking at me. "Want me to walk him?"

"No."

"Okay," I tell her, but I grab the leash anyway. She grumbles the whole time I hook the dog up, but I know she wants me to do it. I still hear her cursing at me when

I go out the door. It doesn't take me long to take care of
the dog and then I'm bringing him back and he stalks off
the same way Lettie did. She has her arms crossed and
won't look at me.

"Thanks," she mumbles. I nod, even though she won't
see, and leave.

Sitting in my car outside of Lettie's house, I tell myself not
to go. I should head home and wait for people to come
over and keep living the life I have been, but I can't.

Instead I turn the key in the ignition and head in the
opposite direction. It's not like I have a choice. The girl
tried to stop my bleeding last night. The least I can do for
her is make it so she's not driving around with my shit
in her trunk all day. Or doesn't have my phone going off
and driving her crazy.

Luckily, I have my notebook and *The Count* just in
case Colt and his girl aren't home. It would probably be
better if they weren't; that way I wouldn't have to try and
explain why I'm waiting around to try and find which
apartment Delaney lives in.

It doesn't take me too long to get there. Casper's car's
parked out front and I wonder if she wakes up with the
ghosts still in her eyes. If they always live there or if a
new day gives her any reprieve.

My fist slams down on Colt and Cheyenne's door.
"Open up!" It's crazy how easy it is to be someone else.
How easily that mask slips into place without even trying.

Grumbling comes from inside before Colt jerks the

door open. His hair's all messed up and Cheyenne's lying in the bed, dressed but looking just as worn out as Colt.

Guilt burrows around inside me, finding another place in my insides to make a home. I feel like shit for interrupting them, for slicing through their limited time together and pulling them apart.

I tap the side of my forehead. "What's the point in knowing shit if you can't have a little fun with it?"

Cheyenne laughs and sits up. Colt doesn't look quite as amused but steps aside and lets me in.

"What's up, man?" I ask.

"Really want me to answer that?" Colt scratches his neck and sits next to Cheyenne on the bed.

"Oh my God. Guys are so gross."

"No. We're honest." I smile before walking to the window. It's got a bench seat in it and faces toward the parking lot where Casper's car is.

Cheyenne's eyes get big when she sees the wrap on my hand. "What happened?"

Colt looks at it, too, before his eyes find me. It's different from the look his girl gives me. She's all concern and with Colt I see the worry, rimmed with a dull, sad blue. It's crazy the things people see if they take the time to look. If they don't only go skin-deep and try to find their way below the surface. In a lot of ways, Colt's a prick. People look at him and that's all they see.

They don't know the guy who has more balls than I ever will. The one who didn't run when his mom was dying. Who stayed and would have burned the whole fucking world to the ground if it would have saved her because she meant more to him than himself or anything else. I never could have stayed and now I just keep running. Maybe not physically anymore, but my mind and heart are backpacking through the darkest corners of the world trying to get further and further away.

What would have happened if one, just one fucking teacher or neighbor or anyone would have opened their eyes? Would have looked deep into that quiet kid I used to be to find the war that raged around inside me?

Maybe...just maybe things would have been different.

So that's what I see when I look at him. That dull, sad blue because I take the time to look below the surface.

"Well?" Cheyenne asks, pulling me out of those thoughts I lose myself in so much.

"Hello, window, meet hand." I smile before sitting down.

We hang out for a while before Cheyenne goes into the bathroom to start getting ready to meet her friend Andy. Andy's her roommate at school, even though Chey really stays with Colt. It works for both of them because it gives Andy time with her girl and Chey time with Colt.

I know they're both wondering what I'm doing here, but they don't ask and I don't offer. Colt has to go to work in a while. Still feels crazy to think those words but he's got a part-time job and is taking a few classes. His schedule isn't as intense as it was before because he doesn't know what he wants to do, which to me means he really does know what he wants—to be happy and not to settle.

Just as Cheyenne's coming out of the bathroom, I see Casper's dark hair as she walks toward her car. I push to my feet. Her brother's motorcycle is here, too, and the last thing I feel like is a run-in with him. "Catch you guys later," I say as I move to the door.

"Great. Now that Chey's leaving, you go," Colt calls from behind me. I know he won't give it another thought, but I can pretty much promise Cheyenne's going to wonder what's up with me running out, so I close the door before she gets a chance to say anything.

I take the stairs two at a time. Casper is walking away from her car. I cross my arms as I walk up to her, smirk, and then keep going so I can lean against her car.

I hear her say, "Oh-kay," before she turns around and takes the few steps back to me. "You're here for your stuff, I'm assuming?" She crosses her arms like I do, but her body is stiff, her voice slightly off, and I think she's trying to sound more indifferent than she really is.

"Maybe." I shrug. "And maybe finishing what we started this morning?"

She's wearing makeup, her eyes painted dark and her lips red, but the lips are natural.

"Adrian...that was a mistake. I...there's so much going on. I just can't."

The urge to ask her what's going on rapidly boils inside me, threatening to spill over, but I clamp the lid down. "Are you sure? It would be fun. Nothing more than that, but a whole lot of fun."

She shakes her head, looks behind her and then at me again. "Why are you pursuing me? I'm sure there are a hundred other girls out there looking for the kind of fun you want to have."

I want to tell her it's because secrets don't reflect in the eyes of other girls. Pain doesn't show, but I've already showed her other little pieces of me, which I want back. I'm not like Colt. I have no intention to stop running.

Anger replaces the urge to talk. Like a magic trick I didn't know I could perform, one is replaced by the other and I don't know how it got there. Or why I'm so pissed. Because she called me out? Because she doesn't want me? Because my body is really jonesing for her? Or maybe because I really want to know about that look in her eyes.

"You make a good point. If you'll give me my stuff, I'll be on my way."

She glances behind her again before going to her trunk and opening it.

"You're acting sketchy and people will wonder what's up," I say. "Not that anyone in this neighborhood would care."

"Sorry if I'm not used to passing drugs to people," she hisses as she digs in her trunk, closes her fist around my stuff, and hands it to me.

I push it into my pocket. "My phone?"

"It's in my house. I'll have to go get it, but my brother's home. Do you mind waiting here?" She's back to that sweet voice. The girl next door that so contrasts the ghosts.

"Really?" I wonder about the hold her brother has on her. Why she would feel like she needs to hide the fact that she accidentally has my phone. "Afraid he'll think you're being a bad girl?"

At that she slams her trunk and I wonder if it's the first time in her life she's ever been mad. The tight lips and narrowed eyes look so foreign on her face.

"No. I just don't want him to know about what happened last night. He already doesn't like the idea that I work nights and that would make it worse. Not that it's any of your business or anything."

She tries to walk around me, but I step in front of her. "Wait. You're going back to work there?"

She sighs and drops her head back. "Oh God, not you too. Do I have 'please take care of me' written across my forehead?"

"No, but maybe you should if you're going back to work there alone. Are they hiring security or anything?"

Not my business. Not my business. Not my business.

"My boss is a tightwad, so I doubt it. It's not as though they're going to rob the same place twice, Adrian."

It's like a little shock to hear my name roll off her tongue. I don't know why. I think she feels it, too, as I see her swallow.

"I wonder what would have happened if I hadn't shown up." What would have happened if I had been a few seconds later, like I had been with Ash. Maybe nothing. Maybe everything. There's only a thin chalk line separating the two—nothing and everything. All it takes is a hand to wipe it away.

"Big strong man saves helpless woman?" she huffs and tries to walk away again. For some reason, it makes me want to smile. I don't know where it comes from, but maybe she reminds me of Casper in more ways than one. It's funny watching the friendly ghost trying to be mad. "If you'll move out of my way, I'll go get your phone."

I don't know what makes me do it, but I step aside. I lean against the trunk of her car. The longer she's gone, the more I wonder why I care. It's her fault if she wants to go work there again. I don't have it in me to watch over anyone. If I couldn't take care of a two-year-old, I don't know what in the hell makes me think I can do it with anyone else.

Or why I would want to try.

I flex my fingers, remembering the care she took on my hand. How her fingers felt. What it would have been like to let myself feel it.

"Here's your phone." She thrusts it into my palm. I didn't even hear her come back.

She opens her mouth to say something, but it's cut off when another female voice pops in with a "Hi."

I groan, wishing like hell I had gotten out of here before this happened. Meetings come with questions and questions have no place in my life.

Delaney turns and standing there is Cheyenne and Colt.

"What's up?" I ask.

"Nothing." Cheyenne looks at me. Delaney. Back at me.

Damn it. It's different with her. Or a lot of people

maybe. There's a difference between trying to look below the surface and trying to see something that isn't there. Cheyenne's going to want the make-believe. She'll want to see something here that's not.

When it's obvious I'm not going to say anything, she holds out her hand. "Hey. We're Adrian's friends. I'm Cheyenne. This is my boyfriend, Colt."

Delaney holds out her hand. "Um...hi. I'm Delaney. Nice to meet you." The girls shake; then she grabs Colt's hand and does the same. My eyes don't leave him and I see the strange look he gives her, the way his eyes study her, and I'm about to ask him what's so fucking interesting when I realize it doesn't matter. I have no say over how anyone looks at her.

"She's my doctor," I tease, but when Delaney whips around to me, I hold up my hand to pretend that's what I was talking about.

Colt's and Cheyenne's stares are all becoming too much. They feel like pressure bearing down on me, making me want to take my backpacking trip even farther.

My phone beeps and I wonder who it is. Want any excuse I can find to get out of here. To stop their stares and cut off the urge to tell her not to go back to work.

"I'm out of here." As I make a move to turn, Casper's hand reaches out and latches on to my arm.

"Wait. I need to talk to you." She studies her hand on my arm like it's a big deal that it's there, and curiosity spikes inside me again, but then she's pulling it away.

"Come on, Tiny Dancer," Colt whispers in Cheyenne's ear. She shivers and I imagine making Delaney do the same thing. There's nothing sexier than making a girl shiver.

"Maybe we'll see you around," Cheyenne says to her.

As they start walking away, Colt looks back. For the first time ever, he taps his finger against the side of his head like I do, like I've done to him a hundred times, especially where Cheyenne is concerned, before turning around.

There's nothing to know . . .

"Please." Delaney's plea pulls my attention back to her.

"You don't have to beg," I tell her.

"That's not what I mean. Please don't say anything. Maddox will want me to quit and without a job, we can't keep this apartment and I don't . . . I can't go home."

That's what does it. The heartbreak in her voice and how it dances on her words and calls to something inside me that I don't understand. *Dance with me,* it says, but I don't do that kind of thing and I won't, so I take a step backward, knowing what I'm going to do and wanting to set the thought on fire.

Wanting to burn or bury this need in me to know why she can't go home.

"I don't know your brother. Why would I tell him?"

"Thank you . . . Adrian. I appreciate that."

I don't let her finish before I'm walking away. I get in my car and drive. When I can't drive anymore, I pull over. Grab my notebook and a pen.

Maybe nothing.
Playing
Front yard
Fine
Screeching
Maybe everything.

Forgotten phone.
Maybe nothing.
Gun in her face.
Maybe everything.

She can't go home.
Maybe nothing.
I can't go either.
Maybe everything.

Ignoring my phone, I drive again. Go until it's late at night and my car's coasting along on fumes again. Ironic that I'm doing the same, but I can't just pull into a gas station and fill up. Can't find a quick stop to make my worries go away.

When I'm not able to drive anymore, I pull into the diner.

Chapter Eight

~Delaney~

We've been crazy busy and I'm thankful for it. Usually it's nice to have a slow night, but being around people is somehow comforting. Actually, there's no somehow about it. I know exactly what it is. It makes no sense that I didn't think it would be scary to be back at work so soon, but it is. It's not often a girl has a gun pointed at her. The whole time all I could think about was Maddox and Mom. What it would do to my brother to lose me and wonder who would help take care of our mother.

I'm not sure he would.

Leaning over the counter, I reach for more napkins for table three. My back is to the restaurant when a loud crash sounds from behind me. I jump, my heart taking the plummet to my feet as I whip around. When I do, I come face-to-face with Adrian.

My hand flies to my chest as I let out a heavy breath.

"It was just a plate." He leans toward me and whispers in my ear. "A little harder to come back than you thought?"

"Yes," I say, not even considering lying. Why fight the truth? It's always there no matter what.

Adrian doesn't look like he's taking the pleasure in it that I thought he would. Instead he sighs and asks, "Are you going to seat me?"

"That's what the hostess is for" is my reply when really what I'm wondering is why he's back. I doubt he usually spends his evenings in diners, yet he's been here numerous nights now.

"I'd rather have you."

The way he says it shows he doesn't mean being seated. I know what it is—that he's trying to make me uncomfortable or to play some kind of sexual game with me. I'm not interested in games. He wouldn't be either if he knew the truth.

"Excuse me, miss?" a customer asks, and I realize I'm clutching her napkins in my hand.

"I have work to do." Before the last word leaves my mouth, I'm already walking away. Out of the corner of my eye, I see Adrian get seated. He's in Lisa's section, which makes some of the tension ease from my muscles. I won't have to deal with him for at least two hours. *What am I thinking?* It's not like he's going to be here for that long anyway.

I stay busy for the next couple of hours. The whole time I'm distinctly aware of Adrian. That he's still here, that he's eating pancakes again. The way his finger plays on the top of the table as though he's writing something with an invisible pen. I think about his poem and if he wishes he was writing one. If that's something he does to deal with life. If he's always written or only since my father took away that little boy.

An anchor lands on my chest, weighing me down with a million tons of guilt—for what my father did and the fact that Adrian doesn't know.

We've slowed down slightly and I'm leaning against the counter, as though that will take the weight away. Lisa steps up beside me, nudging me with a smile and having no clue the storm of emotions twisting inside my head.

"He a friend of yours?" she asks.

"No" pops out of my mouth. How can we be friends with so much between us? "I don't really know him."

"It's a shame. He's gorgeous."

And he really is. All his features are dark—dark hair and eyes and even a bronze shade to his skin. Darkness lingers in those eyes and the set of his jaw. One look at him and you can tell he walks around with a bruised soul.

"Looks like he'd be a good time."

Her words make me wonder if she doesn't see what I do when I look at him. Maybe it's like those ghosts he said he sees in my eyes. We're bound together by this tragedy and even though he doesn't know it, he still sees that thread tying us together.

"Hello? Earth to Delaney?" She snaps her fingers and I look at her.

"Sorry. I guess I'm still a little shaken up from last night."

"I know, right? I can't believe you guys got robbed. What's worse is that we're open the very next day and there's not even any security here." At least Hugo's the cook tonight. It feels good having a guy around.

"Are you out of here?" I ask her.

We keep a second waitress until 1:00 a.m. tonight. After that, it's just me.

"I am. Have a good night!" she says, and then Lisa is gone, the hostess, too, leaving Hugo and me.

Glancing at Adrian's table, I decide I should check on him. It's my job, after all. My feet feel like they're made of lead as I make my way to the table.

His plate is cleared away by now, leaving only a cup of coffee in front of him.

"Need a refill?" I ask and then realize I'm an idiot and left the carafe behind the counter.

"From your invisible pot?" A small smile tugs at his lips.

I cross my arms. "I didn't plan to come over here and stopped on my way."

"Sure." He shrugs, surprising me. I expected something more, so I'm a little taken off guard.

"Oh...okay. I'll be right back."

I grab the carafe and then head back to his table, filling his empty cup. I'm about to walk away when the question I try to bite back climbs from my mouth. "What are you doing here, Adrian?"

His name strikes me for a second. This is Adrian. I've known his name for four years. My father killed a member of his family and now he's sitting in front of me and his name is rolling off my lips. It's strange and confusing and something I thought was a good thing, but then… why haven't I told him? Why are we playing this back-and-forth game while I'm wearing this façade he knows nothing about?

"Now? I'm drinking coffee. Earlier I was eating pancakes. Have you ever had the pancakes here?"

I don't know why his words make me smile. "I'm serious."

He takes a drink of his coffee and I cringe. Yuck. He drinks it black with no sugar. Finally, he replies, "Trying to get in your pants."

I know that's partially true. He's a guy and I'm a girl and he's made it obvious what he wants, but there's more to it. It turns me inside out, amps up the guilt until I feel like it's frying my heart—I know he's also here because in his way, he's keeping me safe. I'm not stupid enough to believe it's me specifically. I'm just a girl he tried to hit on, who he ran into again and later happened to be in the right place at the right time.

And now…well, maybe he's a good guy. My brother would do something like this. He'd never admit it, but I could see him sitting in a restaurant keeping vigil for a girl. Thinking that it was somehow his job to keep her safe. Or to make her feel safe, even if she didn't want to admit her fear.

"Thank you," I tell him.

And when he studies me, looks at me like he's working out a puzzle in his mind, I know that he understands what I'm saying. That he realizes I know what he's doing too.

"You better get back to work." Adrian nods and I look over my shoulder to see Hugo standing in the kitchen doorway watching.

Without another word, I top off his cup again and walk away.

All night my eyes find him. As I'm helping customers or serving food or filling up saltshakers. As people come and go, I'm always aware of Adrian. He pulls out his notebook and writes sometimes. Pulls out his book and reads. Every time I walk to the table, he'll cover whatever he's doing. I wonder if it's the same book or if he moved on to something else. If reading is something he does often or if he's passing hour after hour with whatever he can find.

He stopped drinking coffee for a while and ordered a piece of apple pie. Around four he asked for another cup and I wonder if he's getting tired again. I should probably tell him he can go. The words play on my tongue, but I never let them free. I like watching him, trying to figure out who he is, because I've wondered for so long.

Hugo asked who he was and I lied and said a friend of my brother's. That Maddox was nervous because of what happened last night, and he seemed to take that as a good excuse.

Hugo also falls asleep between customers, so I guess he figures Adrian being here lets him off the hook.

With each minute that ticks by, I tell myself we need to talk. That I should tell him who I am. That's what I came here to do, so why not just get it done? But I can't really do that while I'm working, and anyway, I'm not sure if I should. I doubt he'll keep coming here and I can always go home and never see him again.

The thought of going home sits heavy in my stomach and I want to stick my finger down my throat as though purging will make it all go away.

When six rolls around, my relief comes. When we're done going over the night, I go to the back to grab my purse, and when I come out, Adrian's gone. Disappointment rolls through me. When I go outside, I see him leaning against a car. I should walk away. Or walk to him and tell him everything, but I know I won't. Not the telling him part at least. It's as though the words are trapped inside me.

Maddox might have been right. What if it is the wrong thing to do and I dredge up something he's found a way to put behind him? How can I risk hurting him on the off chance that karma will work in favor of my family?

"Hey." I look at the ground. Kick a pebble, nervous to meet his eyes.

"Hey."

"I thought you left."

"Nope." There's a hint of humor in his voice that makes me look up. He doesn't look away from me when he continues. "How am I supposed to get in your pants if I leave before you get off?"

I'm slightly disgusted, but there's another part of me that blushes. Who feels tingly at the thought of him being where he wants to be. "Do you get a lot of girls that way?"

Adrian shrugs. "At least I'm honest."

I shake my head. "I guess there's that..."

He steps toward me and I know I should walk away. *Back up!* I tell myself, but my feet refuse to move.

"I can see you're still skeptical." His voice is low... seductive. "Here...let me try something."

It's as though he has me in a trance, hypnotized the ghosts I didn't know about until him. I nod as Adrian puts a finger under my chin and tilts my head up.

"Your lips are so sexy," he says as he rubs his thumb over the bottom one. His mouth comes down much slower than the first time, like he's trying to keep me in suspense. I've never been so excited to find out where a story was going until this moment.

He starts the kiss out slowly, brushing his lips against mine. His tongue slips inside, pulls back out like he's teasing me, playing a game of hide-and-seek, and I suddenly want to find him.

He pushes a hand through my hair and he's still tilting my head back as his mouth comes down harder on mine. He's really exploring now, and he tastes like coffee as I swallow the little moan that fights to climb up my throat.

This is wrong. So wrong. I have no right to enjoy this. No right to want it, but as his mouth moves against mine and his other hand goes to the small of my back, easing me against him, I don't remember ever wanting anything more. Needing anything more.

God, I used to be such a romantic. All the girls at school with boyfriends and I imagined someone swooping in and taking me away from the hell my life had become. That person isn't Adrian. He's living in hell, too, but when he's kissing me, I can almost pretend.

His mouth slides down my neck and it doesn't matter that we're standing in the middle of a parking lot. I can almost forget that I'm me and he's him and that it's not okay to let this invisible thread tie us together even more tightly.

When he gets to my ear, I jump when his teeth bite gently into my lobe. "Come home with me, Casper."

I put my hand on his chest, feel his heart beat against my hand. "I can't..."

"Then let me go home with you. I want you."

I shake my head and make myself take a step backward. "I *can't*." I send up a silent prayer that he hears it in my voice. Not that I don't want to, even though it would be scary as hell. Not that I wouldn't like to be swept away if only for a night, but I really can't. It's not right. I know in his way he wants to use me as a distraction to the pain he's feeling. For a split second I consider doing the same thing. Maybe forgetting would help us both, but I can't.

"Are you sure? I won't ask again," he says.

No. "Yes."

Adrian pulls away. I want to knot my hands in his shirt and tug him back to me. Tell him everything and see if it chases our ghosts away.

"I'll see you later." He gets in his car and I notice the window is down. He looks nonchalant, as though it doesn't matter at all that I turned him down. Maybe it doesn't.

"Where are you going?" I ask, not really sure why since it's not my business.

"I've been up all night, so I'll probably go home, smoke a joint, and go to bed."

"You shouldn't smoke like that. Or at least not tell the whole world. You don't know me."

He grabs a pair of sunglasses off the visor and puts them on before looking at me. "It's who I am."

Adrian starts the car, and I blurt out, "Are you a writer?" A tic forms in his jaw and I wonder if he's going to pull away. If I shouldn't have let myself ask him that.

Instead he says, "Do you want me to tell you a story?" He doesn't wait for me to reply before he starts talking again. "Once upon a time, there was a guy. Not a real good guy. Some would probably call him the villain. He didn't care, though. He knew it was true. Knew he used people and other shit to forget. He didn't plan on changing either. Knew he couldn't. That was who he was, so he might as well acknowledge it, right?"

"How did he know he couldn't change?" I ask, my heart chipping away, bit by bit, the pieces falling into oblivion.

Adrian pauses and I'm not sure he's going to answer. "Because," he finally says, "real life isn't made of happily-ever-afters."

As Adrian pulls away, I vow to do everything to make a liar out of him. To find a way for us to all have some kind of happily-ever-after, regardless of what we've been through. Maybe if I tell him, we'll all discover some sort of peace.

I feel like a stalker. I've never done something like this. Never found a roundabout way into someone's life, but I figure our chance at a little bit of peace is worth it.

Half of my day has been spent outside cleaning my car, the inside only because it's cold outside. Telling Maddox I'll take out the trash, check the mail. Whatever excuse I can come up with I use. If it's not that, I'm watching the window. I've seen Adrian's friends come and go, though I didn't realize who they were until he introduced us.

I'm hoping they'll be able to help me.

I'm hoping I run into only the girl.

See? I'm a total stalker.

It's for a good cause. It's for a good cause.

I'm taking a walk right now, bundled up in my jacket and gloves.

"A little cold for a walk, don't ya think?"

I jump, grab at my heart, and turn around. "Jesus, Maddy. You scared the crap out of me."

He's smoking a cigarette. I hate the habit and wish he wouldn't do it. I know our parents hate it, too, and wonder if that's why he started.

"I'm not ten anymore, Laney. You need to stop calling me that."

I choose to ignore those words. "What are you doing?"

"Looking for you. I'm about to head out."

It's on the tip of my tongue to ask him where he's going, but I don't think he'll answer me anyway. He's always been private, but even more so since everything went down.

As I'm about to tell him bye, I see her getting out of her car. She's really pretty and for a second a tiny bit of jealousy sneaks up on me. I wonder if she and Adrian have ever had anything, but then I think about the blond guy and how they looked at each other.

The same way my mom used to look at Dad, like he was the most important person in the world.

"I have to go." I try to walk around Maddox. I've been at this all day and there's no way I'm going to back out now.

"Wait. I—"

"I can't wait. I have to go. I'll call you in a little while." I pull my arm out of my brother's grasp and that's when he looks up and sees the girl. That quickly he knows. I've never been able to hide much from him. "What are you doing, Laney?" Concern weighs on his voice.

"Nothing. Just talking. It's not a big deal."

"Lane—"

"Don't. I have to go. I'll . . . It'll be okay. I'll talk to you later."

He curses but doesn't try to stop me as I jog away. Jog toward this girl—Cheyenne—to try to get information on Adrian.

She's almost to the building as I catch up with her. "Hey! Cheyenne!"

She turns and at first, I'm worried this was a bad idea. She looks like she wants to take me out, but then recognition lights in her eyes and she smiles at me. "Hi. You're Adrian's friend. What was your name again?"

When I reach her, I stop and return her smile. "Delaney. My brother and I just moved in here."

"*That's* who he is. I wondered after I saw you with Adrian. He's got half the girls in the building freaking out over him."

I shake my head. "That doesn't really surprise me."

"I'm sure it doesn't. So, what's up? I have a two o'clock class, but I'm meeting Colt for lunch real quick."

The way she smiles, I'm sure she's meeting him for more than that. Again that jealousy tries to creep in. I've never in my life had someone to meet for something like that.

"Oh. I don't want to keep you. It's just..." I can't believe I'm doing this. I feel like such an idiot. "Adrian... we kind of had a little disagreement earlier and... well, I want to see him, but I'm not sure I could find his house again, and—"

"Say no more," Cheyenne interrupts me. I'm surprised when she reaches out and touches my arms. "What are you doing tonight?"

Giddiness I have no business feeling builds inside me. *It's only because I want to help him. Because I want to help us both.*

"It's my night off," I tell her. "So I have no plans at all."

Cheyenne smiles and something about that smile tells me she likes getting her way. Not in a rude way, but a real one.

"You do now."

I do now.

Chapter Nine

~Adrian~

I don't try and sleep today. Know there's no way I could. When your mind starts cross-country running, there's too much in the brain for it to settle down. My hand still hurts, but not enough that I take anything. Nothing you can buy in the store at least.

I watch as the smoke floats around my living room and wonder what it would be like if it could really transport me away. Lift me up and not stop going until I'm gone all together.

"Fuck." Slouching, I lean back on my couch. I hate these thoughts. Hate living a lie between what's inside me and what I show to everyone else. I want the weed to help me like it used to.

I start to wonder what Casper's hiding. If it's dark inside her like it is me, but then I try to push those thoughts away.

A few hours later, there's no room in my brain to think of anything except the music beating in my veins.

The crowd of people in my house who will always come if they know there's a party, and I count on that. Count on the distraction I know they can provide for me.

I'm sitting around the kitchen table with people whose names I don't even know. Names I won't ask because they really don't matter, just like half of them probably don't even know it's my house they're partying in right now.

My fingers itch to write and my mind itches to be transported away, but instead I laugh and fucking talk and pretend to see the future when some chick tells me she heard I'm psychic. What a joke.

"I need a drink." Pushing up from the table, I head to the fridge. My hand touches a bottle of beer, but then I glance at my cell before I grab it. It's after ten. Delaney's at work by now and I think about the fact that in about three hours she'll be there with no one out front if something goes down.

Closing the fridge, I lean against the counter. People go around me, through me, but all that's in my head is that I need to stop seeing that girl. She's not my problem and if she wants to work by herself at the same place someone held a gun to her head, it's not my business. There's one person in my life I really could have protected— Mom won't ever leave Dad, so there's nothing I can do about that. Angel got out the second she could. My sister was always stronger. She never needed me.

That left Ash and I let him die, so what the fuck do I think I'm doing pretending there's anything I can do for Delaney?

Hell, why do I want to?

"Hey, Adrian." I hardly get a chance to see who it is when the girl steps up to me.

"Hey, Trish." I smile at her. She's got dark skin and these sexy little braids that I've had my hands in more than once. "What took you so long to find me?" I ask.

She smiles, stepping right up next to me. "Maybe I was waiting to see if you'd come looking for me?"

And even though it should be all right, somehow this game feels wrong. It always has, but it's vibrating through me a little deeper than it usually does. An earthquake below the surface and I wonder if it will cause a tsunami to drown me. I'm so fucking tired of it all. I want to step back into the quiet of the diner where I can pretend to be someone else. "Sorry...I'm not really looking to hook up."

She frowns, but it looks more like confusion than annoyance and I know she catches my drift. I don't want to play tonight.

"Oh...okay." Trish still looks confused but doesn't say anything else. Or maybe she doesn't get a chance to, because Colt is pushing his way over to me. It's surprising as hell to see him here and I'm about to tell him when he speaks.

"What the fuck, man. I've been texting you all night. Answer your fucking phone once in a while."

"Miss me that much?" I tease him.

"No, though I guess your psychic ass should already know this, but..." He looks at Trish.

"Eh. I have better things to do than listen to you guys

gossip like a bunch of girls anyway." With that she walks away.

"Chey showed up with your girl today."

What? "My girl?" I ask. "I know I'm good, but not good enough to handle girls I don't know I have."

"You wish, man. Chey thinks she's playing matchmaker. Thought I'd try to warn ya."

I don't know what it is about those words that makes everything click into place. Before I have the chance to think about it much, Cheyenne and Delaney walk up to us. Her cheeks are pink and she doesn't really look at me. Questions start falling down on me, but I don't ask any of them. I'm in the mood to see what it looks like to watch that pink spread. I definitely didn't expect her to come searching me out and I'm not ready to let myself think about what that means either. She's not like Trish. She wouldn't walk away, not giving a shit the way Trish did.

And there's the fact that I still want her.

"If it isn't Casper the Friendly Ghost." I cross my arms and dare her to meet my eyes, which she surprisingly does quickly.

"Casper? What the hell's that?" Cheyenne says over the music.

My eyes don't waver from Delaney's. I'm daring her to look away. To give in first, but she doesn't. Her gaze is strong.

"The name's our little secret, isn't it, Casper?" Inside, I'm begging her to back down. To walk out of here, because the fact that I'm playing this little game with her, that I'm still wondering what she thought of the poem or if she believes in happy endings means she's gotten inside my head when I'm usually so good at keeping it on lockdown.

"You're totally trying to intimidate her. Colt, your friend's being a dick," Cheyenne says. Colt laughs.

"'Bout time someone other than me gets called that," he replies.

One of Delaney's eyebrows rises. Is she issuing me a challenge too? Can I take her up on it?

"He's not intimidating me," she says.

"I like her," Cheyenne jumps in.

"I like *you*," Colt says back to her. It's then I glance over to see her smile at him as he drags her away.

"Looks like it's just us." Pushing off the counter, I stand next to her.

"Yeah, us and the hundred other people in your house."

"Eh. You learn to block them out." She looks at me, like she's not sure what I said, so I lean closer to her. Put my mouth by her ear. "I said you learn to block them out."

She doesn't reply to that. Instead, Delaney turns to my ear and asks, "How's your hand?"

"I don't know. Do you want to check it for me?"

We're fucking close and she smells good. Apples and cinnamon.

"Sure...I want to help you."

Her answer's strange, but I don't let myself think about it. Don't let myself try and figure her out because I'm not sure I want the answers. Instead I nod and grab on to her shirt, right by her side. She jumps a little but doesn't struggle as I lead her through the mass of people in my place. She tries to stop at the bathroom, but I keep going. Lead her to my room, unlock the door, and close it behind us.

"I'm only checking on your hand," she says.

"That's all I asked you to do." I grab my first-aid kit off my dresser and sit on the bed. I glance at my pillow to make sure Ash's shirt isn't showing.

Delaney stands there, looking around. "Did you just move in?"

Through her eyes, I can see why she'd think that. I have a small bed, a table, and a dresser. There's one desk lamp on the table that I use at night and a few notebooks stacked on my dresser. Those are the only things in my room that are out in the open.

"No. My interior decorator's a little backed up."

Sadness creases her eyes when she looks at me. I hate that fucking look, but still I find myself saying, "My sister used to go to this field when she was younger. She brought me there once. All I could see was what looked like weeds to me. No flowers. Just weeds. Dead ones at that. I asked her why she came and she told me to keep following her, so I did. Right in the middle of the field was one tall flower. Almost like it came from fucking nowhere. I told her it was lonely. She said it was beautiful. That there was nothing wrong with being strong, alone."

I didn't agree with Angel then and I don't now. I'm not even sure why I told Delaney that. It doesn't really have anything to do with my room because there's nothing beautiful showing here. And I'm not strong in my loneliness.

"You really are a poet" is how she replies.

I shake my head. "That wasn't poetry. I don't know what it was. I'm fucked up. If you don't hurry and check my hand, I might pass out on you. Unless you think of a way to keep me awake…"

I can tell by the set of her jaw that I've disappointed her, but it doesn't matter. I'm used to it. It should be no different with her…and yet it is. I do care that I've let her down, but I don't know how to fix it, how to step out from behind the mask.

Delaney sighs and sits on the bed. She's so gentle as she takes my bandage off that I can't help but study her. People aren't usually careful with me. Dad wasn't careful when he beat my ass, unless you count being careful not to leave marks that could be seen.

Ash was the only one who was ever gentle. He used to get pissed if I'd kill a bug. We would bring spiders outside to set them free so he wouldn't cry.

I close my eyes, willing Ash out of my mind. I just want a break, some kind of fucking reprieve from myself and my past.

"All done," Delaney says. Somehow she'd inspected my hand and wrapped it again without my noticing. "The swelling's going down. It's starting to heal."

"Let's get out of here." I don't let myself think about the words.

She looks at my hand and bites her bottom lip.

"I thought you were going to pass out."

Got her. "Then I guess it's your job to keep me awake."

"What about all the people in your house?" Delaney asks as she follows me out.

"It doesn't matter if I'm here or not. They'll still have a good time." We get to the sidewalk and I hate it. Every time I stand out here, I remember pulling up and seeing Cheyenne and Colt on the ground. Thinking my best friend was going to die because I couldn't get him to the hospital in time. That he was going to die in front of me the same way Ashton did.

"Think fast." I toss my keys and Delaney catches them easily. "You gotta drive. I've been drinking."

"What about your friends?"

"I don't think they're drinking, but they're not out here or going with us."

I hear her chuckle. I can't see her too well despite the streetlight. It makes me wonder how she caught the keys so easily.

"That's not what I meant and you know it. Isn't it rude to leave them? And Cheyenne drove me. She'll wonder where I am."

"Colt'll know you're with me."

"But—"

"Why did you come here tonight, Casper?" I cut her off.

"To see you...I want to be your friend."

"And you've seen me. If you want to see me any more tonight, this is the way to do it. You can go home if you want. I don't blame you, but my thoughts are going to eat me alive if I stay in there right now."

That's never been the case before. It's always worked to put the pipe to my lips and inhale the smoke. To be around music and people so loud they drown out the voices in my head. Right now, I can't do it.

Delaney steps even farther into the dark toward the driver side of my car. "Which way am I going?"

We drive out to the middle of nowhere, up above town where you see the lights of the city. Not that there's a whole lot of city down there, but enough activity shines below to make it feel like I'm a hell of a lot farther away than I am.

Delaney kills the engine and I push the seat back so I'm practically lying down. Silence fills the space between us, half comfortable and half wanting to shove me out of the car.

"So you wanna be my friend, huh?" The laugh in my voice is hard to hide, not that I'm trying.

"Don't make it sound like that! There's nothing wrong with wanting to be friends with you."

"That's not what most women want from me."

"I'm not most girls."

I don't reply to that because I have a feeling she's right. More silence bears down on us. She takes a couple breaths and I feel the mood changing. "Listen, Adrian. I—"

"Are you in school?" I ask. I don't want to hear whatever she was going to say. Don't want to keep hearing her say that she doesn't want me or whatever the hell else she planned to tell me. Tonight, it doesn't really matter or not if I get to feel her beneath me. If I don't get to taste her, because right now, I just want to fucking talk. "Talk to me, Casper. You said you want to be my friend. I'm asking you to talk to me."

And maybe I'm manipulating her in a way, too, throwing that back at her, but I can't make myself stop.

I hear her breathe. It's sexy as hell and for a minute I pretend I really do get to touch her. Kiss her lips and take off her shirt and explore every inch of her with my mouth. It would be an even better way to lose myself than talking.

"No...I'm not in school. Just the job."

"Why not? You're not into college?"

"I definitely want to go. It's just not something I'm able to do right now. My brother Maddox and I...we have a lot we're dealing with."

Without seeing her eyes, I know that's part of what haunts her. I want to ask but know there's no way in hell I'm telling her about myself, so I don't.

"What about you?" she asks. "You don't want to be a writer, or whatever?"

I remember being younger, burying myself in books and school to take me away from everything else. I used to fucking pretend I lived in the stories. Or I was one of those characters with enough balls to do something about my life. I used to dream about being Edmond from *The Count* and how I would make it through all the shit life threw at me and come out of it better. "Life doesn't work like dreams…"

"What?" she asks.

"I said, nah. No college for me. Cheyenne goes. Colt too."

"Is that how they met?" she asks.

So I tell her. Tell her how Colt used to live with me and about how his mom was dying. How he met Cheyenne and they wanted nothing to do with each other at first, but how they both found a way to make things better for each other. How that led to them making things better for themselves.

I even tell her about Colt getting hurt and how Cheyenne stayed by his side the whole time.

"And you," she says when I'm finished.

"And me, what?"

"You were there too…"

I shrug, because it doesn't really matter. It's not like I did much. "What about you? Where are you from? Why'd you move here?"

She gasps and I know I hit a nerve. It almost makes me snatch the question back, but instead I turn to look at her, watch her face, as so many expressions play across her feminine features.

She's really fucking beautiful.

"I'm from Stanley."

About an hour from where I grew up. "And why did you move here?"

Delaney pauses. "My mom tried to commit suicide," she finally says. Her voice is the softest I've heard it.

"Shit...I'm sorry."

"It's not the first time. I'm hoping it'll be the last. I just...Have you ever wanted to believe you could make it better? That you have the power to fix so many people's lives, so you set out on this path and then you're not so sure? Don't know if you're doing the right thing, but you're already on the path to making it happen, so you have to find a way to see it through?"

Delaney turns her head and looks at me. Her eyes are wet and I feel like shit for bringing all this up. "No," I tell her. "Absolutely not."

She laughs and I realize that's what I wanted. That I'd hoped she would find humor in my semitruth. "I mean, I *know* I'm just going to fuck it up."

"No!" She covers her face with her hands, but I can hear the giggle behind it. It's a mixture of a real laugh, laced with seriousness.

The moon is bright, giving us unexpected light. When she pulls her hands away and looks at me with those haunted-house eyes, and I see that sexy little mole on her face and her pink tongue sneaks out and licks her plump lips, blood surges through my body. Heat comes alive beneath my skin and I know I'm going to try to kiss her.

I lean closer. Put my hand on her cheek.

"Adrian..."

"Shhh. It's okay. I just want to taste you again."

I pull her toward me and I don't have to pull very hard before my mouth is on hers. She somehow tastes like apples, too, and I suck her lip, bite it gently, and let her explore my mouth.

In two seconds flat I'm hard. I want nothing more than to bury myself inside her. To lose myself in all that sweetness.

"Can I touch you?" I ask her. "That's all. I promise."

"We shouldn't... This isn't what I came here for. God, it's just..."

I feel like shit because she moved here to try and deal with her mom's issues. Or maybe she ran like I did, but it doesn't stop me from wanting her. From seeing that same need reflected in her, but there's more there too. That's what scares me. She's attractive and a distraction, but she's intriguing too. I think of the way she cared for my hand and the fact that I keep opening up to her. It makes me unsure if I want to keep going or get out of the car right now.

I've never claimed to be strong, though, so instead of walking away, I ask, "Do you want me to touch you? Don't think about anything else. Just tell me if you want it."

Slowly, she nods.

"Then take it. Take what you want." I have a feeling she doesn't do much for herself.

This time, it's her lips that come down on mine. Not wasting any time, I palm one of her breasts. "I can't feel nearly enough with your jacket on. Turn the car on."

She does and I turn up the heater before I unzip her jacket. She eases out of it and for the first time, I thank God for good luck because she's wearing a button-up shirt.

"I want to see you," I tell her as I push one, two, three

buttons from their holes. When she doesn't stop me, I keep going until her shirt is open, and a pink lace bra cups her breasts.

"You're so pretty," I say as I trace the swells of each breast with my finger. Watch as goose bumps follow the same path.

She's breathing hard, and shaking a little. "And you're good at this."

"I'm just getting started." Soon it's my tongue tracing the same path my finger did. I unhook her bra and watch her breasts spill free, before my tongue tastes each pert tip. We spend the rest of the night alternating between kissing and talking. Turning the car off and on. We end up in the backseat but don't talk about anything important. I spend a lot more time with lips taking voyages over her body, traveling her land. Somehow I know if I go for her pants, she's going to stop me, so I don't.

Tonight, this is enough. It's been a long time since I've done nothing but make out with a girl. When I went to live with Angel at fifteen, I was free for the first time in my life. Away from my dad and finally living, so I went wild for a while. I did a lot during that time, messed around with a lot of girls, but none of it felt as good as it had just kissing her tonight.

"I've never watched the sun come up." She stares out at the pinks and oranges looking like watercolors in the sky.

"You work graveyard."

"I didn't say I've never seen it. I said I've never watched it. There's a difference."

Maybe, just maybe, she might be right. "Then we'll watch."

It only takes a few minutes for the sun to come up and we don't talk or touch the whole time. Soon I'm driving her home. Colt and Cheyenne's car is here. I wouldn't be surprised if they went home right after we separated.

"You're up all night again because of me." There's laughter in her voice. I consider kissing her good-bye, but I don't.

"Doesn't matter. Sleep in the daytime or at night is all the same. It's still sleep."

"Yeah, I guess." She pauses. "Am I going to see you again? I don't mean that in a clingy way. I know what this is, but . . ."

"You said you wanted to be friends, right?" It's the only way that I have to say yes.

"Sure . . . friends."

Delaney gets out of the car. I wait as she walks toward the apartment, but then she stops and looks back at me. "I don't know if it matters, but I don't work tonight."

And then she's gone and I sit there, trying to figure out if it does matter, and I think it might.

Chapter Ten

~Delaney~

"Mom?" I walk into the house after school. Fear clings to my spine at the mess inside. The pictures that have been ripped off the walls. The faces torn out. Photo albums strewn around the room.

Bump, bump, bump, bump.

The drum of my heart almost rivals the music, Simon & Garfunkel, that's blasting through the room. She and Dad used to sing them all the time. Loved the song "The Boxer," but I don't get the same feeling as I used to when I hear it. Now when I do, I know she's thinking about him.

"Mom?" I say again, hoping she'll come out. Hoping that even if her face is tear-stained or she's still wearing the same clothes she had on yesterday that she'll come out. It's only when she doesn't want to leave the room that I know the depression has its claws in her again. That it's pulling her so far under that Maddox will stop leaving her alone with me again, taking up as my savior and bodyguard.

He's not here.

She's not coming out.

I let my backpack drop to the floor and leave the door open as I take slow steps toward the hallway.

This house is so much smaller than our old one, so it's only about twenty steps later that I'm at her bedroom door. "Mom?" My voice shakes. Even if she is here, she probably can't hear me over the roar of the music.

I peek inside. It's empty.

Two more doors stand closed in the narrow hallway, mine and the bathroom. Maddox sleeps on the couch. Knowing she's not in there, I still check my room first before turning to the bathroom.

It's okay. She'll be okay. I don't have to be scared to go in.

Only I know it's not okay and there's no way to stop being scared, but still I push the cracked door open.

"Oh my God! Mom!" My foot slips in the blood running down her arms and making a pool on the tiny bathroom floor.

"Mom!" She's on the ground, her head to the side, lying on the tub. One arm over it and the other limp to her side, and her eyes are closed.

There's no focusing on my heart or my breathing or the fact that she did this right before I came home. Knowing Maddy would be at work and I'd be the one to find her. Not that I'd want my brother to find her either, but I know she did this for me.

I grab towels from the rack, fighting my hands to stay steady enough to try and wrap her wrists. "I'll be right back, Mom. It'll be okay."

Running from the room, I rush to my neighbor's house and bang on the door. When she doesn't answer right away, I push it open to see her walking my way. "Call nine-one-one. My mom is dying!"

And then I'm gone. Running back to her. I'm holding her head on my lap and sitting in blood. Petting her hair and trying to hold the towels around her wrists. Even though she tried to leave us. Even though it didn't matter that I'd walk in and find her this way. I won't let her be alone. Won't let her die alone . . .

Later she rolls over in the hospital bed and looks at me for the first time. It's hard as a diamond and cuts me deeply. "Why did you save me? You want me to suffer, don't you? First you tried to take your father away from me and now my peace. I'll never forgive you for saving me, Delaney." And still I don't leave her.

"Laney, wake up. Wake the fuck up!"

My brother's voice and the hand shaking me breaks my sleep, makes me jerk into a sitting position. I don't need him to tell me I was crying in my sleep. Even if I didn't feel the wetness on my face, I would know. I sit up and lean against the wall, pulling my knees to my chest and wrapping my arms around them.

"Shit," Maddox says, before he climbs into my bed and sits beside me. "Why do you let it get to you, Laney? Why can't you let it go? They obviously didn't care about us."

I put my head on his shoulder. "Why do you think she let me find her? I mean, why not do it in the early morning after we left? Do you think she wanted to punish me for the close relationship I had with Daddy?"

"Don't do that. Don't try and make sense of it or blame yourself. She had nothing to blame you for."

"You blame yourself."

He doesn't answer that.

His voice is soft when he says, "It was about the time in the bathroom?" I nod and he continues. "You shouldn't have been alone. I can't believe she did that knowing you'd find her."

"Would it have been better if you did? It wouldn't have changed anything."

He's quiet for what feels like an eternity. "It would have changed you seeing it. Would have kept you from still seeing it all these years later."

I grab his arm and hold it tight. "You have enough demons inside you. Seeing her would have given you more. I don't want that for you."

Maddox curses again and I know he's about to shut down on me. "I gotta get ready for work," he says, standing up. "Do me a favor and let me know if you're going to be out all night again on a day off."

"The way you'd tell me?" I taunt.

He runs a hand through his dark hair. "Did you tell him yet? Things don't seem magically better." There's a sharp edge to his voice.

"Don't be a jerk."

"Why? You need me to wake you the hell up. You think you're going to go to this guy and tell him your drunk dad, who was a lying bastard with a shitload of gambling debts, drove up a curb with his car and killed his nephew and he's going to tell you it's okay? And it'll make Mom somehow wake the fuck up and everything look like it's perfect? I have news for you, Laney. It never was perfect and it never will be." The venom in his voice isn't really directed at me. I know that, but it still pisses me off.

"What?" I stand up too. "It would be better to walk around pissed at the world? To try and pretend I 'let it go' when I haven't? I have news for *you*, Maddy—you haven't let anything go. You're drowning in it even worse than I am. Almost as bad as she is!"

That last line is like a slap to his face. I see the hurt, the sting. See him bite back his anger because no matter how upset Maddox is, he would never really let himself take it out on me. But still…when he and Dad stopped being close, he got closer to Mom. He took care of her and I know his anger at her has clouded that. I know that what I said hurt him.

"Fuck. You." I reach for him, but he jerks his arm away. "It must be nice living in a fantasy world, little sister. Not all of us have that liberty."

Maddox slams my bedroom door behind him. I hear the front door do the same a few seconds later.

I hate that he's probably right. That I'm just deluding myself and that I had the perfect opportunity to tell Adrian last night, but I let it slip through my fingers. Or maybe *let* isn't the right word. I think I wanted it to, which makes me a shitty person. I let him kiss me and talk to me and the whole time this secret is rotting away inside me. Something he deserves to know. Something that if he did know would have probably kept him from touching me.

A touch I enjoyed way too much.

I used to run. It wasn't something I started until after everything went down with my dad, but it somehow helped me through it. I think I imagined I could somehow find a way to run away from it all. Or maybe not even away. Maybe I could run so fast, so far, and so long that I could make it to the past and stop everything from exploding before it did.

I could ask Dad what was wrong when he had long days at work or not want the best clothes or cell phones when I was too young because all those things were just one more thing to pay for. One more thing to stress him.

Eventually I stopped running. I don't know why. It

could have been because I knew I'd never get anywhere or maybe it was because I thought it would help to finally stop running. Whatever the reason, I don't do it anymore.

After hours of hanging around the house, I'm still so upset about my argument with Maddox that I need to run.

There's no doubt I'll regret it the second I step into the cold weather, but still I push running shoes onto my feet and gloves on my hands. I grab my brother's beanie and a pair of earmuffs and I'm outside where the frigid wind bites my face.

My leg muscles start to ache in about two seconds, but it doesn't stop me from keeping pace. I try to run from my truth with Adrian. The fact that there's something about him that tugs at me, but I know I need to sever that pull. I need to stand up and confess our past and see if there's some way we can work through this. Find a way to heal.

You see stuff like that all the time—where people from the same tragedy heal through each other. It could happen. We deserve that.

My mind runs to Maddox next. How much pain he's in and how mad he makes me and how I wish I understood the extra shadows living inside him. Why he handles our past so much differently than I do.

By the time I make it back around to the front of the apartment complex, my chest aches and plumes of steam puff out of my mouth with each breath.

"You should dance. It's a good way to exercise and you can do it inside, where it's warm."

I jump at the sound of Cheyenne's voice. "Shit. You scared the hell out of me."

Cheyenne laughs. "Sorry. You must have been out there. I figured you heard me walk up."

It's something I probably should have heard but wasn't really paying attention. Since darkness is making its descent across the sky, it wasn't very smart of me either.

"It's been a long day. There's a lot going on."

"I hear ya. Colt had a doctor's appointment today and those always freak me out. He's out right now. I was planning on having a drink. Wanna come up?" she asks me.

I want to, even though I shouldn't do it. Shouldn't push my way into Adrian's life any more than I already have, but I like her. She's cool, and God, what I wouldn't give to have a friend around here. I miss having friends. Back home everyone knew who I was and what had happened, which made it difficult.

I guess it wouldn't hurt to hang out if I don't talk about Adrian.

"Sure," I tell her. "Which apartment are you in? I want to run home and clean up real quick." I hate admitting the giddiness inside me. I'm eighteen years old. This is what my life is supposed to be. Hanging out with friends instead of dealing with a suicidal mom and a brother who might be losing himself too.

Cheyenne gives me her apartment number and I tell her I'll be there soon. After jumping into a quick shower, I change into a pair of jeans and a sweater. I run a brush through my hair and leave it hanging free before picking up my cell phone. There's a text from Maddox telling me he won't be home tonight. That he's "out," whatever that means. I hate it when he gets pissed and disappears.

Pushing those thoughts aside, I put my shoes on before heading over to Cheyenne's. A girls' night is exactly what I need.

I'm holding my third drink, watching the grains of salt drift from the top of my glass and into my margarita.

"Hehehe. I think my salt is having a race," I say, and then Cheyenne laughs.

"Oh my God. That's the funniest thing I've ever heard. I wonder whose salt would win in a race, mine or yours?"

At that we both start laughing. She's sitting on the bed in the small studio apartment she shares with Colt. I'm at the table, which hardly has enough room for the two chairs sitting at it.

But I love it. Their apartment is perfect because you can tell how happy they are in it. There's pictures on the walls and Colt's clothes mixed with hers in a basket and it's so perfect I want to cry. I know for a fact how things can *look* perfect but not really be that way. Somehow I know that's not the case here. Or maybe I only want to believe it.

"How long have you and Colt been together?" I ask her.

She gets that dreamy look in her eyes and my heart flutters for them.

"Honestly, we haven't been together very long. Just since the beginning of the school year, but it doesn't feel like it." She sets her cup down and pulls her legs up under her. "I'm still working on this talking thing..."

It takes her a few minutes, and I give them to her. Understand what she's going through because though I've never been one who has a hard time saying how I feel, I have experience with people who do.

"I wasn't really in a good place when I met him. Colt wasn't either. We didn't plan to fall in love, but—"

"I think that's maybe the best kind of love. I'm sorry. I didn't mean to interrupt you."

She gives me a kind smile. "What do you mean?"

I don't let myself think before I speak. "I think falling in love by accident is special. I remember my mom telling me when she met my dad that she knew he would be hers. I used to think that was kind of romantic, but... that turned out horribly. I think when love sneaks up on you, when it grabs on to you when you least expect it, maybe that's more of a sign it's real. That it's meant to be and nothing could stop the two of you from falling for each other."

I'm drifting away, looking at a picture of Cheyenne and Colt sitting on their bedside table. He's not looking at her. He's staring off into the distance and Cheyenne's behind him. Her head against his shoulder blade and I swear I feel it between them. Feel the connection welding them together.

"I think maybe you're right." I hear the smile in her voice. "He's helped me through a lot. I don't know if

I would have made it without him. The cool thing is, and this might make me sound a little conceited, but I don't care because it's true. I know I do the same for him. Things aren't always easy, but I know in here"—she touches her chest—"that we belong together."

I take a drink, trying to give myself a little bit of space from the mood that's turned slightly somber, but also full of hope. I want that hope. Want it to spread from Cheyenne's life and into my own.

"What about you? Have you ever been in love?" she asks.

Automatically, I shake my head. That's an easy one. "No." My mind then turns to what Cheyenne said. About not being able to talk and I want to do that. I want to open my mouth and tell her everything. I've never really done that—just spilled my secrets for someone to dissect. But I know I can't. I can't tell her before I tell Adrian. I don't even know if she knows his past. That his nephew was killed and that he ran from his family afterward.

"Okay, seriously, we're getting all mopey. I hate girls who get drunk and depressed. We're supposed to be having fun," she says.

At that I smile. I really like this girl. "You're right. I have a question for you..." I swore to myself I wouldn't ask her about Adrian, but after the drinks, I can't help it. I want to hear something, anything to get to know him, but then the door pushes open and Colt comes in. Man, he's incredibly sexy with his messy blond hair and this cocky edge about him.

"Hey, you!" Cheyenne leaps off the bed and jumps

into his arms. He catches her and her legs wrap around his waist.

"Hey, Tiny Dancer." And then he laughs. "You're drunk as fuck, aren't you?"

She giggles a yes and then my breath backs up into my lungs when Adrian steps into the doorway behind them. His eyes are tinged red, and I take in his strong jaw and his dark hair. Holy crap is he sexy too. My heart starts to race and I silently beg it to take a breather.

When his eyes find me, he grins. There's a storm in his gaze that I feel rain down on me. Adrian puts his arm on the opposite side of the doorway. "Well, what do we have here?"

His voice is sexy, which I know he's doing on purpose, but the alcohol invites it in, lets it seep through me and into me, warm and inviting, before it drags my memory to his kisses.

Kisses I can't let happen again.

Maybe this is a good thing, fate that he showed up here when I have liquor to give me a loose tongue.

Tonight, I tell myself. Tonight will be the perfect time to tell him.

Chapter Eleven

~Adrian~

It's cold! Close the door!" Cheyenne says, her head hanging over Colt's shoulder as she looks at me. It's the first time I've taken my eyes off Delaney. I definitely didn't expect to see her when I walked in. Now I'm wishing I didn't get high as hell before I came.

I look back at her and she's still giving me the same sexy, flirty little look that I don't think she realizes is on her face. She's gorgeous as hell. I'm pretty sure she's not one of those girls who's hot and pretends not to know it, but she also doesn't strike me as the real flirty type. There's this air of innocence dancing around her that should make me turn away, but instead it intrigues me.

I don't hang around many innocent girls.

"Adrian! Stop staring at Laney and close the door before I kick your ass," Cheyenne shouts at me again. Colt's laughing and walking over to the bed with her in his arms. I shut the door.

I don't say anything about staring because we all know I was doing it, so instead I look at her. "Laney, huh?"

"Yes. Her name is awesome, but it's long." Like hers isn't.

"It's okay." Casper shrugs. "Most people call me Laney."

"I don't call you Laney," I say, because I know she won't expect it and won't have an answer.

"Why do you do that? You're always trying to fluster me."

Her ghosts are hidden right now, her eyes glassy portals to her soul. "You're drunk too. Were you guys having a party without us?"

"When did you ever need anyone to wait for you?" Colt's got Cheyenne on his lap now, his hand on her hip.

"You're right. Where's the booze?" I stand up and walk over to the kitchen, which is obviously in the same room we're already in.

"You don't need any alcohol. You're always drinking or smoking something." Cheyenne watches him.

"I forgot how that was your business," I reply at the same time that Colt whispers to her, "Hey. Don't."

"Why? He's my friend now, too, remember?"

She's right on that fact. We are friends.

Colt keeps his eyes on her, though. "Okay, fine. Have a drink. And get me another one while you're at it," Cheyenne adds.

I look at her and wink. "Stop trying to get me all liquored up."

Everyone laughs as if on cue and I want to make a comment about it but don't. I'm still shocked to come in and find Delaney with Cheyenne. I know they came to my party, but this feels different. If she's friends with Chey, that means I'll see more of her...

"Did you get any sleep today?" Delaney asks me.

"A little. I do some work with a mechanic friend of mine and I had to help him out." I'm sure everyone wonders where my money comes from. The mechanic thing they know about, but I don't really talk about Lettie.

She gets that womanly look on her face. The one that says she's concerned or worried when really it's not that big a deal at all. She doesn't know me well enough to be concerned anyway. I don't deserve her concern and I definitely don't want it.

"Be careful. You look at me like that and I'm liable to think you like me."

"I thought we were friends? Doesn't that automatically mean I like you?" she tosses back at me.

"No." I lean closer. "I mean really like me. You do, don't you? I see it in your eyes. You want me." I watch as pink starts at her hairline and then makes the descent down her face. I want to make the same journey down her body, covering and tasting every part of her along the way.

"You're such a player. Do you ever stop?"

At that, Cheyenne jumps in. I'd almost forgotten they were here. "He's horrible! I'm always telling him that. Though usually—" When I give her a dirty look, she cuts off. "Not to say I think he's just using you," Chey tries to cover.

"Smooth move," Colt tells her.

"Don't worry about it. It's not as if it's some big secret." One of Casper's eyebrows lifts as though she's daring me. Like she wants me to make a liar out of her. Little does she know I'm the biggest liar of them all.

When I say nothing, the expression on Casper's face changes. It's the way I wonder if people think I'm looking at them...as if she's trying to figure me out. Like I'm words on a paper she needs to decode. The need in her sets my desire aflame. I don't remember ever wanting a girl as much as I want this girl sitting in front of me.

"Do you wanna get out of here?" She uses almost the same words on me as I used on her last night. Only she's asking, like there's any fucking chance I'm going to tell her no.

Pushing to my feet, I glance at Colt and Cheyenne. Before I can say anything, Colt looks at me all cocky like he has some shit on me he's about to spill. "I thought you had people going to your house tonight. You can't hang out long, ya fucking liar."

I know exactly what he's doing. Not long ago we sat around my kitchen table and I told him he was different with Cheyenne. I can see it in his face. This isn't like that, though. I just want her, and that's all...isn't it? That's all it's supposed to be and she knows that. "Maybe I have something better to do now."

"I hope you're not talking about me?" Casper says with a smile on her face. I didn't expect that one.

"Oh my God! I love this girl. That totally sounds like something I would say," Cheyenne adds, and I think she's right.

"Are we leaving or what?" I ask before they can break into girl time.

"We're leaving. Thanks for inviting me over, Cheyenne." Her eyes wander over to Chey, who gets off Colt's lap to hug her.

"Have fun. Be good," she tells Casper before turning to hug me too. It catches me slightly off guard. "Be happy," she whispers in my ear.

Happy. I pull back and look at her, really look and know she sees more than I show. It's not as if I'm perfect at hiding it, but most people don't take the chance to look. Colt knows something's up with me, but he'd never say anything. We're just not like that, but she's different.

"I can't," I say before pulling away. Delaney is putting her shoes on, so I know she didn't hear, but I feel Colt's eyes on me. I know he heard, so without looking back, I head for the door, open it, and wait for Delaney to walk out.

"Where are we going?" I ask her when we get outside.

She looks unsure when she asks, "Want to go back to my place? Just to hang out and talk or whatever? It's not...I don't..."

"We're good. I'm not going to jump you as soon as we get inside. Well...unless you want me to."

"Do most girls want you to?" she asks as we start walking.

Inside, I'm saying, *Fuck*, because the last thing I want

to do is talk about other girls when I'm with one, but then she speaks again. "I shouldn't have asked that. I don't know why I did."

For some reason, that makes me want to answer. There's something so real about her that opens me up. She's done it before and it scares the hell out of me that if I keep hanging around her, she'll do it again. "I'm not going to lie and pretend I've been an angel. There have been girls. There will be girls, but I also don't fuck around. I don't let anyone think there's something going on that's not there."

"How very noble of you." Her voice is bitter like a lemon, but also with a little sugar sprinkled on top. She doesn't like it, but she doesn't hate me for it either.

"You asked and I was being honest. Haven't you ever just had a good time with someone?"

She stops in front of an apartment and unlocks the door. "Will I lose cool points if I say no?"

She's looking down at the key in the doorknob and not at me. It's then I realize she's serious. She's the girl who lost her virginity to someone she loved. I was fifteen years old, when I didn't know how to be a man. Christ, what the hell am I doing with this girl? "Maybe this isn't such a good idea." So much like her words a few minutes ago; mine taste like lemon.

"I thought we were friends? Just because I don't screw around with a lot of guys, we can't be friends?"

"I didn't say that, but you know I want you. That only makes things more . . . difficult."

Delaney sighs and I feel like an asshole.

"I am so lucky I've been drinking right now or I'd never say these things. First, I do want to be your friend, Adrian. I want that a lot. Things are...complicated for me, but I think we'd be good...as friends."

"But?" I step closer to her, thinking I know what she's going to say.

"But...I think after last night it's pretty obvious I'm attracted to you too. And while I'm not like the girls you pick up at parties, it doesn't mean you have to pretend I'm going to break or I'm not up to your standards."

With that she starts to open the door. I put my hand on hers, stopping her. She's soft and warm even though it's cold as hell out here. "Hey, I don't think you're not up to my standards."

"Thanks," she says, and I don't add that she's way better. That in a world full of people who are just as fake as me, there's something about her that feels so fucking genuine.

Delaney steps inside and I'm right behind her. "Your brother's not going to lose his shit, is he?" The door clicks closed behind me.

"He's not here. He won't be back all night. Plus, I'm an adult. He doesn't have a right to lose his shit."

"Doesn't mean he wouldn't."

"Are you hungry?" she asks instead of answering.

"Yeah, but I don't know if you can top the diner..."

She rolls her eyes. "You eat there because you don't work there. My pancakes are way better."

"Hmm." I step up to her while she's at the sink. "Care

to make a little wager?" One hand is on each side of her, flat on the counter as I box her in.

"No thank you. I'll just cook for myself if you don't want anything."

She shrugs and I bark out a laugh at that. I never know what to expect from her and I like it. "Fine. I'll help. Scoot over and I'll wash my hands."

Casper moves and I take off my jacket and toss it on the table. The kitchen's small, but that's okay. It keeps me closer to her.

As I'm washing my hands, she gets ingredients from the fridge and a box of pancake mix, before starting to read the directions.

"What the hell are you doing?" I ask her.

"Seeing how many eggs to use and how much water?" Her gray eyes crinkle at the corners. It's sexy as hell for some reason.

"Tell me you're shitting me. You have to be." I grab the box from her hand. "Grab a bowl for me, would ya, Chef?" A smirk peeks through. She grabs a bowl but doesn't let go when I reach for it.

"Do you want me to show you how it's done, or what?"

"You're being different," she says.

And I am. I know it. I think I might want to keep on pretending for the next little while, so I pull the bowl out of her hand without replying. "The secret to the perfect pancakes is not giving a shit what the box says. Stand back while the master shows you how it's done."

I show her my secret pancake recipe, flipping them perfectly, and then we pile our plates and fill two glasses of milk, before she starts walking down the hall. I'm a little shocked, but I'm definitely not going to tell her I think we should stay in the kitchen.

I follow her into a bedroom and leave the door open, not really sure if she wants to be boxed in with me, but after setting her glass on the bedside table, she closes it.

Another thing I'm not going to complain about.

Her room is somehow exactly what I'd expect—everything matches. It's all purple and gray. "Can I sit on the bed?" I ask.

"Unless you want to sit on the floor."

"Wow. Tequila turns you into a smart-ass." My glass joins hers on the bedside table. Casper kicks out of her shoes and I do the same before we both sit on her bed. We're quiet the whole time we eat. I keep looking over at her. Studying the way her mouth moves when she chews and how her neck moves when she swallows. I watch her tongue peek out of her mouth to lick some syrup from her lip. Fuck, this girl turns me on. It has to be the innocence and the fact that she feels so impossible to get, but that doesn't make it easier to deal with.

"So?" I ask her when both our plates are clean.

"They were all right..."

"What the fuck ever."

She laughs and I pretend to push her before grabbing the plate from her hand. "I'll put the plate away from the pancakes you hated but ate all of."

She doesn't stop me while I walk into the kitchen and put our stuff away. It doesn't take long before I'm heading back to her room and she's sitting on the edge of her bed. Somehow the air in the room has completely changed in the thirty seconds it took me to walk to the kitchen and back.

I feel pulled to her. A little poem beneath my skin that's called by her rhythm, but I hold it back. Don't let my pencil try and etch the words because it feels too close.

"Can I ask you a question?" she asks.

I shrug. "Sure."

She tries to smile, but there's something fake about it, like she's changed her mind about asking me what she originally planned to.

"What do you like so much about pancakes?" she asks.

Her question shoots a bullet through my chest. BBs jetting out from the round and hitting every major organ inside me. She had me in her sights and didn't even know it. It's not the question she wanted to ask. It's supposed to be light, funny, but it brings back images of big brown eyes, looking up at me from the table. *"Cakes! Cakes! Cakes!"*

I see Ash's chubby hands clapping. His eyes so big and happy.

My vision blurs and I suddenly want a lungful of smoke to wipe it all away. "Do you mind?" I ask as I pull out my pipe.

"Kind of…"

I shove it back into my pocket. "They're fucking good. What's not to love about pancakes?" The words hurt to come out, like I'm screwing with Ash's memory by not telling her about the little boy who loved my pancakes.

"I have another one for you. What would you do if... if you knew something that could hurt someone else. Not physically I mean, but emotionally. Would you tell them?"

This question takes me by surprise and I have to think about it. I wonder what's going on in her life, but I won't ask.

It hurts so fucking bad to think about Ash. To miss my sister so much that I would do anything not to think about it. To be able to forget. "If they're doing fine without knowing, why screw with them?"

And now the time for talk is over. I want to forget about everything else, so I step toward her. I get so close that when I look down, I can see her pulse in the base of her throat. See it beat like crazy. I want to lick it. Hold my finger to it and count the beats just to feel connected to her. "What are we doing here, Casper? Are we gonna keep dancing around this?" Reaching out, I cup her cheek. Run my hand through her hair. "Are you going to let me stay, or do you want me to go?"

Please tell me to stay.

Chapter Twelve

~Delaney~

I asked. I asked and he said I shouldn't say anything. That it would be screwing with someone to tell them the truth, which in a way is exactly what Maddox said too.

"Your ghosts are back, Casper." His voice is low but somehow echoes through me. Fills me up until he's all I hear, or know, or think. Adrian's thumb brushes my face, right below my eye. "Let me help you forget about them. We can forget our ghosts together for one night."

A shiver jolts through me. I said before he was good, but *good* doesn't begin to describe him. Two voices are battling it out inside me: logic, who's telling me to make him leave. Or to tell him the truth. To do anything other than let him stay with me. It's telling me to be strong. That staying with Adrian is almost as bad as being like my mom. That I'm weak and giving in, but *God*, do I want to give in. I want to listen to that other voice, which tells me I—no, not even just me—*we* deserve to try and chase each other's ghosts away. Which is what I came here to do. To try and make things better.

It's a stretch. I know it, but my body buzzes to feel his hands on me. I want to feel his words, poetry on my skin, because those secret words he wrote were beautiful. And I want to see more. To know what other magic he hides inside him.

We've both had so many things taken from us that I think we deserve to give something back to each other. Whatever we can.

"Stay...," I whisper. I try to look away, but Adrian doesn't let me. The hand on my face gently holds it in place.

"I need to know how drunk you are right now."

"Kind of late to ask that, isn't it?" Fake laughter forces its way from my mouth.

"It's too late for a lot of things, but not that."

He's right. Adrian doesn't know it, but that's exactly what I need to hear. I think it's too late. Too late to walk away and too late to pretend there's not more to my reason for being around him. There's something about him that I don't want to deny. Something that speaks to me, *me*. When others feel like this foreign language I'm trying to work out, I somehow understand Adrian. Not all of him. I'm not that stupid. I also know it could all be in my head, but it feels real and I like him and it's too late to turn back.

I don't know if it was the food or our conversation, but when I speak, I know my words are true. "I couldn't be any more sober right now."

He gives me a small nod and walks over to the bedroom door, flipping the lock. Adrian drops to his knees in front of me, putting us at eye level. "I don't know what it is about you that makes me want you so fucking bad."

They might not be the words a girl longs to hear, but I cherish them. Because they're real and real is better than a pretty lie.

Adrian leans toward me, his body fitting between my legs. I think he's going to kiss me, but his tongue circles the hollow spot at the base of my throat. Tingles start in that spot and shoot through me.

"I could see your pulse and I wanted to taste it."

Before I have a chance to swoon over his words, his mouth comes down on mine. I expect it to be urgent, frenzied, but he takes his time, letting his tongue stroke my own. His hands move to my neck, push through my hair, and it's so soft that I want to cry, but it feels so good I almost can't help the moan that slips out. His bandages scrape against my skin, which makes my pulse skyrocket, to feel that small bit of rough in all of Adrian's softness. I wonder if that explains him. If he's made up of rough and soft, each giving and taking, unsure which will overcome.

"This shirt has to go," he says when his mouth pulls away from me. Adrian grabs each of my arms, his hands running up them as he tugs mine in the air before he starts to lift my shirt. There's a brief moment where I think I should be embarrassed. This is different than the darkened car, and I know our journey will take us farther too.

But I can't. Not when he's throwing my shirt to the floor, his mouth kissing the swells of my breasts, his skin so warm. His kiss is electric and I find myself wishing my bra was gone too.

Without my having to ask, deft hands make quick work of the clasp. His mouth is on mine again, tasting of syrup as he slides my bra away. His eyes trace me, like he's reading me. Like I'm the paper he writes on or the book he keeps hidden but must be important to him.

"Jesus, you are so hot." His fingers trace the freckles on my shoulders. "I want to connect all the dots. See every spot on your body," he tells me.

My heart drums. Heat burns through me. "Girls stand no chance against you, do they?"

He laughs at that. "I pay attention," he says. "You like to be touched. Anywhere. Skin to skin makes you smile." Adrian traces a path down to my hips. "Or blush. I bet it makes your heart race too. I feel you shiver every time I touch you."

I can't help but to close my eyes. I'm afraid I'm going to cry because he's right. It makes me feel close to someone and that's what I want. I want to feel close to him.

"I don't have condoms with me, Little Ghost." The name shocks me. It's different than Casper...somehow more intimate. He's placing closemouthed kisses to the corner of my lips now. My jaw, my neck. It's almost too much for me to think, but his words push through.

It's another thing that should scare me. The fact that I'd be willing to give him something tonight that

I've never given to anyone else. That I want to. "But I thought..."

"There are other things we can do. I don't go there without condoms. Ever. I'll still make you feel good, though."

There isn't a second I doubt those words. I look at him and smile. His hands are on me when I do and I wonder if he thinks it's because he's touching me. That's not the only reason.

"Stand up." Adrian scoots back enough for me to stand. He's still on his knees, and I know when he does what he's about to do. His face will be...

"Should we lie on the bed?"

"We will," he says. And then he's helping me to my feet. His fingers work the button on my jeans. My zipper goes next. Adrian's slow as he pulls my pants and panties down my legs. He looks up at me. At *all* of me, his eyes reading me like they do and his hands running up the curves of my calves, behind my knees. I want him to see my story, but I want to cover myself too. It's too much. Too painful and embarrassing.

"This is going to kill me, but it's not a bad way to go."

His words make me laugh, taking away any urge I felt to hide.

His finger brushes over the apex of my thighs and he mutters, "So pretty," making heat run the length of me. No one has ever, ever talked to me like that before.

Adrian stands up. His mouth molds against mine and his hand pushes through my hair again. He's more urgent now. More needy as he backs me up so I have no choice but to lie on the bed. He comes down on top of me, his lips traveling my body: lips, neck, breasts. His tongue traces one pebbled peak and then the other, before sucking each into his mouth, one at a time.

My fingers tighten around his hair as I arch forward, my body begging for the things my mouth could never say.

"I'm getting there, Little Ghost," he says, a chuckle in his voice.

"I want to feel you too," I say, and he rips his shirt off before sliding down my body. I don't look at him. Can't. Just let my hands touch his shoulders and back and hope the feel of me gives him some of what his touch gives me.

My eyes close. In this moment, I can do nothing but feel. Feel his mouth slide lower, across my belly, my hips, and then he's right at the spot that's aching for him.

"I want to taste you."

"Please," I rasp out. He could do anything to me right now and I'd let him.

The first lash of his tongue sends a jolt through me, passion and pleasure shooting in every direction.

I arch when a finger pushes inside, his tongue still driving me wild. My hips rotate, trying to get as close to him as I can as that ache builds higher, higher until I'm afraid it's going to make me come apart at the seams.

And then I do, my body exploding from the touch of a man for the first time in my life.

My breathing is heavy and I still can't open my eyes. "That was amazing."

"That wasn't enough."

And then he does it again.

And I come apart for the second time.

My body's limp, completely weak, when Adrian pulls away. "Wait," I say. *Open your eyes.* But I'm tired. So very tired.

"I'm just turning off the light."

I can tell when the room goes black. I hear Adrian shuffling and I know he's stepping out of his pants. He crawls behind me in my small bed. I feel his bare legs, his bare chest, and I want to wrap myself inside him, feel him all over my body.

"I should..." I can hardly get the words past my lips. It's not that I don't want to. It's that I never have. And I also don't know if I can move. "I should...you know, for you too."

"Next time," he whispers, and I'm not sure if I should do it or not, but I decide to risk it. I cuddle close to him and lay my head on his chest.

"I feel your heart," I tell Adrian.

He pauses. "I thought it ran away." His words break my heart. I try to sit up, but his arm wraps around me and stops me. "It was a joke."

I know it wasn't, but I can't make myself call him on it. Not right now. If I do, he'll pull away. I hope I'm doing the right thing.

"Adrian—"

"Sleep, Little Ghost. No more haunting tonight."

His words flip a switch inside me. Open a door to him and pull him inside. "Tell me a story. A happy one this time."

"I don't know any happy stories." He runs his hand over my shoulder and I wonder if he's trying to connect my dots. Or write on my skin.

"Yes, you do. Tell me something." He doesn't answer at first. My eyes are so heavy. I'm drifting…falling, deeper and deeper when I hear his voice in the dark:

Skin to skin
Breath to breath
Touch to feel
Body to soul
But only
To chase
Away
Your ghosts

A loud banging sound jerks me out of my sleep.

"What the hell!" Adrian's voice yells from the hallway. "Back the fuck up, man."

Oh no! I grab the sheet, because it's the only thing close to me, and wrap it around myself as I dart for the hallway. Adrian's left eye is swollen as Maddox stands there, his body stiff and his hands fisted.

"What the hell are you doing in there with my little sister?" His voice is so angry, so sharp that it scares me.

"I would have thought that was obvious," Adrian tosses back at him. Totally the wrong thing to say. My brother lunges at him, but I grab him just in time. It's the first either of them see me.

"Maddox! Stop it! What are you doing?"

"Is this him?" he seethes. "What the fuck is he doing here, Laney? This wasn't part of—"

"Stop it! It's not your business!" My heart is a herd of elephants stomping across the earth.

I know my brother can get out of my grasp, but he doesn't. He wouldn't risk hurting me like that. But I also don't trust him not to say something to Adrian. *You're fighting to keep the secret now. That's not right.*

"We'll be right back," I tell Adrian as I'm pushing my brother into the bathroom. That's when I see it. I knew Adrian had a few tattoos, because they're on his arms, but the second my eyes land on his chest, it's like a fist grabs me around the throat, cutting off my breath. On his chest, over his heart, is a tattoo of a hand. A little baby hand with a heart in it. Adrian's heart.

And it's for Ashton. I know it is. The little boy my father killed.

Tears choke me. Adrian's giving me that look that says he sees something's wrong and is searching me for the truth.

I look at him, standing in my hallway in his boxer-briefs, with a black eye, a messed-up hand, and a tattoo on his chest for a dead little boy who he loved.

"Are you okay? He's not going to hurt you?" he asks.

"Kiss my ass, motherfucker. She's my sister."

"It's okay. I'm okay," I tell Adrian as I close the door.

Everything in Maddox's demeanor changes as we step inside. He's still mad. I can definitely see that, but now the worry is breaking through. "What are you doing, Laney?" He keeps his voice low and for that I'm thankful.

Still, I say, "Shhh. It was a mistake. I didn't plan it but..."

"But what? You're hooking up with him 'cause you feel guilty?"

"No! It's not about that!"

"Fuck." He drops his head backward, lets it hit the door as he looks up. "You like him?"

"I don't really know him."

"Don't bullshit me. Now's not the time."

God, he's right. "I do. I didn't mean to, but I do." I'm standing in the bathroom with my brother. I'm only wearing a sheet wrapped around me and the boy whose family mine ruined is in the next room, hurt from my brother. Hell, and from me. His hand wouldn't be messed up if he hadn't tried to save my life.

"Oh God. I'm making a mess of this." I fall onto the closed toilet.

"It's not your job to fix it, but you have to know this isn't smart. What do you think he's going to do when he finds out?"

I shake my head, not wanting to hear it. "He said he wouldn't want to know the truth."

"He also didn't know what the hell that truth was, did he? You're fucking naked with this guy, Laney."

My eyes start to water, but I wipe the tears away and

stand up. "I don't ask a lot out of you, Maddy, but please, *please* stay in here until he leaves. And don't say anything to him, okay? I'll fix it. I'll find a way to make it right for all of us."

As I did a few seconds ago, he shakes his head this time. He looks much more glum than I did. "I see it in your eyes. Don't do this. Don't get close to him. If you do, we're even more fucked than we are now. You know this can't end well, Laney."

I hate that I don't know if he's right. Those two voices fill my head again. One that says Maddox knows what he's talking about. That says this can't help Adrian. That it might hurt him. But then there's the other voice. The one that lives in my heart that wants to think this is right. That wants nothing more than to try and save Adrian, to try and save us all.

I still don't know which one to listen to. "Let me handle it." The door clicks behind me. When I step inside my room, Adrian is dressed again.

"Your brother has a good right jab. He's lucky my hand's fucked up and I'm not a big enough bastard to kick his ass in his own house."

"I'm so sorry. When he's out like that, he doesn't usually come home so early. I didn't think I would sleep so well. I thought I could have had you leave before he got home."

"Have to ask his permission for a sleepover?" There's venom in his voice I've never heard before.

"That's not fair. He's my older brother. I think any guy would be like that."

"Guess we don't get to play doctor this time."

His eye is swelling more. "I'm sorry. I'll get you some ice."

"Don't worry about it. I have to go." I try to grab him, but he dodges me and walks to the door, but then stops, his hand on the knob and his back to me. He doesn't move for what feels like an eternity. And then he turns around, touches my face, his finger drifting down my neck and over my left shoulder.

I don't even realize I'm smiling until he says, "There is it. Just one touch. Don't ever lose that, Little Ghost." And with that, he's gone. I watch the door long after he's walked away. I think about what Maddox said. Think about last night, Adrian's caresses, his words. And the mask that started to slip away. The same mask he wore when he told me good-bye. I want to show him how beautiful he is without it. Maddox is wrong. He has to be. And I'm not letting Adrian run away anymore either.

Chapter Thirteen

~Adrian~

I can't believe I'm here. I don't know what the hell I'm doing at this place. I never come to Ash's grave. Can't fucking do it, but instead of going home after leaving Delaney's house, I just drove. The whole time I told myself this wasn't where I was going, but I'm here, so it's only another lie to add to the million I tell myself every day.

My weak ass still can't get out of the car. My eyes burn and not from getting hit in one of them. My mind rides the smoke to the little boy in the grave. The one who loved me. *Me*. He didn't look at me like he wished I was man enough to save him like Mom did. Didn't look at me with disgust like Dad. Didn't know he needed to save me like Angel. He believed in me for no other reason than the fact that I was me.

And I'd shattered that to fucking pieces. Didn't take it seriously. I cared too much about living my own life for the first time and waiting for my friends and *partying*, like I do now, to protect him.

Get out of the car, get out of the car, get out of the car.

I can't even make myself do that. So instead I read my stupid fucking book like I always do. Remember reading to him like he even knew what the hell *The Count* even was. Another way I screwed up with him. Why the hell would I read a book like that to a kid? Didn't matter that I cherry-picked what I read. I still did it.

When it's painfully obvious I've failed him again, I start my car and drive back home. Angel's birthday is coming up. I wonder what she's doing. If she'll be with whoever that guy was at the cemetery with her. I know that as much as Delaney's brother pissed me off this morning, I would have done the same thing if some bastard had been with Angel. That's what family does—they protect. He's doing it a hell of a lot better than I do. It's good he chased me out of there today. I don't need to let myself get close to a girl with problems. I have my own and I'm doing a shitty job of taking care of them.

Once I get home, I put the water in the shower as hot as I can handle it, letting myself stand under the spray until cold starts to take over. My body aches from her brother shoving me into the wall. Tiredness lives in my bones now, swims in the marrow, and I can't ever seem to get it out of my system.

My cell rings, Colt's number lighting up, but I don't answer it. I put money on it being Cheyenne and I don't want to play the friend game with her today. Don't want to remember seeing the wheels turn in her head or the hope in her voice that someone's going to come along and save me the way she did Colt. He wanted to be saved. I don't.

When knocking comes from my door hours later, I almost ignore that, too, but something about the gentle *rap, rap, rap* lulls me, calls to me until I stand up, walk over, and jerk the door open.

My eyes travel up from the pink, fluffy jacket to Delaney's face with the unsure smile and eyes she's trying to shield from me. There's nothing there. Not the pain or the desire, and I think about the words going through her head right now. Wonder if she's trying to talk herself out of her thoughts, hoping not to show them to me.

And as much as I don't like to admit it, as much as I want to bury this part of myself, deeper than the earth covering Ashton, I can't. I'm glad she's here. Glad she came because I wanted to see her and I wouldn't have gone to her. But it's not my fault she came to me. When I wanted to have her, to take her, that was different. It's not like I don't still want that. Want to swallow all those little cries of pleasure. Taste the sweetness she offered to me last night. There's a part of me that feels a little less alone right now, and alone is all I've known for so long.

"It's cold out here. Think you could let me in?" she asks.

"I could." My arms cross and I slip back into my façade. "What are you doing for me if I do?"

Instead of answering, her hand moves toward my face. "Your eye..."

"Eh." I step back and open the door. "It's not like I've

never been hit before. My dad was an even better shot than your brother."

"Adrian..."

"Don't. It happened, can't change it. There's no point in pretending words will make it go away." I close the door behind her. Delaney walks into the room but doesn't sit down. I go right back to where I was on the couch, putting my arm on the back as springs creak under the cushion.

"Maddox can be a jerk, but you have to admit, you didn't do much to plead your case. You made it sound like more happened than it did. You're lucky he didn't do more, and honestly, I don't really appreciate it either."

She crosses her arms, and Christ, as much as I don't want to, I smile. She looks like a marshmallow, her arms puffed up because of her jacket. "Come here." When she raises an eyebrow at me, I say, "Please."

Delaney walks over and stands between my legs.

"Just last night I was standing in front of you this way."

"I remember." Her cheeks squeeze in and I think she's trying to hide a smile. Sitting forward, I reach for the zipper on her jacket. A sharp gasp slips past her lips.

"Don't worry, Little Ghost. I'm only taking your jacket off." The name came out when I was talking to her last night, but it fits her more than Casper really did. It feels like it's her, even though I don't think I should be giving her any kind of name like that. I don't need to be close to her. I shouldn't be close to anyone.

We both study the teeth of her zipper pulling apart.

She's wearing a sweater, but it's short, showing me a sliver of her stomach. She's thin, but soft, too, little dips and valleys that I remember exploring. After pulling the jacket off, I toss it to the couch. I'm hard already but try and stamp it down. As much as I want her, I don't think she's here for that right now. "What's going on?"

She fidgets, transfers her weight from her right foot to her left, showing me her nerves and that she knows what I'm asking.

When she doesn't answer, I again say, "Come here."

"I'm here" tumbles from those cherry-red lips.

"Not close enough." I tell myself it's because I want to touch her. She's gorgeous and feminine, and what guy wouldn't want to get close to that, but there's more. I'm hoping when we're closer, she can't keep her secrets from me. Can't cover the windows into her soul.

I take her hand and give it a gentle pull. It's all I need and she's climbing on my lap, straddling me. My cock's nuzzled right between her legs and I know she feels it, feels how much I want her, and fuck if her heat doesn't seep right through me. My hands hold her hips and I wish we were both bare. Wish we were skin to skin because bodies don't lie the same way mouths do.

"What are you doing?" She turns her head. Every time she does, I move mine the same way, not letting her escape. Funny how I don't want her to retreat, how I want to be inside her and know everything that lives there, though I know there's so much of me she'll never see. So much I'll never show her.

"Your eyes don't lie. Even when this"—I rub my thumb across her bottom lip—"doesn't want to talk, your eyes do."

"Why is it fair that you get to know what's going on inside me if I don't know about you?" She doesn't shield her face from me this time, like she wants me to know she's serious.

"It's not fair...but..." The words I want to say won't leave my lips.

"Maybe you will...be able to."

"What are you doing here?" I should tell her I'm glad she came. I am, and it makes me feel like an asshole grilling her like this.

Delaney shrugs, playing at a nonchalance I don't think she feels. "I work tonight...I wanted to make sure you were still coming. You know...to keep me safe."

"Your brother seems to like protecting you." My hands squeeze her hips and I pull her a little closer.

"I don't want him to protect me."

With that, I fuse my mouth over hers. Her arms wrap around my neck. Each time she moves, my cock jumps at the feel of her moving against it. I don't want to want her this much. I don't know why I do, but instead of pulling away, I kiss her deeper. Suck her tongue into my mouth and move my hips with hers.

Christ, my whole body is on edge because of her and I don't know what I'm feeling. "I should tell you to leave," I say against the skin of her neck. "I need you to leave." But I don't stop kissing. I take her earlobe into my mouth and suck it gently before nipping it with my teeth.

Laney's head drops back, giving me more room to explore. "I should go. I didn't mean for us to end up this way again."

My hands move to the curve of her ass. I grip her, go to turn her, when her cell rings from the couch beside us. Delaney stiffens, and I know the moment is over.

"I have to get that. It could be my mom." She scrambles off my lap, making it feel empty, the way I should.

I can tell by the conversation it's not her mom. It's a quick call but enough to part the lust in my brain.

"I have to go," she says reluctantly.

"I'll be there tonight," I tell her, not sure how I feel having said it.

"Okay. Thanks." She stands and pulls her jacket back on. Grabs her hat and slides it into place next.

She gives me a quick gaze before walking to the door.

"Hey," I say when she's halfway out. She turns and looks at me, really looks this time. "I'm glad you came."

A smile.

And then she's gone.

"We are *so* slow tonight."

I look up at Delaney as she leans against the bench seat across from me. I've been at the diner for the past few hours. I ate pancakes and watched as she cleaned every table twice.

"I've noticed." I close *The Count* and set it on the bench next to me. I almost try to hide it, but it doesn't matter. She knows I read it and I'm not sure why I don't feel the need to pretend I don't anymore. "And your cook hasn't come out of the kitchen once to check on you. That pisses me off."

It's my excuse for being here. What if something happens? What if the assholes come back? But I also know that's exactly what it is. An excuse for being in the one place I've felt sane in a long time. I don't want to consider why that is.

"He knows you're here."

I let those words sink in. Let them feel good when they shouldn't. They might not know it, but I do a shitty job of protecting people.

"Want to sneak in the bathroom with me?" I tease.

She rolls her eyes. "Not going to happen."

"Sit with me." I nod my head across the table. Delaney looks around as though she needs to make sure the empty diner didn't suddenly fill up with people while she wasn't looking. When she's sure it's okay, she sits down, watching me. Both of my elbows rest on the table and I hold my hands out, palms up. She studies me for only a second before her palms rest on mine.

We hold each other, as though neither of our eyes can divert away. Questions dance in her eyes. I let myself smirk before I jerk my good hand out from under hers and lightly smack the top of it.

"Oh my God. You're a cheater. You didn't tell me we were playing!"

"Wasn't it obvious?"

She laughs. It's soft, but you can tell nothing's more

real. It starts in her stomach and builds until it rolls out of her mouth. I want to catch it, to do the same thing.

"Considering I haven't played the slap game since I was twelve, no." Another laugh. I lift my middle finger and rub it across her palm, to tell her we're playing again. Or just to feel her shiver.

"What about your hand?" she asks.

"It's fine. It's healing. I only keep it bandaged up so you'll baby me."

At that, she straightens in her seat. Gets a cutthroat look in her eyes that tells me she's ready to take me down. We sit there for an hour, playing the slap game, thumb wars, whatever else we can think of. I count her laughs, memorize the sound and wonder if she's keeping track of mine too. It's stupid. So fucking stupid, but it feels good and I don't remember the last time I felt good. More than just physically, at least.

When a customer comes in, the little ghost gets up and does her job. I watch her seat them and take their order and bring them drinks. The sway of her hips when she walks and the curve of her ass drive me crazy.

Soon her shift is over, and I'm walking her out. I back her against her car, cup her cheeks in my hands, and say, "We're still dancing around this. I want you. Come home with me."

Because that's the only thing I can admit. The only thing I understand—a physical want.

She sighs. "I want to...I just don't know if I should."

"Because of your fucking brother?" I ask. It takes her

a minute to reply. I expect her to tell me I'm wrong. To give me another reason. Maybe to say because it's me.

"You don't understand. I'm his little sister. He thinks he has to take care of me. We're all each other has. I haven't talked to him since you left and I can't not go home. He'd worry."

Funny, I almost get what she's saying. Even though it was Angel protecting me, covering for me and fixing my mistakes, I always thought I would be able to do the same thing for her.

Only, I left instead. Left her alone with the memories of the little boy she loved so much.

Emotion fights to get to the surface and I want nothing more than to shove it down again. I'll do anything to make it go away. Leaning into Delaney, my body holds her against her car. "Are you ever going to let me inside?" I ask, grinding into her so she feels the hard length of me. It makes me a prick, falling back on this time and time again, but being a prick is better than cutting myself open and letting my secrets leak out.

"Are you?" she tosses back at me. "Doesn't feel so good, does it? You throw sexual stuff at me, because you know it builds up those barriers. Maybe I should do the same with the truth."

I respect the hell out of her for calling me on it. For not letting me get away without knowing that she sees this game I'm playing with her. So I let a tiny seed of truth slip out. "It hurts too much to let myself bleed." Those words are more than I've given any other girl.

They're a truth I wouldn't share with anyone, but yet I gave them to her.

"Sometimes we need to bleed to heal...and...I just want..." She covers her face with her hands. I don't move away from her and don't pull her hands away either. I let her fight whatever battle she's waging because it doesn't work that way. She can't fight mine and I can't fight hers. "I like you." Her hands slide away. "I can't believe I said that. It probably sounds stupid, but I do. I didn't expect it and I don't know how to deal with it, but I just want you to be okay."

Jesus, she's honest. Honest in a way I've never been. Not when I was hiding Dad's bruises or cleaning up puke while he raped my mom in the bedroom. I wasn't honest about Ash.

"I'll never be okay. This is it for me."

"Delaney! I'm glad you haven't left yet. Can you come back inside for a second?"

I don't look behind me at the sound of the female voice coming from the diner.

"Umm. Yeah. I'll be right there." Delaney tries to look at me again, but I take a step backward. She follows, moving toward me before her lips come down on my swollen eye.

"I'm sorry Maddox hit you. I'm sorry for everything. All I want is for it to be okay."

She's such an optimist that I want to laugh, but I don't.

"Tonight," she tells me. Honesty mixes with sincerity on her face.

If I were a real man, I'd walk away. I'd tell her no and never show my face again. Or better yet I'd open my fucking mouth and spill the truth. How I let an innocent little boy die and I let Angel save me and let Mom get hurt and how I left my sister behind despite everything she did for me. But I can't do any of that. Instead I kiss her ear. "You haunt me."

I squeeze her hand, walk to my car, and drive away.

Chapter Fourteen

~Delaney~

I hardly hear the other waitress as she rambles on about the schedule change. That the manager called and they caught the people who tried to rob the diner. One of them confessed, she says, but her words don't register.

When I get home, I struggle to remember the drive there. The whole time I think about Adrian and I remember what his breath felt like against my ear. For the first time, I know I got a partial glimpse of the real him. Yes, I knew he hurt. Obviously. I know there are demons and pain and regret in his past, but listening to him speak, seeing the loneliness in his features and even in the way he touched me—no, I never realized how very deep it ran.

Which does nothing to wipe out my guilt.

And it also makes me connect to him more. *"You haunt me."* His words so soft in my ear. They did something to me. I like him. That much is true, though I can't believe I admitted it so bluntly, but more than ever before, I feel that invisible thread between us. Feel it tighten and

strengthen and not just because of the past we're both
linked to.

Because of *him*. There's something special about
him. And it's scary. Scary as hell. But not as scary as the
fact that I need to tell him. That I owe him this and I
don't know how to do it.

Instead of going straight to bed, I soak in a bath. I fill
it with bubbles and let it try and wash away my thoughts.
It doesn't work and I think maybe, maybe I might be
glad of it.

When I get out, I dress in my pajamas. Maddox is
sleeping on the couch, so I'm quiet as I walk back into
my room. Unease gnaws at my stomach as I dial the hospital to talk to my mom. I've tried before and she won't
speak to me. I'm not surprised, though; she never wants
to talk to me, but I can't stop myself from seeing if she's
okay.

When the operator answers, I ask for her room. She
patches me through and Mom's groggy voice comes over
the line on the third ring.

"Hey, Mom. It's me."

"Who else would it be? It's not as though I have a
husband anymore. And my son doesn't give a shit about
me." Her voice is harsh. It's not a good day, though when
it comes to me, I guess it never really is.

"How are you? How are things going?"

She skips my question completely. "Where's your
brother? I want to speak to my son."

My heart aches at her words, aches because even
though she loves Maddox more, I don't get why she can't

love me. Because I was suddenly a daddy's girl and that has somehow turned me into a monster in her eyes and Maddox into an angel?

Which I could handle, if it gave her—or him—some comfort, but I know it doesn't because Maddox wants nothing to do with her, the same way she wants nothing to do with me.

"He's not here. He's——"

The line goes dead. I try not to let the empty air squeeze through my pores and find its way inside me. I don't need it there. Not anymore. I would do anything to bring our family back together. Why doesn't she see that?

I will the tears away, not wanting to shed them today. I cry too much. For now, I only want to sleep. Sleep and pretend nothing is the way it is.

"I need you to call Mom," I tell Maddox when I wake up. He's sitting on the small balcony, smoking a cigarette again.

"Good morning to you too." He takes another pull on the cancer stick.

"I'm serious, Maddy. I called to check on her this morning and she hung up on me. You know she would rather talk to you. We need to make sure everything's okay."

"If she hung up on you, that says she's okay. That she's like she always is."

"You know—"

"No, actually, I don't know what you mean." He

stands, leans against the railing, and looks at me. "You say I take too much blame, but look at you, Laney. You think you're going to save us all. You keep pushing, trying to fix her when she treats you like shit. You're getting close to that prick, thinking you'll make it better, when you know he's just going to hurt you."

I refuse to hear the truth in his words. Refuse to discuss Adrian with him. "Just call her. Two minutes. That's all I ask."

He sighs. "Why do you do this to yourself?"

The way he looks at me breaks my heart. I know he loves me. Know he feels like he has an obligation to take care of me because Mom was so mad at me, so hurtful after Dad went to prison. Her words try and find their way into my head, but I slam the door on them like I always do.

"I know we've been fighting a lot and I hate that. You're my brother...my best friend. I know I push you and we don't understand each other, but I need this. I need you to check on her and I need...I want us to get along. I don't want to fight with you anymore."

He closes his eyes tightly. I see his jaw tense. "You're too good for the way she treats you. I hate her for that. You didn't deserve any of this, little sister."

Taking a step forward, I hug him. Hug him even though he stinks like cigarettes. The embrace doesn't last long and then he's pulling away. Dialing the phone and grunting a hello into it when she answers. And then he listens as she talks. Asks how she's doing. She doesn't hang up on him. She doesn't yell. It's Maddox who says he has to go a few minutes later.

I hear her voice through the phone when she says, "I know you only called because of *her*. Your father was the same way. She's so spoiled. No one could ever tell her—"

Maddox turns off the phone. "I'm not doing that again."

My chin quivers as I shake my head, telling him I won't ask him to.

"Don't fucking listen to her, Laney. None of this was your fault." He ruffles my hair like I'm ten years old and then goes into the apartment. And I know that he thinks it's his fault, but he'll never tell me why.

Maddox had gone to work less than an hour when the banging starts on my front door. It scares me at first, and I pick up my phone, ready to call someone if I have to, when Adrian's voice breaks through the thin wall.

"Fuck," he mumbles, and I give a small smile, wondering if he hit the door with his injured hand. My heart jumps, shocked that he's there, but then it does a free fall because it's probably not a good thing that he is.

I open the door, seeing a shadow of stubble on his face. The swelling has gone down in his eye, and it's mostly only the purple ring.

"I need to get out of here." His voice is calm, but I sense the urgency beneath his words.

"What happened? Are you in some kind of trouble?"

He shakes his head. "I know it doesn't make any

sense, but I need to go. I need to fucking breathe and I'm suffocating here. My phone rings every ten minutes and people show up at my house and I called…"

He doesn't finish.

"Called who?"

"You've been crying." He studies my face, slightly cocks his head like he does sometimes.

"I'm fine. It's just stuff with my mom. Who did you call?"

Again he ignores my question. "I want to get lost. Have you ever wanted to get fucking lost? That's all I want. I'll be back. I just didn't want you to think I bailed on you. Maybe your brother can—"

"They caught them. My boss got a phone call. One of them confessed, which is why they don't need us to identify them. They were young kids, but even if they hadn't been arrested, I wouldn't need my brother to protect me."

"What happened with your mom?" His eyebrow rises and I know he's doing what I did when I asked again who he called.

"She hates me for not letting her die." The way his lips curl down and his jaw tenses, I know he didn't expect the answer. "Though I guess if I'm being honest, I'd admit that she had issues with me before that."

As I'm standing here talking to him, I realize I can breathe too. That after speaking to Mom and fighting with Maddox so much, I was feeling the exact way he does—like I'm suffocating.

"Let me come with you."

He takes a step backward and fear hits me. I'm scared

he's going to say no and I'll be embarrassed I asked, and I realize how much I really do want to just...go. I've never been able to do something like this. Moving here is the closest I've come to something like that, but even that was with Maddox. It was, in my own strange way, for my family. Going with Adrian would be for me.

But he doesn't tell me no and he doesn't keep walking away. Instead he grabs my hand and pulls me to him. I recognize his scent now—all outdoors mixed with boy. His heat is familiar. The way he lines up against me is familiar and it shouldn't be. Not on the level it is.

"You know if you go with me, there will be no escaping me anymore? That I'll make you mine."

And I know he doesn't mean his to keep, but it still pumps all sorts of happy electricity into me. The kind of static I think we both deserve.

"What if..." *Say it, say it, say it.* "What if I don't want to escape?"

"You should," he tells me. "But I'm bastard enough to want you to stay."

I expect him to kiss me, but he doesn't. Instead he walks into my house and I follow him. "We'll only be gone a day or two, so pack what you want."

Giddiness pumps through my veins. This is the one thing I have that's something I want and not just for me, but for him. For *us*. Because I think he actually wants me to go. An adventure no matter how short-lived. "Where are we going?" I ask as I grab a bag out of my closet.

"We can just drive for all I care, I just need out."

It's what he does. I'm not stupid enough not to see

that. He ran from what happened, from his sister, and when he needs a break, he continues to run, even now. Does it make a difference that he's bringing someone along this time? That he's not going for good and he's trusting another person with that part of him? I don't know, but I really hope so.

"You know you don't have to do this." He sits on my bed as I'm putting clothes into the backpack. "I'll be okay. I'm always okay. Don't go because you feel bad for me or because—"

"Maybe I'm going for me because I need to get away too."

He gives me a simple nod and I finish packing my clothes. I move to the bathroom next, gathering my toiletries.

"You need to tell your brother."

It doesn't surprise me that Adrian says that. He has every right to hate Maddox since he's sporting a black eye because of him, but there's a heart in there. A big heart that cares about people.

"I'll leave him a note."

He's going to freak. I know it, but there's also no way I would leave without telling him. He'd lose it.

After scrawling a quick letter to Maddox, I'm locking the door behind us. I've never in my life done something like this and I'm doing it with Adrian.

The man who doesn't know his life is a mess because of my father.

Not now. Don't do this now.

We decide to take my car because it's in better shape

than Adrian's. I toss him the keys and tell him he can drive. He has to scoot the seat back so he fits well. I'm shaking as I try to buckle my seat belt, my hands jumping so bad I can't get it in. Adrian touches me. Grabs the belt and clicks it into place.

"Thank you," he says.

It doesn't matter that he helped me, not the other way around. I know exactly what he means. "You don't have to thank me."

"Such a friendly little ghost." And finally, *finally* he kisses me again. It's a possessive kiss, so different from each of the ones he's given me before. Those felt like they were to prove something, to accomplish something, but as his tongue slow dances with mine, I know this is much more.

Because I'm falling for him. There's a lot I don't know about him, but I don't think that matters. What counts is how I feel, and Adrian makes me feel things deep inside in places I didn't know existed.

And I hope I'm able to reach those places in him too.

Hope that it's enough to save us.

Chapter Fifteen

~Adrian~

It's so fucking strange sitting in the car with her. Disappearing with someone else instead of just the secrets that chase me. When I was a kid, I was always by myself. I lived inside my head, inside my words and with books. The older I got, once Angel moved out, the more I realized I needed to hide, so I started hanging out with people, partying, meeting girls. Lots and lots of girls, but it was never something like this.

No one knew about the words that live in my head, begging to spill on paper. About *The Count* or the bruises or the cries from Mom that will never find their way out of the maze inside my mind. They didn't know that there were times I needed to disappear...to run before the loneliness inside me threatened to fucking eat me alive. Even the people in my life now, Colt and Cheyenne, they only know the Adrian I want them to. It's crazy how being alone with people can sometimes feel emptier than being alone on your own.

But now this girl is here. She's beside me as my hands tighten on the steering wheel, because I don't know what else to do with them. After I called my sister, didn't speak, and then hung up when she said my name, Delaney's seeing me run. That's one of the many things that are mine. That I keep locked inside me because they're weak and I don't want anyone to see how fucking weak I really am.

I don't want her or anyone else to see those parts of me...but I'm also glad she's here. There are a million and one different reasons I don't want to dissect that, but it's hard to turn off my brain sometimes. "I'm not going to have to worry about your brother putting a fucking APB out on us or something, am I?" Talking is better than thinking. I have more control over what comes out of my mouth than what goes on inside my head.

The little ghost laughs. "Honestly? Maybe. No, he won't go to the cops. Can't since I'm eighteen, but I wouldn't be surprised if he thinks he can hunt me down himself."

I think about Angel and what I would have done if she took off with some guy. I can't blame him. "That's cool...."

Another laugh. She's nervous. Not scared, I think, but unsure.

"If you say so. He has this hero complex. Maddy thinks he has to take responsibility for everything—or at least me. Ever since..."

Her words die off. Sadness bleeds into her features, her eyes looking down. I don't like to see the look there. She's too fucking beautiful to be so tortured.

"He lets you call him that? *Maddy?*"

My question seems to chase some of the sadness away. It feels good, being a bodyguard against her ghosts. I'm shocked when her hand smacks my arm.

"Don't even!" she says. "There's nothing wrong with calling him that, though I know he agrees with you on that one. Didn't your sister—I mean, if you have one—didn't she ever have a nickname for you?"

The question brings back the past I try too hard to forget.

"What were you thinking, Shakespeare?! You are sup-posed to get out of here. That's why I took you in—so you could have a life!"

"I know. I fucked up. Don't you think I know that?"

I don't know why a memory of Angel being mad at me is what I pull out. Hell, it's one of the only times I think Angel ever really got mad at me. My brain shuts down before I go any deeper into that train of thought.

"Nah," I tell Laney. "I only have one sister and we weren't really that close." The words sting my tongue, making me feel like shit because she's the only person in my life besides Ash who ever loved me.

"Oh." She looks at me, the sadness creeping in again. "That's too bad...I don't know what I would do without Maddox. I bet your sister feels the same way about you."

The way she says it, the sureness in her voice makes me want to believe her, but I can't. Not when I've done nothing but fuck things up and cause pain. "Maybe once, Little Ghost, but not anymore."

I flinch slightly when she reaches over and grabs the

hand I let fall from the steering wheel. She holds it lightly at first, and then with strength. I've never held hands with a girl in my life. It's not really my thing but I let her hold mine. Eventually, I even squeeze back.

We drive until around six, until my life feels far enough behind me to muffle the voices inside.

It's already dark outside and the temperatures are dropping. "Wanna find a room?" I ask her. It's not what I usually do. Usually I drive, sleep in my car, or stay up all night, but I won't do that with her. She deserves to be in a bed somewhere tonight.

"Sure."

I don't even know the name of the town sitting off the freeway. It's here when I need it, so I take the next exit. "What about food? You need to eat?" I probably should have thought of that earlier, but I'm not used to being with anyone else on these little trips.

"It's the only cure I've found to quiet my stomach growling."

I laugh. "Smart-ass. You should have told me you were hungry. I would have stopped."

In the dark, I see her head turn toward me, then back to the window. "It felt good to drive. I didn't want to stop either."

There's a strange sort of magic to her voice, which finds all the cracks, all the slivers in my armor and works its way through. I want her out, want to get her out of my system any way I can. To purge until she's gone if I have to, but…fuck if I don't like having her in there too. If I don't want to binge on her until there's nothing else there, because the storm inside me doesn't feel as fierce when that magic in her voice speaks to me.

I probably should, but I don't reply to what she said. "Where do you want to eat? I'm not sure how many options there are." A few places are scattered around, a Denny's, pizza, China House, and a few local places. "There's probably more if we drive around, but I wouldn't want to be blamed for starving you all day."

I wink and then remember she can't see me. Christ. What the hell is wrong with me?

"We could just find our room, if you want. It looks cold outside. I'm sure we can order something."

I want nothing more than to get her to a hotel. Want to finish what we started the other night. I tell myself it's because ever since I met her, I haven't touched another girl. My fingers itch to explore her body. My tongue wants to taste her again. I tell myself it has nothing to do with it being her. I need it to be true.

"You know I still want you, right? That if we're going to be alone in a room all night, I'm going to want to do more than taste you this time." Sex is one of the few things in my life I'm completely honest about. I can pretend to be a good guy, pretend I'm not going to want her, since I know that's all I'll give her, but we both know who I am. Or she knows as best as she can.

I stop at a red light, the glow enough so we can see each other. It's one of the few times I can't really make out what she's thinking. There's a lot going on behind those shadowed eyes of hers, but I don't know what it is. Or maybe I don't want to know.

"If... if I didn't want you, too, I wouldn't be here." Her chin juts out and damned if I'm not proud of her. Innocence radiates from Delaney. She tries to hide it under a mask, but it's always there, peeking out from behind her words and reminding me how different we are. But just now, she owned what she said. It turns me on, turns me inside out in a way I don't want to think about.

"Good to know." This time when I wink at her, she can see me. A honk comes from behind me and I pull away, pretending she's not fucking with my head.

It doesn't take us long to find a hotel. It's not the best place, but it's also not a piece of shit either.

We get out of the car and grab our bags. When we get inside, Delaney says, "I need to run to the restroom real quick. Here..." She starts to dig in her purse.

"I got it, Little Ghost. You're here because of me." Before she can reply to that, I walk up to the counter. The guy working there can't be much older than Delaney. Probably eighteen, maybe nineteen if he's lucky. Not that at twenty-two I'm that much older than either of them, but I think the little ghost and I have seen a lot more than this kid probably has. I eye him as he watches her walk away. I know her jeans are hugging her ass because I saw them earlier. I get why he's staring, but he needs to stop.

"Something interesting, man?" Not that it's any of my business.

"My bad." He doesn't look at me when he asks about the room.

I open my mouth to tell him a single king room, but then all sorts of thoughts that aren't usually in my head start to slip in. She isn't like other girls and I don't want to push her, no matter what I said earlier. And what if she needs space or something like that?

"Just gimme two queens." I give him my card and get it back with the keys a few seconds later. I turn around to see Delaney sitting next to a little girl in the lobby. She's helping her tie her shoe, while the mom is corralling another kid.

Ashton would have been about this little girl's age. As soon as I think about it, I see his brown eyes and think about the shirt in my bag that I usually keep under my pillow. Red clouds my vision. Blood. So much fucking blood. Suddenly I'm pissed. Or maybe it's hurt that's clawing its way into my chest. I don't know, but whatever it is, I want to evict it. I'm so fucking tired of feeling this way, but should I have a choice?

Ashton didn't have one...

I watch Delaney smile at the girl. Watch as the mom says thank you and Delaney replies. And when she turns to look at me, the feeling in my chest multiplies. It's like she has her heart in her hand and it's broken. She's holding it out and showing me all the little pieces. Or maybe it's my heart. Just another thing I don't know. The only thing that's clear is she looks sad, like she can read my emotions and somehow knows I'm wrecked. It feels good to have someone see it, to have someone really get something in me, but I want to hide it from her too. Hide it because I can't handle the idea of anyone knowing.

"Got the room?" Slowly she walks toward me. Instead of replying, I hold up the key cards and head back outside to take the stairs to our room. We're silent as we make our way upstairs. I hold the door open for her as she walks in, letting it close behind us.

"Two beds?" She sets her bag down.

The urge to smile tries to fight its way through. "It's all they had." We both know it's a bullshit lie.

She turns around to look at me. "I'm going to take a shower."

It's her way of giving me space. This girl is fucking incredible. "Thanks. What do you want to eat? I'll go get it and come back."

We decide on pizza. I jump in the car and head to the restaurant I saw on the way in. The whole time I'm thinking about her. I see her with the little girl, but that's only a second of it. I think about how she just let me off the hook. People give me shit about being psychic, but it's her who's the reader. At least when it comes to me. No one else would have known I wanted space like that.

While I'm waiting for the food, I don't know what makes me do it, but I pull my cell out of my pocket and call Colt. We don't do conversations for no reason, so when he picks up, the first thing he says is "I'm with my girl. I'm not partying tonight."

"I'm not even in town, man."

"Where is he?" Cheyenne asks, which tells me she's sitting close enough to Colt to hear everything I'm saying.

Fuck. Why the hell did I call him? "I don't know. Some town a few hours away...with Delaney."

There's a rustling sound like Colt's covering the phone with his hand. I hear him tell Cheyenne, "I'll be right back, Tiny Dancer." More moving around and then the sound of a door closing. Maybe I'm not as unreadable as I thought because Colt knows I wouldn't want to talk around Cheyenne. Not that I have anything to really say, but still, he knows.

"I remember sitting around that little fucking table in your kitchen not too long ago when you told me I was different with Chey. I thought you were fucking crazy. Or maybe I didn't and I was just too big of a pussy to admit it, but you still told me."

"Is this where you pretend to return the favor? I'm not you, man. I can't." I shut my words down there, not willing to go any further. What am I supposed to say? That I run away from everyone because I can't handle shit? That I let a helpless little boy die because I only think of myself? Not going to happen.

"Fuck that. It doesn't matter. You think I was the type to fall for someone before Chey? No matter how much you might want to, you can't control that."

Yes, I can.

"The fact that you're away with her now...hell, the fact that you're calling me about this proves it."

Can I?

"Listen, bro, I'm standing outside freezing my balls off while I'm talking to you. Then I'm going to turn around and walk back into my apartment. I'm going to crawl into bed with a beautiful fucking woman. I'm going to make love to her and then I'm going to talk to her and she'll make me laugh and then we'll probably get into an argument and then we'll do it again. When the worst shit in my life was happening, I had that girl with me. She never left me even though I probably didn't deserve her. I've never had something like that and let me tell you, it's fucking incredible. Way better than that other shit. I don't know what's going to happen with Delaney, but don't be a pussy. Don't fuck it up before it has a chance to happen." The line goes dead. Not that I'm surprised. That's Colt.

I twist my phone around in my hand as I think about what he said. For once, I want to do it. Just let go and not in the helpless, I-don't-give-a-shit way, but forget the past, even if it's only for a little while.

She dropped everything to come with me. She took care of my hand and kissed my eye and talks to me and has read my words. She's gorgeous. And I left her in the room, naked and under the spray of a shower while I pretend to mentally check out, like I always do. When really, my mind is always, *always* going. Even if it's for this night I want some peace.

They call our order. I grab it and speed my ass back to the room. I needed space this weekend, to clear my head, and I have the chance for even more than that sitting in the room waiting for me. I'm not talking about sex either. That night in the car and then in her room, I definitely enjoyed her body, but it was the first time in a long time I've really talked to anyone.

I want to talk to someone. No, not just someone—I want to talk to *her*.

Not about Ashton or Angel. I can't go there, but fuck if I don't want to open my mouth and say something. Tonight I'm going to wear someone else's life and try to make myself believe things are different.

Chapter Sixteen

~Delaney~

What am I doing here? I'm scared to death this is wrong. That all I'm going to do is make things worse. I don't have a right to be here...but I want to. Want to more than I ever thought I would. There's something about Adrian that feels good. Feels right. I see the pain in his eyes and I want to extinguish it. To fight it until there's nothing left to hurt him.

But it's more than that, too, and that's what scares me. I told him I like him, but the warmth he spreads through my chest and the pull I feel toward him are more than that. I can't even blame that thread anymore. It's just... Adrian. The words in his soul and his quiet nobility and the way he smiles. He's special and I feel it in every part of myself.

And once he finds out...I'll probably lose him. *But do I really have him?*

A rattle at the door tells me he's here. I'm sitting in the middle of the bed that doesn't have our stuff on it.

My wet hair's tied up in a ponytail and I have a sudden urge to run into the bathroom and put makeup on. It would look ridiculous to put it on after a shower, though, so I don't. I did put a bra back on, but I'm wondering if I shouldn't have.

I don't sleep in them. And he said he wants me, but—

"You okay?" he asks. "You're spacing off with a look of fear on your face."

I hadn't even realized he'd come in! "Yeah . . . fine. Just tired." And scared, excited, nervous, and needy too.

"I got some Mountain Dew. I can go to the machine if you want something else. I don't know what you like." He sets the pizza, soda, and paper plates on the table.

"Mountain Dew's my favorite." I pull my legs out from under myself and stand up.

"Maybe I really am psychic, then. Or just really fucking good." He gives me a grin and it slams me right in the heart. It's playful, and though Adrian's sometimes playful, it never really rings true. This grin? I feel it in my toes and my stomach and my heart and I think maybe that means he really feels it too.

We make our plates and Adrian fills cups for both of us. I'm not sure where we should eat, but then he steps out of his shoes and climbs onto the bed I just left.

"Sit with me, Little Ghost."

Those words, that name sends a shudder of pleasure through me. I love to watch his mouth as he says it.

My heart is going crazy as I climb next to him. Looking at him now makes it almost possible to forget the ache in his eyes when he saw me with that little girl today. I want nothing more than to make that look go away forever.

"Why aren't you in school?" he asks me.

Adrian's not really one to ask a lot of questions. He doesn't talk, but he's trying to talk to me now and I'm not sure exactly what that means. "Money, I guess." I shrug. "And my mom. Though that's not really a good excuse. It's not like she really cares if I'm around anyway."

The thinker in him comes out. It's almost a shift when he's trying to figure out something in his head.

"Do you want to go to school?" is his next question.

I take a bite of my pizza, using it as an excuse for some time. I'd always planned on going away to college. Maddox too. He was going to be a football star one day. We all knew it, but when he and Dad stopped being close, Maddox stopped playing.

I wanted to help people. "Yeah...I want to be a nurse. I've always wanted to be one." The words make the urge come to life inside me again. My dream. Don't I deserve my dream too? Doesn't Maddox and Adrian? Why did my father's action get to take that from all of us?

"You'd be good at that. I can see you sneaking extra lollipops to little kids if they're good."

That makes me smile. It sounds like something I would love to do. "That would be very nice of me," I tease.

"So sweet and innocent."

"Hey!" I set my plate down and pretend to be annoyed by crossing my arms. "There's nothing wrong with being nice." Turning my head, I poke out my bottom lip.

Adrian's hand cups my chin. In a smooth movement he's turning my head so I face him again. "I never said there was anything wrong with how you are. And if you stick your lip out again, I'm going to bite it."

His words are a syringe, injecting a pleasurable heat into my veins. I want his mouth on me again so, so much. "What...what about you?" I ask.

"You can bite me, too, if you want."

I throw a napkin at him. "You know that's not what I mean."

"You know what I want. I write." He doesn't make eye contact with me as he grabs my empty plate, tossing both his and mine into the trashcan before coming back to sit on the bed again. Two urges bubble up inside me and I'm not sure which one to go with. I want to ask him more, want to ask him everything so I know every piece of Adrian, but I want to be quiet too. To wait...and listen in the hopes he'll give those pieces of himself to me without my having to pry.

"When I was younger"—he takes a deep breath—"I wrote all the time. Read and wrote. I thought if I disappeared enough into the words, they would become my life instead of the one I was living."

Oh God, oh God, oh God. That is a piece of him he never would have given me before. It makes me feel buoyant, invincible, but also like a fraud.

"It doesn't work that way, though." There's seriousness in his voice.

I feel him starting to shut down again and I want to

do, to say, anything to bring him back to me. To open him up. "Maybe it can.... Your words are beautiful, Adrian. The poem you left at the diner was wonderful and the one from the night at my house too."

"You like them? Do you want me to tell you another story?" His voice is gravelly, husky, but manages to pour over me as smoothly as honey.

"Yes." My voice sounds funny as well. He's looking at me so intensely, as though it's impossible to turn away. My heart is suddenly going crazy again and my skin tingles, burns, whatever else it can possibly feel.

He leans forward. "There once was a beautiful girl. She was sexy as hell."

Closer. With each second that ticks by he gets closer to me.

"She met a guy. Of course there was a guy and he wanted her so fucking bad he could hardly stand it."

I want to back up.

I want to lunge for him.

"And for one night, she was his."

Adrian's mouth comes down hard and fast on mine. Tender mixed with hungry need as his tongue is stroking and exploring my mouth. My arms wrap around his neck. Adrian leans me back on the bed, my head on the pillows as he lies on top of me.

"Tonight she was his," he says again, and then kisses me thoroughly. His lips tantalize every part of my body. Somehow I feel him everywhere. Our lips the epicenter, but my whole body is under the same assault.

All the feelings from earlier hit me again. They're harder and stronger, full of excitement and nerves and fear. I push the others aside, making room for more excitement and desire because no matter how scary this is, I've never wanted anything in my life as much as I want Adrian right now.

"Please..." slips out of my mouth.

"Whatever you want." And then he's pulling my shirt over my head and I'm pushing his up too. He sits up, straddling me, and I slide it over his head. His tattoo is there and I want to kiss it but don't know if I should. Instead I let my hands travel over his tanned skin. Feeling each sinewy muscle as he constricts in what I hope is need.

"You drive me so fucking crazy," he says before his mouth is on mine again. His weight so deliciously perfect on top of me. I only tense for a second when his hand pushes under the waistband of my sweats and then my panties. Nerves threaten to push in again, but I remember he's had his mouth on me before and this is Adrian and no matter what, I know he'd never hurt me.

My body arches toward him as he pushes a finger inside. My nails claw at his back as I move with his hand.

His mouth leaves mine long enough to say, "So tight," before he's kissing me again. This time down my body, lavishing first one and then my other breast. And we're moving together as his finger works me. Pleasure is climbing higher and higher inside me. My body yearns to cry out, but I don't know if I should, so instead I dig my fingers in tighter until I'm coming apart at the seams beneath him.

He leans his body forward and we're pressed together. I'm sweating and he's not, but I can't find it in me to care right now.

"So beautiful."

"So tired," I gasp.

"So not done."

The promise in his voice reignites the fire inside me. Adrian stands up, his hands going for the button on his pants.

"Can I?" I ask, thankful I didn't let myself think about the words before they came out.

"You can do anything you want to me."

I tremble as I sit up and he waits.

My fingers move slowly as I push his button through the hole. I'm sure he's used to girls being much better at this, but he doesn't say anything. Risking a glance at him, I look up and his eyes are just as smoldering, just as intense as they were earlier, maybe more.

Adrian touches my cheek. Pulls the band out of my hair and runs his fingers through it. I work his zipper next, seeing the bulge he's hiding behind it. My breath catches.

"Keep going, baby. I want you."

And I do. He steps out of his pants after I push them down and then I hook my hands in his boxer-briefs, sliding those down too. Adrian's length springs free. This time I almost swallow my tongue. Granted, I don't have anything to compare it to, but he looks really big.

"You started this. You have to finish it," he says, so I do. I push his underwear all the way down and he steps out of those too. Fear spikes inside me when he begins to step away, but he only bends down, pulling his wallet out of his pocket and then a square package from there.

Adrian opens it, but this he does for himself. I can't take my eyes off him as he rolls it down.

He lays me on the bed and takes off the rest of my clothes. Lies down on top of me, and even though there's space between us, I wonder if he can feel my heart beating.

His fingers drift over me. "Still wet for me," he says.

"Go slow." My voice sounds like a plea and I hope it doesn't scare him.

"Whatever you want."

And then he's pushing in. Slow...so very slow and I'm arching toward him, but tensing up too. *I can do this, I can do this, I can do this.*

A small burst of pain makes me cry out and Adrian freezes above me. *In* me.

"Why didn't you tell me, Little Ghost?" His forehead drops to mine.

"Because it doesn't change anything. No matter what, I want to be with you."

He gives me a small nod. A light, soft kiss on my forehead before he starts to move. With each stroke the pain is wiped away and all I feel is pleasure. Adrian. I wrap my arms around his back again. Sweat slicks his skin now and I revel in the fact that I can get him that worked up.

Each time he pulls out, I gasp, wanting to feel him deep again.

Words fill my head. I want to call his name. Want to

hear him say mine, but I don't know if it's right or if he'll hear the need for him in my voice, so I don't say anything. Try to let my body tell him how good this feels. How good he feels as I move with him and clutch the strong muscles of his back.

His lips take my own and all I can think is we're joined in two incredibly important places. That's all it takes for the pull to start building in me again. Adrian seems to sense it and moves faster, kisses deeper, and that's when I can't hold it back anymore. I bite my lip as wave after wave washes over me.

"Christ," Adrian hisses, and then he tenses above me. I feel him jerk inside me and know he's finishing too. Veins spring to life in his neck before he pulls away. I miss the feel of him instantly. I'm scared I'm going to cry. I don't know why. Don't know if it's because that was more than I expected or because as beautiful as it was, there are lies between us because of me. Lies that I need to come clean about before they ruin us both.

I try to stand up, but Adrian says, "Don't go. Stay here. I'll be right back."

He disappears into the bathroom and I hear water running. He's back in a few seconds and I can't keep my eyes from his gorgeous, naked body.

"Let me clean you."

It's so sweet and so unexpected that I'm again scared the tears will come. I try not to be embarrassed as he cleans me with the washcloth. His condom is gone and when he's done, he puts the washcloth away, turns off the light, and crawls back into bed with me.

He doesn't touch me at first, making me wonder if he's going to pull away again. If somehow what was so beautiful to me could have been a mistake for Adrian.

"Come here, my little ghost." As he says it, he's pulling me to him, my back to his front, out bodies naked and molding together. He wraps his arm around my waist, his mouth by my ear. All I can do is feel him and hear him. He didn't just say *little ghost*...he said *my*. It's thrilling and wonderful and another reason to feel guilty all wrapped together.

"Do you want to know more of the story?" he asks, holding me so close.

"Yes."

"It was about more than just wanting her. The girl... she was amazing. So giving. She gave the man something he didn't deserve...but he was really thankful. He treasured it."

In the dark, I let the wetness in my eyes brim over. "What happened next?"

"I don't know," he says after what feels like forever. "I don't know the end."

Another truth I would prefer over the lie. No promises.

Adrian doesn't say anything else. I can tell when he falls asleep, when his breathing evens out, his body as relaxed as I've ever felt it. But I can't sleep. Guilt churns inside me.

Quietly I slip out of bed. I grab my short robe from my bag and slip it on before walking over to the window and opening the curtains to look out. *Please don't wake up.*

You can see the coldness in the air. I look at the stars. They're so bright, so never ending and so far away from all the hurt that I envy them.

The tattoo on Adrian's chest shows in my mind and again the look on his face when he saw the little girl. The pain that is so dark and lonely in his eyes and how when we came together, I could have sworn it disappeared. Tears stream down my face. How can I feel that way when I know it's a lie? When I know he'll never be able to look at me without seeing the nephew I took from him, once he finds out?

But I have to tell him. After what just happened, something that I will always treasure, I almost feel dirty. It was like he somehow knew and tried to clean it from me but couldn't because it's my secret sin he doesn't know about.

I wipe my eyes, trying to hold all these feelings at bay. I have to tell him and I don't deserve to cry before I do it.

"She stands amongst the stars of night..."

When I hear his voice, I jump but don't turn around. I can't.

"They look back at her and envy her light. For none of those stars shine as bright as she..."

I don't move. His words are beautiful music in my head.

"That's all I can think of right now," he adds. I don't know what it is about those words, but they break me. All I can think of is it's perfect exactly how it is. He doesn't need more, because I don't think it can get any better.

I can't hold back the cry that pulls out of me. It's not loud and I bury my face in my hand, but still he knows. I feel him behind me, so close but not reaching for me.

"I'm sorry."

I hate that he thinks I'm crying because of what we did. He might not be able to touch me right now, but I need my hands on him. I turn, grab him around the neck, and bury my face into his chest.

"It's not because of what we did. I loved being with you."

Finally he holds me back, squeezes me to him. Probably because I'm breaking down, but the reason doesn't matter.

"Adrian...I..."

"Shhh. It's okay."

Without knowing it, he saves me from telling him I know about Ashton. That my father ruined their lives.

We stand together, holding each other for what feels like hours. Adrian turns to the side so we can both look out the window and watch the stars.

"You're wrong," I whisper. "It's not me who shines so bright. It's you."

He doesn't answer, but I could swear the beat of his heart picks up against my cheek.

Chapter Seventeen

~Adrian~

No matter what's going on around me, I've always known one thing. I show what I want to whoever I want to see it, but my thoughts have always been mine. I may not like where they go sometimes, but I'm good at keeping them locked in there and knowing what they mean.

Right now I have all sorts of shit taking space inside my brain and I don't know what half of it means. I don't like that—the loss of control or the mixed feelings and they all stem from the beautiful, naked girl lying upstairs in bed.

I don't like to be scared. I spent my childhood living in fear and under the control of my dad. I keep my feelings in check because getting close meant being afraid and losing that control. The only people I let go with were Angel and Ashton and then I let Ash die and ran from Angel. It's been easy to keep my distance since then. Even with Colt and Cheyenne, they don't really know me.

I think I want my little ghost to know me.

I think she already does.

She knows my words, which are part of my soul, a part I've never willingly let anyone else see, yet I show them to her. I write them for her. She knows those parts of me—the only parts of me that aren't a lie.

Would she still be here if she knew the rest?

"Hey, you. You disappeared."

I turn toward the sound of her voice, rough with sleep. She's in her pajamas as she approaches me in the corner of the lobby.

There's a lie there. An excuse waiting to come out, but in this, this one little thing, I choose to give her a truth. At least as much as I can. "Sometimes there's so much shit going on up here"—I tap the side of my head—"that I have to have some space...or be alone so I can work through it."

Which probably makes me sound like an asshole. Or weak, but she doesn't look at me with either of those feelings in her eyes. Not really pity either. Just understanding tinged with sadness.

"Oh...okay. I'll go back upstairs, then. I don't want to—"

"Come here." Looking at her, all sexy from sleep, her lips swollen from my kisses and her skin blushed with red, probably from remembering what we did last night, I wonder why I ever left her. Why I didn't lose myself in her again instead of everything in my head.

She steps closer. I'm leaning against the wall and I pull her to me. She fits right up against me and damned if she doesn't quiet some of the voices. *Tell her you don't want space from her.*

Instead, I tilt her head up and kiss her. She tastes like cinnamon toothpaste and melts against me, making me smile against her mouth. My hands fit perfectly on her waist as I let my fingers slightly bite into her skin.

"What are you doing to me?" I ask into her ear before pulling away. She opens her mouth as if to reply, but I shake my head. I needed the question out there so she knows what I'm feeling, but I can't contemplate the answer. Can't let myself think about the fact that she's here and I want her to be or that I'm holding her and kissing her when usually those aren't the things that are important when I'm with a girl. It's all about the act, but with her it doesn't feel like an act and that's another thing that scares the hell out of me, that I don't want to think about right now.

"What do you want to do today?" I ask her. It's not like there's probably that much to do around here, but I want to do something with her. She's the girl with ghosts in her eyes, but she's the most level person I know. She deserves a good day and I want one—to pretend I'm just as level as she is.

"Nothing."

"What?" I kiss her neck as though I have a right to kiss her when I want to. I know I can't give her more than this. I've never wanted to with anyone else. Those things aren't inside me anymore, but for another day, I think I'd like to pretend. To wear a different façade than the one usually in place. "Nothing?"

I let one of my hands travel up her body and stroke the soft skin of her neck.

"Okay...maybe...I can't think when you do that." Her voice is breathy, the way I like it.

"Fine." I pull back so my mouth isn't tempted to taste her again, but keep my hands on her.

"Maybe not nothing, but...why don't we just hang out? Walk around? It's more of an adventure if you don't plan it." She looks down as though those words embarrass her.

"I love how real you are." I brush my thumb across her cheek. "You're honest, but also...so fucking innocent. You're different than the other girls I know." She makes me want to be honest with her.

She closes her eyes, making me think I said the wrong thing. Did the wrong thing. "What's wrong, Little Ghost?"

Delaney opens her eyes, shadows creeping in on them. For the first time since I was a dumb-ass kid, I want to try and win a battle for someone. I never could growing up, so I learned to stop trying. I don't like those shadows in her eyes and I wonder if it would be worth it to try again. To go to war with whatever plagues her because at least *someone* I care about should be happy. Since it won't be me, I think I'd like it to be her.

"I'm not that honest."

That's what she thinks. Her little white lies can't compare to the ones I live every day.

"Neither am I, so I can't fault you for that. But you're innocent and it's sexy as hell."

It's so strange, being with her like this. Being with

anyone like this. What I just told her sounds like a line, one I would have used on another girl, but with her it's true. The words come out without my having to think about them or plan them or paste that fake-ass smile on my face.

"Oh God. I can't believe this is happening." She covers her face with her hands. It's still pretty early in the morning, so even though we're in the lobby of the hotel, it's empty.

"I never expected..." She shakes her head.

I feel her pulling away. This is where I should open my hands and let her go. Set her free because she deserves to fly and I never will, but instead I touch her hands, gently prying them away from her face. "Don't think. Don't stress. Just...laugh until those ghosts disappear from your eyes. They do, ya know? They're not always there. I can't make promises, but we're here now. Let's just..." Ashton slips his way into my head.

"I Adrian... you Ash."

"No, no." I shake my head at him. "You're Ash."

"Let's play. I wanna be like you."

I remember standing there in awe because this little guy wanted to be me. No one ever envied me for anything. Girls wanted me, Dad liked to hit me, Angel protected me, but here was this little kid who wanted to *be* me. It was fucking incredible.

"Let's pretend to be someone else. Pretend we don't have anything to worry about except right now." And I need that. I didn't think I needed anything anymore, but standing here, I realize I do.

"Okay."

"I'll make sure you don't regret it," I say against her ear. She shivers and it transfers to me. Damn, this girl affects me.

We go upstairs to our room. "I need to take a shower," she tells me.

Yeah. That sounds good to me too. "Want some company?" I ask, and damned if she doesn't blush.

"I don't think that's a good idea if we want to get out of here."

There's something else to her voice that tells me not to push it. It has nothing to do with being out of here on time because we don't have a specific time to go anywhere. She has her boundaries, just like I do, only mine aren't physical.

I nod, without breaking eye contact so she knows I'm hearing her. I learned that growing up. Even if I don't understand something or I know it's a lie, or on those rare occasions I get it and it's real, look someone in the eye when it's important. When Mom was hurt, she could never do that. That's how I knew it was a lie, even if the bruises couldn't be seen.

While she takes a shower, I unwrap my hand. It's healed enough that I don't need to keep the bandage on anymore. Even though my eye isn't as purple as it was, I still have the strike against me. Having my hand bandaged feels like another one. It's one of those signs that something's wrong that people notice but don't fucking act on.

I don't want to look like that when I'm with her.

I shower after she does. I come out of the bathroom

with a towel wrapped around my waist. Delaney's standing by the mirror, looking into the glass, but I know she's really waiting on me. It's in the way she stands and the way she turns to look my way and fuck if I don't get hard seeing her gaze at me all innocent in nothing but a bra and a pair of jeans.

"What?" I ask her.

"That was ridiculous, right? We had sex last night and we both needed to shower. I could have..."

"Don't." I step toward her and she looks up at me. This girl does something to me. Makes my gut twist and makes me feel on edge. I'm not stupid enough not to understand it. Not to get that I'm falling for her when I've never fallen for anyone else in my life, but I know I have nothing to give her either. Not permanently.

"Don't what?" she asks.

"Don't ever feel like you have to do something because I want it, okay? If I'm pushing you, tell me to fuck off and don't ever feel bad about that. I'll respect the hell out of you for it."

I know it's Dad's fault and I will always hate the bastard for what he did to Mom, but there's a part of me who's angry at Mom too. I don't get why she couldn't tell him no. Why she couldn't sneak away with me and Angel the same way my sister had the guts to leave. Even when I flirt or make my intentions obvious, I never want a girl to think I'm pushing myself on her, the way Dad did with Mom.

"I know you would never try to force me into doing something I don't want to. It just feels..."

"Like it doesn't matter." I trace the swells of her breasts with my fingers. Palm their heavy weight, covered by cool satin. "We have time, if you want to. If not...well, hopefully you'll let me have a taste again. Will you, Little Ghost?" I pinch her nipples and she cries out. "Will you let me?"

"Yes..."

Jesus, she's hot. I kiss her forehead, then her lips. "If you want to leave this hotel room, you really need to get dressed right now."

Then she fucking giggles and it's so crazy. I've never been one to go for girls who giggle, but it's different with her. And even though she's happy, I know she still has clouds in her life. She doesn't smile as much as she should and damned if it doesn't feel good to give her that. I'm suddenly trying to think of ways to do it again, which is just another of those strange things I have to file away in my brain.

"So sweet...so innocent," I tell her before I pretend to nip at her neck, which makes her laugh again before backing up. As much as I want to keep going, to kiss her again, I don't.

We make it out of the hotel a few minutes later. We're in one of those little towns that look perfect, like the one I grew up in. I wonder what secrets it hides, because they all have them.

It's cold, so we're both bundled up. There's a sign on a pole outside a Winter Celebration, and even though I've never been to something like that in my life, and I'm honestly not real excited about the idea right now, I think it's something she would like.

"What about this?" I ask. Happiness eclipses any of the remaining shadows in her eyes and I know I asked the right question.

"Really?" she asks, and she looks so fucking happy that it almost makes me feel happy too. Or maybe it does and it's too hard for me to admit it, but I think I'd do just about anything to hold on to that feeling.

Chapter Eighteen

~Delaney~

He's smiling and I wonder if he notices. It sends this electric sort of feeling through me. Like I've been shot through the heart with a lightning bolt, but it doesn't hurt. It shocks me to life and makes me feel more alive than I ever have.

This feeling can't be wrong. What I'm doing can't be wrong if it makes him smile so pure. If it makes me feel like this. But I know that's not completely true. I need to tell him. The words are there in my mouth and on my tongue all the time, but I can't make myself push them out because I'm scared of losing him and scared of hurting him when all I want is for him to be okay. It might have begun as a hope of absolution for my family, but that's not what it's about anymore. It's about the man standing in front of me and the warmth that spreads through me when I'm with him and the jolts he shocks into my heart.

"If you don't mind being cheesy with me, I think the festival sounds fun."

"I've never done cheesy before. Might as well give it a try."

We walk to the car and this time I drive. It's not hard to find because half the streets are closed down, directing all the traffic in the same direction. Luckily we find a parking spot quickly and head to the festival. It's only midmorning, but it's already busy. The air is crisp, but everyone's walking around like us, bundled up, though they have steaming cups in their hands.

"It smells like apples," I tell him. "I love the smell of apples. There's something comforting about it." I shiver, but then feel a sudden burst of warmth when Adrian puts an arm around me.

"I don't want you to get too cold on me. I have plans for you later on today...though it might be fun to warm you up."

Another laugh tumbles from my mouth. He chuckles, too, and I nuzzle closer to him as we walk. I love this side of him. That's almost so carefree, even though I know it's another mask for the pain inside. It feels real, though. I want it to be real.

"Do you have a childhood memory with apples?" he asks. It takes me a minute to remember that I'd just mentioned them.

"No..." A ghost of a memory floats into my head. "You know what? I never even thought about it, but I do." It all starts to form in my brain and I can't help but let it out. "I was about thirteen. My dad had been away working for over a week. Or we thought he was working. He traveled a lot and I always missed him…"

It had all been a lie. I hate missing him and knowing how much I loved him when none of it had been real. When he'd lived a double life and hurt all of us.

"Where was he?" Adrian asks.

"With his girlfriend."

"I'm sorry."

Not as sorry as he would be if he knew my dad and the same woman were in a car together, driving by his house a year later.

"What happened?" Part of me doesn't want to tell him. Doesn't want to share anything positive about my dad with Adrian because of what my father did to his family. But I want to talk about it. I want to open up with him whenever he asks because I don't want there to be secrets between us. I'd like to find a way to reveal them all and for us to be okay.

"He came home and saw me sitting in the window watching for him. He didn't even come in the house. He just called me out and we jumped in the car and he took me to the fair that had come to town and we ate caramel apples. He made me feel special. After him being gone, I wanted that time with him. We laughed and he told me about his trip and we talked about Maddox and trying to get him to play football again."

At the time, I'd thought it was perfect. My best day. Yes, I'd been Daddy's girl for a while now and I'd always thought that was good. That it was okay, but now I hate that part of my past.

"It sounds like it was a happy time. What changed, Little Ghost? What ruined that day?"

My head snaps up to look at him. "How did you know?"

"You let your emotions into your words. I think you have a big heart that's been bruised, but you're better than me because you keep letting it beat. You let it get stronger. So tell me, who ruined your day. Who bruised your heart?"

I stop walking. There's people all around us, but it feels like we're the only two in the world. Everyone else manages to fade away and as I play his words in my head and as I feel his intense stare, I know there is absolutely no man in the world as beautiful as he is. Yes, he's closed off and freely admits to using sex and drugs to hide from the world. Yes, when we first met he told me he wanted in my pants, and yet he makes sure I know we go at my speed. That I should never do something I don't want to do for him. So despite his shortcomings, to me, he's beautiful. His heart is more scarred than mine ever could be, but he cares. He might not know it, but he feels for people. It's so easy to pretend to listen, but he really does. I don't think anyone listens and really, really thinks about my words the way he has. Like each one of them is important.

He walks forward, which makes me walk backward, and we're suddenly leaning against a tree.

"Let me bandage your heart the way you did my hand."

My eyes fill with tears. Who would have known this boy who is so hard on the outside could be filled with such beautiful words?

"My mom...she was angry when we came home. She'd been planning a special afternoon for them, but it was too late for them to go by the time we got back. She told him it was okay and smiled and hugged him, but when he went upstairs, she told me it was my fault. That I was always trying to get all the attention and that I was selfish. She said I ruined their day on purpose. I didn't know, Adrian. I swear I didn't."

He pulls me to him. My arms feel at home around his waist, with his body so close to mine. His chin rests on my head, and his arms are around my shoulders.

"You went when your dad told you to. There was nothing wrong with that. If she said that to you, she didn't know you. Not in the way that matters. Your heart beats so strong, I feel it against my chest. You make mine want to catch up, to match the rhythm."

His words are too much. They're everything and as much as they build me up, they break me down too. I do the only thing I can think to do, what I need to do, and close my mouth over his. It's the first time I've been the one to kiss him and I can tell he's holding off, letting me take the lead. I wish I could feel him, really feel him through all our clothes and jackets, but his lips are the perfect tease. The perfect prequel to Adrian and how he feels and what I know he can and will do to me later.

He moans and I think it's probably the sexiest sound I've ever heard. But then he's pulling away. I want to grab him. Yank him closer and never let him go, but people are walking next to us now.

We find the source of the apple smell, and it's a booth with the longest line. We wait in it and people talk about how they make the best hot apple cider in the United States. Adrian chats easily with people in line around us. It's a different side of him. He talks to them differently than he does to Colt, Cheyenne, or me. He holds me against him as he does it, so I can't see his face. I try and study the sound of his voice the way he seems to know mine, trying to gauge if it's another of his masks or if for this moment in time he's really opening himself up. If he's really trying to pretend to be like everyone else.

When it's our turn, he orders us both cups and we walk around, sipping it like all the locals do. There are booths and games. We play some, and he doesn't vow to win me a stuffed animal like you always hear about. I think I love that about him. Love how real he is.

Most of the booths are made up of locals: crochet blankets on sale, handmade hats, gloves, and painted coffee mugs.

We look at everything. I know this can't really be his idea of a good time, but he's here and I love that. There's nowhere else I'd rather be than with him right now.

The air starts getting colder and the pull to the hotel room and being alone with Adrian becomes stronger. "Do you want to go back now?" I ask him.

He looks at me, promises of pleasure in his eyes. "To be alone with you? Do you have to ask?"

Laughing, I say, "Yes, I know. You've been trying to get into my pants for a while now, and you finally made it."

The words were meant to be a joke but there is a change in his look. The playful smile I've started to get used to fades before he says, "You know that's not all this is about, right? I'm not one to make promises I don't know if I can keep. I won't insult you by doing that, but...it's not just about that."

"I know." The words come out steady and strong because they are. "I'm not asking for promises. And I know how honest you are. Maybe in the beginning that's what it was about, but I can see the change."

In that moment, I could swear he's stripped bare. That he's proud. I want him to be that. Want him to be proud of who he is because he deserves it.

"Full of so many surprises." His finger skates down the side of my face.

"It's true...I owe you that. I owe you more truths than that one."

"One at a time. That's all we can do is take it one at a time."

We're quiet most of the way back to the hotel. During the short drive, I wonder what's on his mind as guilt hammers down on me. Things have gone too far. It's been too long for me to have any kind of real excuse for not telling him. The thought of hurting him makes an ache build inside me. One so strong and fast-moving that I feel like it's breaking me apart. The words are there and I need to get them out and hope, hope there is some way to make him understand. Some way that this won't hurt him.

We take the last corner on the way to our hotel. "Adrian. I—"

He's not looking at me when he says, "Oh shit!"

From there everything happens so quickly it's hard to follow. Adrian jerks the car into a nearby parking spot, jumps out while it's still running. The door hits another car and he leaves it open. And runs. I look up ahead of us and see cop cars, an ambulance, someone on a stretcher, and people all over the sidewalk. My heart drops.

Turning the key, I jerk it out of the ignition and run. Run to find Adrian.

Chapter Nineteen

~Adrian~

I can hardly breathe as I push my way through the people. My breath doesn't matter, though. I don't know what happened or who's hurt, but it's not important. All I see is Ashton. I feel him. Red clouds my vision as I try to work my way through the crowd. I see the ambulance that came to our house. The people who tried to take him from me.

Please don't be dead, please don't be dead, please don't be dead.

I remember Colt and walking up to the house to find him on the ground. Knowing I was too late. That he would die like Ash. *Ashton.* Oh fuck, pain pierces my chest again. I'm shaking and people are crowding me and I can't get through.

"Watch where you're going!" someone says, but it doesn't stop me. I have to save them. *Don't die, don't die, don't die.*

Please Ashton don't die.

My vision blurs. My chest aches and my legs beg me to fucking stop. What can I do? Who the fuck am I? If I couldn't save a helpless little boy who only wanted to be like me, who wanted me to protect him, what the hell do I think I'm going to do here?

I push through the front of the crowd and I see him. I see that little boy with the big eyes as they look up at me. He's bloody and hurting, the light gone from those eyes that looked at me like I was something. Like I was somebody.

"Ash!"

The image morphs and it's not Ashton anymore. It's someone I don't know, lying on a stretcher.

"Adrian?"

The sound of Delaney's voice brings me back to the past. Ashton and blood and a broken little boy. *Why couldn't you save me?* I rub my eyes. I'm fucking cracking up and I know it. Ashton hadn't said anything, but I know it was there. I thought it as I held his bloody little body, memorizing the injuries as though that could make them mine instead of his. "I'm sorry."

I'm so fucking sorry. When will it ever end? Do I deserve it to end? Why did I have to screw up so bad? He was perfect and innocent and I still see his blood on my hands. Fuck, I want to be clean of it, but I deserve to wear it. Deserve to see it every day because he's in the ground and he would have loved me. He *did* love me and I killed him.

"It's okay. You don't have anything to be sorry about."

She touches me and I shake it off. "He's dead. He's dead. He's dead."

Even to my own ears I sound insane. Maybe I am. Maybe I've always been. But he's fucking dead because I should have been protecting him.

"He's okay. Look. He's talking to EMTs."

Ash is gone again. The guy is probably my age. He's on the stretcher just like I thought, but he is sitting up and he is talking. There's a car and a bike and I know he must have been hit, but there's no blood. No empty brown eyes, locked on me.

I'm fucking losing it. I hate that she sees me like this. Hate that I'm *like* this.

"Come on, Adrian. Let's go. Come inside with me."

"Adrian! Where's Ashton? What happened to Ash?" Angel's voice slams into my head now.

"Adrian?" Delaney.

"Adrian?" Angel.

I push my way through the crowd. I need to get the fuck out of here. Delaney's on my heels, but I can't make myself stop. Up the stairs, down the hall, unlock the room. It's all on autopilot. She storms in right behind me as I'm grabbing my bag and shoving stuff inside.

"What are you doing?" she asks, out of breath. Christ, I'm being an asshole to her. She doesn't deserve this.

"Leaving."

"Why? Stay. Talk to me."

Honesty finds its way out of my mouth. "Leaving is what I do. My feet itch to run and my hands itch to write and my mind is going and going and I can't fucking shut it down." Stopping, I turn to look at her, which is a huge mistake. It makes me want to stay. "Sometimes I feel like I'm taking so much in and I can't stop it. It overloads my fucking head and I can't forget. I just want to fucking forget."

"If you go, let me go with you." She steps closer. "If you need to write, I'll be your paper. I have no idea what I'm doing here. I don't know if this is the right thing, but whatever you need, if you need to try to forget, let me help you."

What I want is to take a really big bong hit and get the hell out of here.

She takes off her jacket. Her scarf. And somehow the voices in my head are quieting. I don't want the weed. Don't want anything but her. "I have no idea what I'm doing," she says again before pulling her shirt over her head. My little ghost drops her arms, and it slowly falls from her hand.

Her breasts heave up and down with her breathing. She's biting her lip and I know she's nervous and I know I'm a bastard for wanting to take her up on this.

"You're too good for that, for me to use you."

"Then don't..." Her voice is so low, so soft, but it's all I hear. "Don't use me. Just make me feel good, Adrian. Let me try to make you feel good too."

"You do." And it's probably the realest truth I've given her. She does. She makes me feel good. There is suddenly nothing that could make me leave this room. My jacket comes off, tossed to the chair.

"Come here," but I don't wait for her. I pull her to me. Her breasts press against my chest and her breath smells like apple cider and I let the scent comfort me the way she said it does her.

"I want you bare to me, my little ghost. I don't know all your secrets and you know none of mine, but I don't want to wear masks with you right now. I want to see all of you. Show me those ghosts in your eyes and I'll try to kiss them away. Let me bare my scars to you and feel your lips on them." Because fuck if I don't need to tear down this façade. I know she sees how broken I am, but to admit it is different. To acknowledge the masks are there—regardless if she knows what they are or not—and to feel her try to comfort me. To give her that in return is a burning need inside me. An ache that can only be cured with her because no matter what, she doesn't push me and that means something.

"I want that, Adrian. I would do anything to take your pain away."

And I believe her. My hands travel over the landscape of her back. I let them slide down until they're under her ass, and then I lift her. Easily she comes to me, trusts me, wrapping her legs around my waist. Her shoes dig into my thighs and I welcome it. Feel her jeans as they stretch across her ass and wish it was her naked skin under my hands.

My mouth trails down to her neck and she arches for me, giving me free rein to explore her. "Such a gift," I tell her as I lick the soft skin there. Taste her, learn her, until she invades all of my senses. She's what I hear, see, taste, and smell. I want all of it.

As if she's just as hungry for me, her mouth finds mine. Her arms are so tight around my neck as though she's afraid I'm going to let her go.

"I won't let you go," I say, though we both know eventually I will.

She shows me her eyes and I see the knowledge there. See her pain and excitement and everything I could want her to show me.

I turn and lay her on the bed. Push my stupid fucking bag to the floor because it's not like I'm going anywhere tonight.

I slide down the straps of her bra. My fingers drift behind her back to the hooks. When it's gone, I drink my fill with my eyes. Kiss each peak with my mouth. When I pull gently with my teeth, she cries out.

"Adrian...oh God..."

I can't stop there, so I kiss my way down her torso. Unbutton her jeans, take off her shoes, her pants, before I start at her ankles and work my way back up with my mouth. Each place I kiss her, touch her, I pretend it wipes away one of her ghosts. Cures one of her aches and relieves some of her pain.

Her legs hang over the side of the bed as I kneel on the floor between them. She's so beautiful. So fucking beautiful that when I look at her, it's hard to remember there's any bad in the world. "Tell me what you want. Tell me what you need."

She doesn't answer. Only cries out as I push a finger inside her.

"You...just you..."

"I'm here." I move up her body, lean over her to take her mouth as I kiss her again. Pump my fingers and revel in the little gasps of pleasure she makes. When her body begins to stiffen under me, she says, "Oh God, oh God, oh God," over and over. I kiss her again, deeper, until her words are lost and she's coming apart beneath me.

I can't help but smile. "You are so sexy."

She doesn't smile back. She's still completely open to me like I ask and so serious when she says, "Let me kiss your scars, Adrian. Show them to me."

There's never been anyone I've wanted to show more. "Yes."

I take my shirt off, kick out of my pants, and then lay on the bed, as bare as she is. Her eyes skate over my body, exploring me with all that innocence and curiosity in her that makes me smile.

"Don't be scared," I tell her, hoping to wipe away her fear.

When she straddles me, her warm, wet heat against me, it's searing. A wildfire raging inside me. She kisses my stomach.

"I lied to you. When I said I wasn't close with my sister. She was my best friend. The only person I used to have in my corner."

I know her mouth can't really take away these scars, but it feels so good to show them. To bare them in a way I've never done.

Her mouth moves up to my chest, kisses the right side.

"My father used to beat the shit out of us. Mom... Angel...and me. We all just fucking took it, but then Angel left and she came back for me."

Her mouth stops moving. "Adrian—"

"No, baby. Don't. Not right now." If she talks, I won't be able to and she deserves to know the things I can handle telling her.

Her mouth comes down again. This time on the little fist tattooed over my heart, the one that holds my heart in its tiny hand.

"There was only one responsibility I ever had. Only one person I should have taken care of...and I let him die."

She freezes on top of me like I knew she would. What other response can someone have to something like that?

"Adrian...no. You didn't. You couldn't."

"Shhh." I run my hand through her hair. See her eyes water and wipe away the tears. "Don't stop, Little Ghost."

Indecision shows on her face. It's not as though a comment like mine wouldn't cause it. She has every right to stop. Probably should stop, but she doesn't. Instead she takes my hand, the fingers that just wiped her tears and she kisses each one of them.

"I need you," I tell her. She's still straddling me as I sit up and grab my bag, pulling out a condom from inside. Her eyes don't leave my hand as I open the package, roll it on, before I push in, disappearing inside her.

"Oh God...Adrian."

I lie back and she goes with me. I thrust forward and her hips roll with mine. We move together, in unison. She's the fire in my veins, the breath in my lungs, and the glue trying to hold each of my scars together.

I've had sex. A lot of sex, but nothing like this. Nothing like it is with her. It's raw and real and fucking incredible.

"You feel so good." I know if it were possible to save me, to make me feel whole, she would be the one to do it. I can't be whole again, but it's nice to pretend.

My hands won't stop moving. I want to know all of her. Use her as my paper, like she said. Her back, her shoulders. Every part of her I explore while we move together.

"Adrian...I'm..."

"I know, baby. Let go," I tell her.

And she does. Quivering above me, she lets go. Lets me catch her and then I'm doing the same.

"I'm hiding! You can't find me!" Ashton tells me. He's sitting on the couch with a pillow in front of his face. Angel's in the kitchen, about to head out to work.

"Ash? Where are you?" I call.

He giggles. "I hide!"

"Adrian. The mail came. You got the placement test results from the college."

I roll my eyes. I took my GED on my own, not wanting to be a dropout, but she pushed me on the college thing. It's not that I don't want it, but who will take care of them? "We're playing hide-and-seek. I'll look later."

"Hide-and-seek can wait. This is huge, little brother."

"Find me! Find me!" Ashton calls out.

"I'm looking for Ash. Have you seen him?" I ask her.

"Adrian!" Angel groans.

"Find me!" Ashton squeals.

Excitement colors Ashton's voice. It drives me crazy sometimes, the way she thinks she's my mom, but then I remember she's the only person who's ever really given a shit and I realize I'm lucky to have her.

"The test results might not matter. What if I don't get the scholarship?"

She crosses her arms. Ashton keeps yelling "Find me" in the background. "You're the smartest person I know. You had to write an essay for that scholarship. You're a beautiful writer, Adrian. There's no way you won't get it."

It feels good to make her proud. Good to know I'll hopefully make them both proud. I've fucked up so much with Mom and then screwing around, when Angel took me in. Maybe this will make up for it all.

"Open it," I tell her.

She smiles and I know she already did. "You did incredible. Just like I knew you would, you

little smart-ass!" She swats me with the paper. "I
have something else for you too. This one I didn't
open."

"I hide! Find me," Ashton's little voice calls
again. My hands shake as I grab the envelope.

"Ashton? Where are you? I can't find you!" I
open the flap, pull out the paper and read.

"We're pleased to tell you . . . Fucking A."

"Fucking A!" Ash calls.

"Shit!" I glance at the little boy on the couch.
"Ashton, don't—"

"Shit!" he repeats.

"Adrian!" Angel groans. "Watch. Your. Mouth.
You have to be careful. We're the only examples
he has."

I look at the words on the paper again. The
ones that say how much talent I have. The ones
that offer me money to go to school. "I'm trying
to, Angel. I'm going to make both of you proud."

She hugs me and then "finds" Ashton on
the couch, before giving him a hug. "I'm going
to work. Have a good day. Oh"—she turns to
me—"if you guys go outside, please bring him
out back. I hate this corner. The front yard's too
dangerous, especially when the roads are slip-
pery, like they are today."

I nod to appease her, my eyes scanning the
paper again. She's always overworrying about
everything.

"Find me!" Ashton says again. When I look at the couch this time, he's gone.

My eyes jerk open when the nightmare ends. Delaney's naked and wrapped in my arms. I pull her close, as close as I can get to her. Why didn't I listen? Why couldn't I have done the right thing by them?

"Were you dreaming?" she asks softly.

"Yeah."

She rolls over so she's facing me. Leaning up on my elbow, I look down at her. It's just now dusk outside. The last of the day, disappearing into night. Here, then gone, like Ashton was.

"Can I tell you something? It's probably not what you want to hear and I know it's not the right time, but I feel it and I need to—"

"Say it," I finish for her. "I want to hear whatever you have to say."

"I know I shouldn't and I know there's so much we don't know about each other and it's probably wrong of me but... but I'm falling in love with you. And I want you to know. You deserve to know and—"

"Say it again." I close my eyes. Focus on the words.

"I love you."

Those words wash through me. Fucking fill me up. She moves closer to me. Buries her face in my chest and I want nothing more than to be the man she deserves. "There have only ever been two people in my life who have loved me, and they both had no choice. And I let them down, Little Ghost. I don't want to break you too."

"You won't, Adrian. God, if you could only see. You're so much better than you give yourself credit for."

I let her think that's true. Wish it was. And I know I should be man enough to return her words, but I can't, so I give her what I can.

"Haunt me,
my little ghost,
Possess me.
Live inside me,
And scare away my sins
Until there's nothing left.
But you."

Chapter Twenty

~Delaney~

In the morning, I don't have to open my eyes to know I'm alone in the bed. The knowledge adds another weight to the anchor already holding me down. I should be floating. Part of me is. I love Adrian. I really, really do. And he didn't freak out when I told him. He didn't say it back and I didn't expect him to. Maybe I'm even partly glad he didn't because I wouldn't want him to admit something like that with the weight of my betrayal between us.

But he didn't run and the words he spoke were the most beautiful to ever touch my ears. Love and life and all the things that matter in this world live inside Adrian and he's shown me those pieces of him. I want to honor them and treasure them and lock them away in my heart forever.

Live inside me, he'd said, and I want to be there, the way he already inhabits me.

Which means I have to tell him right away and hope

there is some way to salvage what we have between us. Because I know when I do, he might hate me. Odds are he will.

The door to our room clicks and I know it's absolutely ridiculous, but I keep my eyes closed, not ready to see him. But it's hard, so very hard because my heart is calling to him and I want to soak in every part of him that I can.

The bed dips next to me and his hand pushes the hair away from my face.

"Don't open your eyes," he whispers, which immediately makes them pop open. "I knew you would cheat." He winks at me.

My heart flips, the way he tossed those perfect pancakes into the air.

He's not perfect, but he's sexy and beautifully broken, inspiring and passionate and *everything* at the same time.

"It's impossible not to open your eyes when someone tells you not to," I say.

"Then close your eyes." His hand moves to my forehead and then slides down, as though it is magical, making my eyes obey.

There's a rustling sound. My lips stretch into a smile and happiness bursts inside me, sending confetti all through me at the sweet scent that hits my nose.

"Open your eyes now, Little Ghost."

I do and they fill with tears. I don't try to stop them as they roll down my face and soak into the pillows we slept on last night.

"You bought me a caramel apple?" My voice cracks.

"Not to make you cry." He wipes my tears and holds it out to me. "You wear your emotions so openly. That's a gift. Don't ever lose that."

"I won't." I can hardly get the words out as I sit up and take the apple from him.

He opens another for himself and we lean against the headboard and eat caramel apples for breakfast, me still naked and him cold from braving the weather.

"Tell me more about you and your father," he says.

As much as the ache in my stomach hurts with his question, I want to share all of my life with him too. "Maddox used to play football. He was incredible. It was his and Dad's thing....That stopped all of a sudden. I don't know why, but then Dad started paying more attention to me. I thought I was lucky. Everything he ever told us was a lie, though. I hate that I looked up to him." This could maybe be the perfect time to tell him, but it doesn't feel right to do it here. To tell him away from home where he doesn't have his friends or anything else familiar to hold on to.

"At least with my old man, I always knew he was a bastard. He only hid it from the world, but not us."

"Maddox has always been there for me, though. He would do anything for me...maybe that's not always a good thing. He never does anything for himself and he carries too much blame for things that aren't his fault."

I expect Adrian to make a sarcastic comment. It's not like Maddox made the best impression. The only time they've really met, he punched Adrian for no reason. Still, Adrian doesn't let anything negative past his lips.

"He's solid, then. Does the right thing for the people he loves. It's so much fucking easier to be weak."

"You're not weak," I tell him. Maybe it's not the right thing to say. Maybe I'm not supposed to realize he's talking about himself, but I do and I hate it. Nerves twitch around inside me, but I ignore them. Turn to him and crawl onto his lap, straddle him, the apple in one hand, and hook a finger of the other under his chin like he's done to me, so I make sure he's seeing me. "You are so much more than you see, Adrian."

"You're naked and on my lap, baby. It's not like I'm looking anywhere but at you." He grins and I know he's trying not to really hear what I'm saying.

"I'm being serious. I'm not letting you deflect this. You're like this live energy that gets under my skin. You make me feel alive. You show me beauty in everything. You brought me a caramel apple," I say again.

"I'll buy you one every day if it makes you look at me like that," he says, and then leans toward me. "And if I get to lick the caramel off your lips." And he does. Then we make love again before I ask him to shower with me.

"If anyone could wash away my sins, it would be you," he says.

Those words grind my heart to dust. "Adrian."

He shakes his head, changes the subject. "I'll introduce you to shower sex."

He does and it's wonderful. I'm achy in so many places, but it's a good ache. A satisfied ache that I welcome. And then it's over and I miss every part of it.

All too soon we're packing our clothes to go home.

There are a million reasons we have to go back. I can't fake being sick another night at work and Maddox is likely to lose it if I don't come home. Adrian has a life to get back to as well. We have to go home so I can tell him and earn his forgiveness. But so badly I want to open my mouth and tell him *Let's stay*. That I don't want to go back.

"It's back to the real world when we leave this room, Little Ghost."

"You read my mind. I wish we could lock ourselves in here and never come out."

He nods as though he agrees and kisses me on the forehead. Without the words, I know what he's saying. What he's thinking. There are no promises when we leave. Especially once he learns the truth.

Adrian pulls up next to his car at my apartment complex. Maddox's motorcycle is here and I can honestly see him coming down and taking another shot at Adrian. Even though Adrian gets it, I don't think he would be so understanding a second time.

"I'd invite you up, but..."

"Yeah. I'm a little too tired to fight your brother today."

We get out of the car. Adrian tosses his bag into the passenger seat and I stand on the sidewalk, waiting, unsure of what to do or where we are. He looks at me and I think he's wondering the same thing. Finally a partial smile teases his kissable lips and he says, "Come here." Only he's walking to me as he says it. Our mouths meet perfectly as I stand on the curb and him in the parking lot.

I wish I could taste the caramel on his tongue. Savor the feel as he deepens the kiss and weaves his hand through my hair.

"What are you doing in the morning?" I ask him when we part. "I was thinking I could come over when I get off..." *Because I need to talk to you. Because I'm telling you the truth.*

"I don't know." He shrugs. "I'll call you."

He's pulling away, but I won't let him. I can't. No matter what, I have to go to his house in the morning.

"I love you," I tell him. "I really do." It's different saying it after sex, I think. I want him to know it had nothing to do with that and everything to do with him.

"You honor me," he says before walking back to his car...and then he's gone.

Maddox jerks me into his arms the second I walk through the door. He squeezes me so tight I can hardly breathe.

"Jesus Christ, don't you ever do that to me again, Laney. You hear me? Fuck Dad, fuck Mom. You and me, okay? Don't pull that disappearing shit again. We have to stick together."

Guilt wraps its hand around me and squeezes, even tighter than my brother is. "I'm sorry. I didn't mean for you to worry. I left you a note."

At that he pulls away. "Fuck notes too. I don't know that bastard and you write a letter telling me you're leaving with him and then don't answer your phone? Christ,

I would never forgive myself if I let something happen to you."

I shake my head and step in front of him when he tries to turn away. They're so much alike and he doesn't even know it. In another life, before my father, they would have been friends.

"I'm a grown woman, not your kid. Nothing happened. Adrian wouldn't hurt me. I can't help but think it would be a different story if you disappeared with some girl for a couple days."

"First, when do I ever disappear with a girl? If I did, it sure as hell wouldn't be with someone who had a family member six feet in the ground because of our father." His words make my stomach turn. The apartment stinks like cigarettes and I realize he's been smoking inside. Probably the whole time I've been gone.

"I'm sorry. Not for leaving, but I should have called you. It wasn't okay for me to let you worry. But... it's not your job to take care of me, Maddy. I'm a big girl. You need to realize that."

The way his eyes narrow when he looks at me, I know something happened. Know there's more to it than the fact that I disappeared with Adrian.

"The same way it isn't your job to take responsibility for Mom? To feel responsible for her not giving a shit about anything except herself? To try and make things better for her when she's the one who owes you?"

"What happened, Maddox?"

"She was never right to you. She was always jealous. What kind of mother is jealous of her own fucking daughter? She left you to find her bleeding on the bath-room floor. It should have been me. I should have had to deal with that and not you."

My heart rate spikes. "What happened?" My voice comes out louder than I meant.

Maddox paces the living room now. "You're just like me, little sister. You say I can't let go and that I take responsibility, but what do you do? You take her abuse when she yells at you for saving her life and you take care of her and you try to help her and you drag us here to meet some guy who's probably even more fucked-up than we are. Or if he's not now, he will be when he knows the truth."

"Stop it!" I grab his arms to keep him still. "You're trying to hurt me and that's not okay. What happened to Mom?"

"She didn't give a shit, what else? Her mandatory thirty days was up, so she left. She knows I don't care about her, but she doesn't call you, the one who is still trying to save her, but she called me."

Flashes of her on that bathroom floor four years ago pop into my head. Of how she must have looked in that hallway on this new suicide attempt. How small she was in that hospital bed. "What happened?"

"I hung up on her."

Oh my God. "Maddox! Where is she?"

He collapses onto the couch, elbows on his knees, hands in his hair, and sighs. "I tried not to fucking go, but I couldn't help it. She's at home. I saw her there, but I didn't talk to her. I knew you'd be freaked out. There's nothing we can do. She's an adult. She's home. Is that going to stop you from trying to save her?"

I feel the pull. She's my *mom* and she just got out of the hospital after trying to kill herself.

And she called Maddox, not me. She told me she doesn't want my help.

I fall onto the couch next to my brother. My best friend. "Why does she hate me?"

He curses. Wraps an arm around me. "I don't know, but it's her issue. I think it was just...Dad started to favor you and she took that as a slight. Then with everything that happened...Knowing that no matter how much she loved him, he obviously didn't give a shit. I think it was easier to lash out at you, but that doesn't make it fucking right. She's your mom and it was always her job to love you."

"I know..." And I do. I didn't make him treat me differently. I didn't make him lie, gamble. I didn't put him in the car with another woman when he was driving that day.

"Laney...I'm sorry, my baby girl. Daddy loves you," he told me as I stood next to the cell talking to him. Maddox was back in the corner, wouldn't come near him, looking at him with angry eyes that haven't left him ever since. And he didn't even try to get Maddox to forgive him. Why didn't he try?

"Delaney! Let's go." Mom grabs my hand and pulls me away.

"Why didn't he try to get you to forgive him, Maddox? Why did he only ask me?"

Every muscle in my brother's body stiffens. Things that should have clicked into place a long time ago start fitting together now.

"Why didn't he ask you, Maddy? Why didn't you ask the same questions I did?"

Why did he and Dad stop playing ball together before any of that happened...Maddox was angrier before that too...and that's when Dad started getting closer to me.

"What are you doing, Delaney? Why are you spending so much time alone with your father? It's not right, at your age. He should be with Maddox when he's home. He doesn't even play football with your brother anymore. You're taking him away from your brother."

"You knew..." whispers out of my mouth. "Didn't you? Somehow you found out. You knew about the affairs. What about the gambling? Did you know about that too?" That his work trips weren't work related. That he disappeared with the woman who would be in the car with him when he killed Adrian's nephew. That there would be debts and secrets that would change all our lives.

Maddox jerks away from me. "He used to fucking take me with him when he gambled and I thought it was cool. That we'd go away and it was a secret you and Mom didn't know. I didn't realize there was anything wrong with it—it had been happening since I was a kid! But then things started getting worse and he would have to go more because he wasn't winning. That's the first time I realized something was wrong and then I met *her*."

Oh my God. My brother met the woman?

"That was it. That's when I knew it wasn't okay, him screwing around on Mom. It felt like a lie to all of us. He fucking bribed me not to tell and I didn't. Where would my college money come from? All I ever wanted was football, Laney."

Oh my God, oh my God, oh my God.

"But he told me he was done. I couldn't keep his fucking secrets anymore and he told me it stopped, but it didn't. He started getting closer to you and then Mom started getting pissed at you, and I had to have fucking *known* it was still happening. I would have had to be stupid not to, but I kept my mouth shut. What if I would have told? Or threatened to tell? Would he have stopped? Would that kid still be alive? Would Mom have dealt better and not treated you like shit?"

It's suddenly too much. A scream builds up inside me. "I hate this! I'm so tired of all the fucking *lies* and *secrets!*" *Guilt and pain.* "When will it end?"

"I'm sorry, Laney. So sorry I screwed up." Maddox is moving toward the door. The pain in his voice slices through me. I grab his arm, barely getting it, but knowing if I don't hold on, he'll be gone.

"It's not your fault! You were seventeen when everything happened. Younger even when you found out. You were a kid! It was Dad's fault." And Mom's after.

"After I told you that, you still want to save me? First Mom, then Adrian, and now me? If you're smart, you'll leave us all the hell alone and save yourself."

With that he pulls his arm out of my hand and slams the door.

I need to go find my brother . . .

I need to check on my mom . . .

I need to tell Adrian . . .

All I wanted to do was save us, *one* of us . . . and I probably just lost us all.

Chapter Twenty-One

~Adrian~

I'm sitting in the car with Oscar and a few other people wishing they would shut the fuck up. Each word they speak or each time they laugh it's like someone shooting a BB gun at my head. It's not killing me yet, just an annoying fucking ache that's driving me insane. That eventually I think will kill me.

I need a distraction. To keep me busy and my mind off my ghost. After being in the hotel room, remembering how peaceful it felt, how much like a fucking *home*, they called and wanted to come over and I remembered that room and thought of my house and I wished like hell I could make it like that.

That my walls weren't tinged with weed smoke and beer stains weren't ground into my carpet. For the first time I wanted it to be my solace, and the idea of people fucking in rooms and dancing on the floors made me sick.

Now sitting in this car with them is doing the same thing.

I didn't want to go to her. I need to cut the ties because I feel her in my chest and it's not right to have anyone there. Not when I can't do right by them.

"Why the fuck are you so quiet up there, Westfall?" some guy in the backseat says.

I don't even know who he is. "Why the fuck do you care?"

Oscar laughs from the driver's seat. "He's always got that quiet thing going on. No one ever knows what he's thinking."

I don't know what it is about those words, but they make me want to hit something. They make me want to bleed because they're true and I've always wanted them to be true, but Christ is it lonely. *I want to be alone...*

And I do. I did. But I haven't felt it lately. Not when I'm with her.

Suddenly every fucking nerve ending in my body needs to be with her. To really *feel* something. I never, ever let myself feel. Yes, I loved my sister, but only her. And then Ashton. Jesus, I fucking loved him, but Delaney makes me *feel*.

And it's an ache building inside me, a need tearing me apart, wrecked by this tornado of what it felt like to be touched by her. Inside and out.

"I need you to bring me somewhere," I tell Oscar.

"What? Where?"

I tell him and he looks at me like he gets it, but he doesn't. He thinks I'm going to get laid, but what he doesn't understand is sitting in that diner, watching her work, writing in my book would be better than this shit.

I'm over it. So fucking over it.

I know it won't last and I know I can't really keep her, but while she's willing, I want to keep this going.

Oscar pulls into the parking lot and I get out. When I don't see her car I tell him, "Hold up for a minute."

"Hey." Jamie, the hostess, smiles at me when I walk inside.

"What's up?" I nod at her, but my eyes are scanning for Delaney, for her gray eyes and sexy smile.

"She's not here. She called in again. Between you and me, boss is pissed. Three days in a row. I wouldn't be surprised if she loses her job."

"It's not her fault," I tell Jamie before walking out. I check my phone and she hasn't called and then I wonder what the hell I'm doing, tripping out because I haven't heard from her and she didn't go to work. She's an adult. She can do what she wants and doesn't owe me a damn thing.

I get back in the car. "Take me home, man," I tell him.

He curses and says something about being a taxi.

"I'll remember that next time you want to party at my house."

He drives and they go back to listening to music and talking about shit that really doesn't matter, but the whole time I'm letting my ghost haunt me. Fuck if I didn't plan on trying to walk away, but then I went to the diner and she's not there. I can't stop trying to figure out why she wasn't there.

It was too much . . . I was too fucking much.
I shouldn't care.

But I do and I don't know what to think about that.

Which is why it's good she wasn't there. To cut the ties now . . .

When we pull up in front of my house, Oscar moves to turn off the car. The thought of sitting in my house with them all night makes me sick. Makes me want to get out of the car and just keep fucking going.

"Not tonight, man. I have some shit to deal with."

The light in his car is broken, so it doesn't come on when I open the door. Without giving him time to reply, I get out and close the door behind me. I don't know what time it is but know it has to be after ten when my ghost goes to work. It's dark out when I walk up to my house. The closer I get, I realize there's someone sitting by the door.

The second I see her, I know I'm in deep. Any thought of why I wanted to walk away from her seems crazy. The fact that I considered not going to the diner to see her tonight, fucking nuts.

She's the rapid pulse in my neck and the welcomed ache in my chest and I want to talk to her and make love to her until there's nothing else there but us.

I want to protect her. I don't want to fail her.

Bending down next to her, I touch her hair. She looks up at me, only shadows in the dark of my porch. "What's wrong, baby?" I ask her.

"How do you know something's wrong?" Her voice is soft . . . too soft.

"Because you're here sitting on my porch in the dark and the freezing cold instead of being at work. Because I can tell you've been crying." Red rings the gray of her eyes. They're swollen and sad.

Her chin starts to quiver, setting off a storm of worry raining down on me. Her tears rival my rain, so I pick her up and her arms go around my neck.

"I messed up, Adrian. I screwed everything up," she says into my chest as I push into the house.

"Shhh...it's okay. We'll figure it out." I can't even explain how incredible it feels to hold her up. To be strong enough for both of us or to be here when she needs me. To be the one she comes to because she trusts me even though I've done nothing in my life to deserve anyone's trust.

Without turning on the lights, I head straight to my room. Once we're there, I lay her on the bed, switching the button on the small lamp on the table. *The Count* is sitting there, but it doesn't matter and I don't hide it.

"Is it your brother? Was he pissed you left with me? I'll talk to him—"

"No." She shakes her head. "I mean, Maddox and I got into it, but it's not your fault. He told me about Mom getting out of the hospital, and at first he didn't know where she was...that brought up some other stuff. He left right after that and I haven't seen him."

"Shit." I stroke her hair as she lies on my pillow. All I can think is it's the first time she's been in my bed, but it feels like it should be hers too. Or that she has a place there. I like the fact that her head is on Ashton's shirt.

That's she's close to him even though she doesn't know anything about him. "So let's go find them." I know this has to be killing her. I'm surprised she's here now instead of out looking for them. She protects and takes care of the people she loves. It's what she does and I suddenly feel like shit for being gone all night and keeping her from what she needs to do.

She shakes her head and starts crying harder. Her hands move up, trying to wipe the tears way.

"It's okay. You don't have to be strong. Break if you need to. Let me help you the way you did with me."

My words seem to be the wrong thing to say because they upset her more. Finally the tears are slowing and she's trying to sit up.

"Do you want to go look for them? Need me to help?"

Another shake of her head. "Mom's at home, last we knew. Maddox told me later. Plus, I need to be here with you. I need to fix things with *you*. They...I'm where I need to be right now."

Her words don't make any sense, but I know it's big. Know it's part of whatever brings those ghosts to her eyes. But I can't figure out what I have to do with any of it. What she thinks she needs to fix with me...Ice crystalizes my spine, giving me this weird feeling where I don't know if I want to let her speak or kiss her until there's no room for words between us.

"Adrian." She reaches forward and puts a hand on my cheek. That ice is spreading. "I wish there was a way for you to see how wonderful you are. You're smart and you have a poet's heart and soul and I never expected to fall…" Her voice breaks off, but she pushes through. "To fall in love with you. No matter what, you need to know I truly did. That I *do* love you."

My muscles start to spasm. Tighten, cement encasing them. I pull back, letting her hand fall. Wanting to grab it again but unwilling to let myself. I have no clue what the hell's going on here, but it's wrong. I feel it. I need her to talk and hold the words back at the same time.

"What are you talking about, Delaney?"

She tries to grab for my hand, but I shake her off.

"No games. What's going on?"

Delaney takes a deep breath. Her hands shake, but nothing like the earthquake that goes off inside me at the sound of her next whispered words. "I know…I know about Ashton."

I push off the bed. My heart thunders. My hands fist.

"Find! me! Find me! I hiding!"

Ashton, Ashton, Ashton.

How does she know about him? What does she know?

"You really need to start talking fast." I'm pacing the room. Suffocating. The walls are getting closer and closer to me. Delaney. My ghost. She knows about Ash.

"I went to see your sister…to see Angel. Maddox told me not to, but I just…It was close to the anniversary and…"

Her words start fading out, but I man the fuck up and find a way to keep listening to her. She knows my sister.

"It was something I wanted to do for a long time. I just didn't know how to do it. Just to say I'm sorry. Just to try and, shit, I don't know what I wanted to do."

She's talking fast. Questions are rapid firing in my brain. Why would she need to apologize?

"I couldn't believe it when she forgave me. That we were okay and I thought... after that I thought things would somehow be better. And then Mom tried to kill herself again and it suddenly didn't feel like enough anymore." Fear darkens her voice. "I had to do something to help make it right. I don't know. I guess if I thought I earned your forgiveness, everything would start to be better."

Forgiveness, forgiveness, forgiveness.

"Forgiveness for what?" The words struggle to squeeze past my lips through my tensed jaw.

"Play! Play with me!"

"Just a minute, Ash. I'm making a phone call. We have to celebrate."

"Cel-bate!"

"When we first came here, I thought... I thought I could try to find you and we could talk and I would tell you everything that happened and how much I hate that my—"

My insides shatter at that. No, not even shatter, they turn to dust, blow away, lonely and lost. "When you first came here you thought you would talk to me? You fucking came here *looking* for me! Looking for me and you didn't say anything? Was this all some kind of fucking game to you?"

"What? No." She pushes off the bed and tries to step toward me. She's shaking all over, but I'm still so confused. How the hell does she know about Ash, and why is she acting like it has anything to do with her?

"Don't. Finish talking."

"I'm going to tell you everything now, Adrian. I promise. But I need to explain something first. I thought maybe we could help each other. Maybe... it would bring us some kind of closure to talk to each other, but then I wasn't sure if I should tell you and the longer I waited the harder it was because you turned into more than just the guy whose life was tied to mine in tragedy. You became... everything."

I stop. My feet won't move. I can't walk as I turn my head to look at her. I feel nothing right now. Empty. Hollow. "How are we tied together? What the fuck ties us together that has to do with Ashton?"

Her eyes are soft and pleading, but it doesn't matter anymore. I don't trust them.

"Don't fucking play games with me. Tell me."

Her eyes water again and there's a part of me that wants to go to her. That wants to try and fix it, but I can't. Not after this. Not when I know it's somehow about to get a whole lot worse.

"My dad was supposed to be working out of town... but he wasn't working. He was with his girlfriend."

Two occupants in the car. Caucasian male driver and a woman.

"Where were they? Tell me where they were." I feel like I'm cracking apart. One minute I can't move and the next I can't stay still. She hasn't said anything, but I don't need her to. I know. I fucking know, but I need to hear it, too, even though I don't *want* to hear it.

She nods. Tears stream down her reddened cheeks. Her ghosts have multiplied, reflecting in each and every one of those tears. "I'm sorry, Adrian. I'm so very sorry."

I fall back against the wall. It holds me up. The room blurs. "Say it. I need you to say it." I don't know where the words came from. How I got them the hell out.

"Adrian."

"Say it!" I yell.

"My dad . . . it was him. He was going too fast. He'd been drinking. His girlfriend distracted him."

I'm shaking. Rocking back and forth. "And?" *"What are we going to do tonight? I need out of the house." I lean against the door while I stand on the porch. I look over at Ash as he walks around the front yard.*

"They were messing around. They weren't paying attention around the curve. They drove into the yard. And . . ." A cry breaks free. I can hardly understand her as she speaks. "And he hit him. He hit Ashton."

A scream jerks out of me. I yell until my throat burns. My legs collapse from under me. My head drops back against the wall as I sit there, legs out in front of me. There's nothing left. I'm gone . . .

All this time, Delaney knew.

"Chase! Let's play chase!"

I look over at Ashton and he smiles. It hits me in the chest, the way he looks at me. It always does. Like I'm the king of the fucking world or something. "I gotta go," I say into the phone.

"Yay! Let's play, Daddy!"

Tires wail. A car flies toward the yard. Ash's smile. His big fucking smile and his big brown eyes that I see every time I look in the mirror, looking at me like I can do anything. So fucking happy just because I'm going to play with him. His whole future ahead of him. Happy. He's so fucking happy as I see the car come at him.

Happy because he thinks we're about to play. Happy because he loves me even though I don't deserve it. Happy because he's perfect, and I didn't protect that perfect. Because he doesn't know what's coming.

"Noooo!" I don't even make it to the porch stairs by the time the car hits him. His tiny body flies through the air, lands in front of me. Blood... so much blood.

"Nooo!" I fall. Pick his little body up. Broken... he's so broken. He's not smiling. He's gone. That quickly, he's gone.

I push to my feet as the driver stumbles around my yard. My fist connects with his face over and over. Wanting him to bleed like Ash. People come out of their houses. Rip us apart. Neighbors scream.

"Ash! Ashton! No. Fuck no! It's not right. He's okay." I get out of my neighbor's hold and run to

him. "Let's play. I'll find you. Wake up. I'll find you if
you wake up."

"Adrian?" Delaney's voice is quiet next to me. She's
kneeling beside me, her hand on my shoulder. "Adrian?
Are you okay?"

"She got pregnant when I turned sixteen. Just some
girl I met. Tina. Another fucked-up decision by me." I
hear my voice, but it's like I'm not controlling it. It feels
like someone else is speaking my truth.

"Who? What are you talking about?"

"I didn't know until she was about to have him. I
was sixteen fucking years old and she comes to me nine
months pregnant and says he's mine."

"Oh God . . ."

"He was always mine . . . I knew just by looking at
him. And then she fucking *gave him to me.*" My eyes are
still forward. I don't move. Don't look at her. I'm not even
sure I'm here. Nothing but words. Words I've never told
anyone. "Angel had to save me like she always did. When
we were kids, she took beatings for me. Then she took
me to live with her. And then she took care of my son.
Just like Tina gave him to me, I fucking *gave* custody of
my son to my sister. Who does that?"

"Adrian. No. I didn't know! But you were there. You
didn't leave him. You tried to do what was best for him."
She's sobbing so hard it's difficult to make out what she's
saying.

"I let him die." Fire laces my words. It all comes back

to me. Her coming here to find me. Knowing who I was. Knowing what happened. Lying. Making me love her. Knowing what I lost. "Your dad killed him."

I push away from her and to my feet. "I let my little boy die! The only fucking person in the world to ever look at me and not see all the things I did wrong. All he ever, ever wanted was love from me!"

My hands fly out as I shove the few things off my dresser, then knock it to the ground. Delaney jumps back.

"Don't. Adrian. Let me help you. I'm so sorry. Let's just—"

"Fucking help me!" I kick over the bedside table. The lamp crashes to the floor, but somehow the light doesn't go out.

I rip the blankets from the bed. Throw the pillow. And grab his shirt. His little shirt that belonged on his two-year-old body. I clutch it to my chest.

And cry. Fucking cry. Wail. Scream.

"I killed him. I let him die. I want him back. I just want him back."

Delaney tries to come toward me. "Get out," I say, and then I'm in a ball on the floor holding Ash's shirt.

"Adrian. I'm sorry, so, so sorry."

I can't look at her. I'm seeing his smile. Still crying. So many tears. I haven't cried since the day I let him die and now I can't stop it. Her dad did it. He was laughing and drunk and screwing around with some woman as he took a corner and killed my son. *My son. My boy, Ashton.*

"Adrian...you all right, man?" Colt's voice.

The light's gone out now. I have no idea how long I've been lying here. I lift my head. Colt is crouched next to me. The light from the hallway shines down on Cheyenne, who's waiting there.

"You okay? Delaney called us."

"Her dad killed my son," tumbles out.

Cheyenne gasps, then covers her mouth.

"Fuck," Colt curses. "Son?"

I see the pity in his eyes and I fucking hate it.

"Come on, man. Let's go. Come with us. We'll figure this out." He grabs my arm and tries to help me up, but I jerk away and sit up, still clutching Ash's shirt.

"I gotta get the fuck out of here." As soon as I'm on my feet, Colt is too.

"Then I'll go with you. We'll take off. However long you want. Chey doesn't care, right, baby?"

"No," she says. "Whatever you guys need, do it."

I've said before how real he is, how real they both are, but I didn't realize how much until this second. He would leave his girl to take off with me if I need it. She would let him. "You're a good guy, man. Real. Stay with your girl. You need each other. Don't worry about me." I just want out. I need to breathe and get away from everyone so I can try and lose myself again. It hurts too fucking much to get close.

I walk away from him. "Don't do this. Don't fucking

bail like this, Adrian," he says, but I know he won't try to stop me. Colt doesn't work that way.

"Please?" Cheyenne reaches for me as I hit the hallway. She grabs my arm, tears in her eyes. "I wouldn't have made it through Colt's accident without you."

"Now you have him, so you don't need me." I kiss her forehead and walk out. Walk away to get lost again, Ash's shirt still tight in my grip.

Chapter Twenty-Two

~Delaney~

His son, his son, his son. How could Ashton have been his son? But then...he'd been sixteen when Ashton was born. He'd given legal custody to Angel. According to the law, she was his. It's not like Mom talked about it. Or that Maddox or I had gone to court with Dad—or if they would have even mentioned something like that there.

His son. My father killed his son. Adrian saw his little boy die. And he has the guilt of thinking he should have been able to protect him like he thought he should his mom.

I jump out of my bed and hardly make it to the bathroom before I'm vomiting. Everything purges out of my stomach until it cramps. Until I'm gagging and dry-heaving and there's nothing left in me.

Flushing the toilet, I lie right there on the cold bathroom floor. Somehow I still have tears left and I let them fall. Couldn't stop them if I wanted to, and the whole time I see Adrian.

His son, his son, his son.

❦

It's been two days and I haven't left the house. Work calls, but I don't answer. I can hardly make myself leave the bed. My brother hasn't come home. I've called him a million times, but he doesn't pick up. He's never stayed gone like this before. Never just *left* me like he did. Maddox always answers when I call. He's always there when I need him.

But now he's not...

Just like Adrian...he's gone.

❦

"Cheyenne?" I ask when she answers the phone one day later. "Hi...it's Laney. Delaney." She called me Laney when we hung out at her apartment that night, but I don't know if she'll want to anymore.

"I know who it is." Her voice is clipped. "Well, I *thought* I knew who you were. I definitely didn't know you were tied to Adrian's past somehow. Definitely didn't know you'd wreck him like you did."

I know I deserve the anger in her voice. I deserve more than that and I'm glad she's doing it. Glad Adrian has her.

There's a part of me that wants to cry, but God, I'm so tired of crying, of folding, but I don't know if I can do anything else.

"Hurting Adrian is the last thing I wanted. I know it doesn't seem that way, but it's true. I love him."

She sighs on the other end of the phone. "What happened? I've...I've never seen him like that. It's like he was gone. His eyes were empty. Adrian doesn't say much, but you can always tell he has so much going on inside him."

I play those words over and over in my head. Let them echo and penetrate each layer, no matter how much it hurts. "I know..." I curl up in the corner of my bed, like it will somehow protect me from the truth. "I did that. I know it, and my intentions don't matter. I just wanted...I wanted to try and find a way we could all make it out of this without so much pain. But I took too long to tell him. How is he?"

"I don't know. He's gone. What do you expect? It's not like Adrian's going to tell us. We didn't even know... he really had a son?"

My mouth opens and I start to talk. I tell her about my family, my dad and what he did. About my mom. Even about seeing Angel. I admit that I came here to find him and that I basically lied...but then I tell her how much I love him. And how he makes me feel and how incredible he is. When I stop, she's crying.

"We never knew....How could he not have told Colt at least?"

Then we cry together. Cry for the broken man we both care about. For the demons he lets haunt him. And for the little boy we'll never meet, who would have grown up to be just as special as Adrian.

I sit outside my mom's apartment complex. It's been a week since Adrian left. Since I've seen my brother, who's texted me a couple times to let me know he's okay.

I didn't tell him I was coming here because I know he would come for me. And as much as I want him by my side before I step into that apartment, I have to do it on my own. It's not Maddox's job to protect me. It's not his job to follow me, regardless of whether he believes in what I'm doing or not.

It's time I do something by myself.

It's time I really face her, and talk to her, because just like it's not Maddox's job to protect me, it's not my job to take care of her. To be her punching bag. I accept her anger and hate of my father and let her make it about me.

If I could look Adrian in the eyes and tell him about my father, I can do this. If I can survive the pain in his eyes, I can do anything, which is why I don't even let my legs shake as I walk up the stairs. I don't stress enough to let my heart go rapid.

And I hope she's okay. God, I hope she is, but I can't make it my responsibility to make her that way. We all deal with our pain in a different way, I realize. Maddox is broken because he takes the blame for Dad. Thinks he should have done something. I want to *fix everything*. I take responsibility for Mom's anger at me. I tried to make it better for all for us when no one, *no one* can fix anything for anyone else.

And Adrian. My heart jumps at the thought of him. He puts more blame on himself than all of us combined. For Ashton. For leaving his sister and not stopping his father. He's lived with this misplaced responsibility since he was a kid. It's been eating him alive ever since.

I grab the railing and close my eyes, willing the tears

to stay back. I miss him. I miss him so much that I had to force myself to leave the bed, but I have to do this.

After taking a couple deep breaths, I finish the walk to Mom's apartment. I raise my hand and knock on the door.

"Who is it?" she calls, but I don't answer. Instead I try the handle, which is unlocked, so I open the door.

"It's Laney," I say as I close it behind me.

"I wondered how long it would take before you came to check on me." She's sitting on the small love seat. The TV's off and she's crocheting. It's so normal that you'd never know she tried to kill herself a month ago. That she's fine and then suddenly she's not. You'd never know she hates me.

"I'm here now." Walking over to the chair across from her, I sit down.

"I'm all medicated up." Mom picks up a pill bottle and shakes it. "A dose of happiness once a day. Everything's better now. You don't have to try and fix me."

Her words sting.

"Where's your brother?" she asks.

I look at the hooks in her lap, a memory floating to the surface. "Remember when I was little and you tried to teach me to crochet? I was horrible. I never could get it, but I still have the afghan we worked on together."

She sighs and smiles a little. "I remember. That was when everything was good. Before your father started chasing women and you started chasing him."

And there's the slap I've been waiting for. "I didn't

chase him. He's my *dad* and I was a child. What kind of person do you think I am?"

She opens her mouth to speak, but I keep going. "You know what? I don't want to know what kind of person you think I am. Instead, I'm going to tell you *who* I am. I'm the little girl who felt special because her father, who'd always been closer to her brother, started showing her attention. The girl who was scared and confused when her mother suddenly wanted nothing to do with her. Who didn't get why her brother stopped playing ball or why her dad started to be gone all the time. Who thought if she got good enough grades and did all her homework and didn't date and just tried to be *good* that everything would be okay."

"Delaney—"

"No. I'm not done yet. I was a scared little kid who suddenly found out her father killed a boy. Whose dad went to jail and her brother, her best friend, drifted further away from her. And you? That whole time you never held me or told me it would be okay or never cried with me. You let me find you bleeding to death. I held you and thought you were going to *die* and then you blamed me for saving you!"

I find myself standing over Mom, shouting while she stares at me, gaping. "And still! Still I thought if I was good enough or nice enough or tried to fix things, they would be okay. But they weren't. You hated me more and Maddy lost more of himself and I tried, tried so badly to hold it together for us all. I went to see the woman

I thought was the little boy's mom! I bet you didn't know that. And I apologized for what Daddy did, and she, this woman I didn't know, cried with me when you never did!"

"Delaney!" she screams, standing up and letting everything fall from her lap.

"No. You don't get to do this. You don't get to stop me from saying this. All I wanted was for us to be okay. To try and be some kind of family after everything that happened. To deserve to be okay again and then I hurt— no, I fucking broke—the only person to ever really make me feel normal. To make me smile and to see that I had secrets and imperfections inside me but to like me regardless of them. I loved him. And I think he could have loved me. *Me*." My closed fist comes down against my chest, over my heart. "*Me*. And I ruined it. I betrayed him and what he meant to me and I'll never, *ever* forgive myself for that."

She slaps me, whipping my head to the side. My hand shoots to my stinging face, holding my cheek as we stand there staring at each other.

"How dare you talk to me like that! He was my husband. *Mine*. My life was ruined because of him. I lost my home and we had debts to pay, debts he told me he'd been taking care of. You didn't have to deal with any of that, so don't make this out like you lost more than me."

Finally, *finally* my tears have dried. I can't shed any more. Not for her or my father. "It's not about who lost the most. It's about trying to make it through it together."

"Get out," she tells me.

I close my eyes. Take a deep breath. Consider saying more, but I can't. It's not in me any longer.

"Get out," she says again.

"I love you, Mom. Take care of yourself. I can't help you do it anymore."

For the second time in a week, I leave when someone tells me to, only this time, everything inside me doesn't wish I could go back.

Chapter Twenty-Three

~Adrian~

I drove until I was almost out of gas, pulled over to fill up, and started driving again before I stopped at some nothing town in South Carolina. I haven't left the tiny, dark hotel room since I got here.

Money's tight and soon I won't have any more, but I don't care. Don't fucking care about anything.

I haven't smoked weed since before I left. Not like I couldn't find it if I wanted to, but it was never about a need for me. It wasn't about addiction. It was about forgetting and now I can't let myself forget. It's there in my head all the time, raining down on me. Flooding me and I'm drowning in it.

I'm ready to let myself sink.

My eyes sting because I don't close them for long. Every time I do, I see Ash. See him smiling at me. See him fucking loving me as the car is coming at him. His little body on the ground and knowing that I failed him.

Except now it's not a guy behind the wheel. It's Laney

and it makes the loss multiply until I feel nothing but the pain.

Daddy, Daddy, Daddy. His voice is in my ears and his face in my head and sometimes it makes me smile because I think it's real. Think I hear his voice or see his face, but even in those dreams or thoughts where we're not standing in that yard, the car always comes and it always takes him from me.

I grab Ash's shirt and push it into my pocket, needing to get out of the room. Pulling the door open, everything freezes inside me at the same time I'm burning alive.

"Motherfucker." I lunge at Delaney's brother as he stands outside my hotel room. My forearm goes straight to his throat as I back him up against the brick wall and hold him there. "What the fuck are you doing here?"

"I've been following your ass through two states."

"How the hell—"

Maddox cuts me off. His voice is rough as it tries to squeeze out from under the pressure I'm putting on him. "I left, but I was worried about Laney so I asked around about where you lived. It wasn't hard to find out. When I got there, you were leaving. I started to follow you and for some reason, I just kept going. When I finally decided to talk to you, it was kind of hard to catch you since you're not man enough to leave your room."

Jerking my arm away from him, I let my fist fly right into his face. Blood rushes out of his nose and I flash to Ash, which gives him the delay he needs to run at me. He slams me into the wall on the other side of the walkway, before he hits me back. With everything I have in me, I push off the wall and we hit the other one, then the ground, both of us swinging at each other. Neither of us getting anywhere, besides trading blows.

"You're a bastard and you don't deserve my sister. She doesn't deserve to get hurt for trying to make things right," he says between punches.

"She fucking lied to me. She was playing games the whole fucking time!" I groan when his fist slams into my stomach.

"If you think that, then you definitely don't deserve her, because you don't know shit about her."

And damned if I don't know he's right. If I don't know those ghosts in her eyes were because she was just as haunted as me. If I don't remember how she touched me and how she looked at me and the gift she gave me... but still, all that time she knew.

I pull my fist back to hit him again and he doesn't try to stop me. He just lies there, and I want to hit him so bad. Want him to feel some of the pain I do, but instead I push off him and sit against the building. We're in an outside hallway. I'm surprised no one came out with the fighting, but don't care either.

"Knowing her or not doesn't matter. It's not enough." I'm breathing heavy. My face and body are killing me.

Maddox curses before grabbing a backpack from the ground. He pulls something out of it to wipe the blood from his face before he sits across from me. Neither of us speaks for a long time and then he reaches into his bag again, pulls out a fifth of whiskey, takes a pull, and hands me the bottle.

It takes me a second, but I grab it, take a drink, and then hand it back.

"She cares too much," he finally says. "She's sweet... despite all the shit we've been through. I know it doesn't make sense, but in her mind she thought it would help. She wanted to believe she had the power to make it better."

I grab the bottle from him and take another drink. I know he's right. Know she wanted to try and fix it. That was one of my favorite things about her, wasn't it? How sweet she was. How innocent. But then I see Ash again and the pain squeezes me so tight I can't breathe. "It's still not enough."

"Then you're a bigger pussy than I thought," Maddox says.

"And what are you running from? Don't sit there and pretend you're not fucking weak too. Don't pretend she's never shed tears over you."

"Touché." He takes a drink. "Did she tell you she found Mom the first time she tried to kill herself? That Mom knew Laney would be home soon. That she'd be the one to find her, yet she still slit her wrists in the unlocked bathroom right before Laney got home. That my little sister was scared to death her mom would die and she sat in her blood with her mom's head in her lap and when she was okay, that same mom yelled at her for saving her. That she was pissed she was alive and blamed Laney."

"Fuck." I drop my head backward. Look at the ceiling. I knew she had tried to kill herself, but I didn't know the details.

"I know you lost someone but you're not the only one. She watched her mom almost die, more than once. She still loves her and cares about her, even though she always gets shut down. She lost her dad that day too. She lives with those memories. Lives with the knowledge that her mom will never love her like she should, yet she's a whole hell of a lot better than we are. She doesn't fucking run. She's stronger than we could ever hope to be."

Maddox pushes to his feet, hands me the bottle, and grabs his bag. "And for some reason, she loves you. Hurting you will be something else she lives with. It will eat her up inside and it will kill another part of her, like Dad and Mom did. Like even I do, but she'll keep on living. I wish I was that brave."

I watch as her brother walks away, leaving a trail of blood behind him as he goes.

 ❦ 

"I hiding! Find me!"

Ash's voice echoes around me. I look at the couch, his favorite hiding spot, and he's not there.

"Hurry! Find me!"

"Where'd you go, little man? You found a new hiding spot. I can't find you." I'm smiling, proud of him for finding a real place to hide this time.

I search the living room, but he's not there. The kitchen. Our room. Angel's room. The bathroom.

"Daddy! Find me!"

My heart is starting to hammer and I'm beginning to sweat. "Where are you, Ash? I can't find you."

I look in the backyard and through the house again and I'm running now. Freaking out because I can hear him, but I can't see him. I have to find him. How can I lose my own son?

"Daddy. Hurry." His voice comes from the other side of the front door. Everything stops. I start to shake. I can't go out there. If I do, I'll find him and I don't want to see him out there.

"Ashton?" I creep toward the door.

"Here, silly," his voice says from outside. My hand shakes as I open the door and he's sitting there, in the yard, eating pancakes. Holding his favorite shirt on his lap.

"Ash. Get in the house. You have to come inside." I'm fucking crying now because I know if he stays out there he'll die. I can't let him die this time. He's my son. He thinks I can do anything. I have to save him.

"Can't." He shakes his head. "Can't go in."

"You have to." I try to grab him, but I can't. It's as though there's an invisible barrier around him keeping him from me. "Ash. Come on, little man. You have to come inside. Come to Daddy."

"Can't," he says again, and he's looking at me with syrup on his face, his big, happy smile.

I try to grab him again, but I can't get within a couple feet of him. I'm panicking now. "You have to try. You have to come in the house or you're going to die!"

At that, his little smile morphs into a frown. And I know he knows. Know he's known since before I came out here that he can't leave this yard. That he's going to die.

"Sorry, Daddy." He grabs the shirt. And then he gets up. He walks toward me and he hugs me. I don't know what happened to whatever kept me from him, but it's gone and he's in my arms hugging me as tight as his little body will let him.

But I know. I know I still can't save him. "I'm sorry. I love you. I wanted to be better for you. I wanted to protect you and do better for you than my dad did for me." Tears are running down my face and I'm holding him, squeezing him tighter than I probably should, but I can't let him go.

"I lub you too."

I look at him and smile.

"Smile!" He claps his hands. "Daddy's happy." And he has that huge grin again. The one that makes me feel fucking invincible. "Play!"

So I play with him. We play chase and hide-and-seek and he laughs and I laugh. We tumble to the ground and I wrestle with him and tickle him. And then he just stops. Stops and looks at me with those brown eyes that are just like mine and the dark hair that's just like mine and he climbs into my lap in the middle of the yard.

"Tell me a story," he says.

So I do. I tell him about a boy who was the coolest kid I've ever known. How his smile made everyone happy and how he makes me love pancakes and how there is no one in the world as important as he is. I tell him how much I love him and how much his auntie loves him and how happy he makes me.

For the first time in any story I've ever told him, Ash interrupts. "Happy?"

"Yeah, little man. Happy."

"I like it when Daddy's happy."

Fuck. I do too. I didn't have a lot of happy in my life, but those two years away from home, living with my sister and with him...I was happy. Knowing I was going to college and that I'd be someone he could look up to, it made me happy.

"I want to be happy."

"Then do!" He smiles. Like it's that easy. Like I should just know that and be able to do it.

"I love you," I tell him again.

"Lub you. I like Daddy's stories." And he wraps his arms around my neck. Squeezes me, and this time when he goes, there's no car. No blood. No little broken body. He's just...gone.

I jerk upward and jump out of the hotel bed. The empty bottle of whiskey is sitting there. It sounds crazy, but I swear to fucking God I feel him. I remember how it felt to have him in my lap and to have his arms around me and to play with him and the exact sound of his voice when he said *I love you.*

"I like Daddy's stories," he'd said, and suddenly my fingers itch to write. I pull open all the drawers until I find a pad of paper and a pen and I start filling it. Writing on the front and back of every page. Writing to Ash. Writing about Ash and life and poems and stories. Whatever comes to my head, I write it.

When the paper is gone, I run out of the room across the street to the corner store and buy every notebook I can find before I'm back in the dark room again writing to my son. About him.

I'm doing it for him. For me. For Angel. Hell, maybe even for my ghost. I only know I have to do it. That I can't stop. With each word I see his smile and I feel him again and I know I'm doing what he would want me to do.

I write that I'd always wanted to be a good dad to him, better than I had been, but I haven't been doing it. I tell him how young I was and I didn't think I was ready to be a father but that I want him to know how much I wanted him. Even if I wasn't ready to at first, he stole my heart and made me wish to be a better man. That if I had it to do over again, I would be different. Would be what he deserved. That all these pages and all these words and my hands that cramp and hurt are my apology. They're my way of being the person he deserved for me to be.

For the first time in four years, I stand in front of the house I shared with my sister. I look like shit. I haven't slept much. I'm screwed up from my fight with Maddox, though in the week I've been writing and then driving here, the bruises are fading.

But I'm here. Looking at a new fence around the yard. The new speed bumps on the street and at the signs that say to go slow. That say traffic fines are double and children are at play.

They have my son's name on them. They're for him.

And I know that's what my sister has been doing to be okay. That's how she's been fighting for Ashton. While I've been running and . . . fuck, *dying*, she's been living for him. It's not like she's ever had much. The house is tiny and it's in a shitty neighborhood, but she still did something. She fought, probably with all she had, for my son.

It took me long enough, but the notebooks full of our story are the start of my fight.

I let myself in the gate and walk up to the front door. That ache in my chest spreads being here. Looking at that spot I held him last and where I played with him in real life and in my dream. I almost can't breathe.

The steps still creak like they used to as I walk up them. There's a weight fighting to pull me back because I need to do this. I have to. For Ashton.

My fist comes down on the door in a knock. It's only a few seconds later I hear my sister say, "Hold on!"

Four years. I haven't talked to her in four years. I left her right after she lost her nephew. What was wrong with me?

Less than a minute later, she opens the door. Her hand shoots to her mouth, covering it, and it's shaking.

"Hey," I say. She doesn't look much different. I notice her hair's a little longer and that she has her ears pierced. She never had them done before.

"Hey...," she replies. And then she flies at me. Her arms wrap around my neck the way Ashton's did in my dream. I hold her back and she cries into my neck. "Adrian...you're home. I can't believe you're home."

"I'm sorry, Angel. So fucking sorry."

She laughs, still hugging me. "You still have a bad mouth."

"I can't help it."

And then we go inside and we sit on the couch. We talk about Ashton and our lives the past four years. We cry and I tell her everything. How I wanted to get lost. How I wanted to forget and live this façade that wasn't real. I even tell her about Delaney and the book in my hands. Then I picture the little boy with my eyes, and I think I'm finally giving him a reason to be proud of me.

Chapter Twenty-Four

~Delaney~

When I hear the front door opening, I run for the living room. I skid to a stop right as Maddox is closing the door. The urge to hug him bubbles inside me, but I shove it away. I missed him and I love him, but right now I'm pissed.

"What the hell, Maddy? I can't believe you've been gone for two weeks!"

He flinches and I feel a small amount of guilt, but then I think of all the times he's given me a hard time. How he punched Adrian when he spent the night and how often he's tried to run my life.

"You disappeared recently too," he says before he falls onto the couch. He looks tired. Bruises are fading on his face.

"For two days, not for two weeks! And not after having the kind of conversation we had before you left. Seriously!"

I'm still mad, but I sit next to him on the couch anyway. "I was worried about you."

"I texted."

"Doesn't matter."

"Shit." He shakes his head, but then looks at me.
"Sorry, little sister. I had something to take care of. It was
important and then...I don't fucking know. I just wasn't
ready to come back yet."

It's impossible to stay mad at him. I know I should,
but he's my brother and out of anyone in my life, I know
I will always be able to depend on him. And I know he's
hurting. Know he's been hurting for years. Reaching over,
I hug him. "I'm not going to say it's okay because it's not.
I'm glad you're home, though...and don't do that again.
Things have to change with us, Maddox."

I take in his dark, messy hair. The set of his jaw.
It looks like he hasn't shaved for a couple days, dark
stubble on his face. He looks like my dad. Only with
Maddox, there's a kindness in his eyes I don't remember
with Dad.

Maddox gives me a small nod.

"You can't keep taking responsibility for me. For Mom
or Dad or anyone."

"Neither can you," he answers back in that rough
voice of his.

"I know. I saw Mom last week. We got into it and
I told her how I felt. She kicked me out and I said I
wouldn't be back. I haven't and I won't." It still hurts to
remember, and the urge to call her, to check in on her is
there, but it's hard giving out love to people who shove it

back in your face. That's not what love's supposed to be about. No, it's not perfect and people get hurt, but it's a give and take. And it should be comfort, not pain.

Maddox takes a deep breath and I know he's trying to calm himself. That he wants to say something about Mom but is trying not to.

"You're growing up," he says, which is ridiculous.

"I'm eighteen. I've been grown up for a while."

"It's different now. Good for you." He tries to stand, but I grab his hand and keep him next to me.

"It's time for you to do the same. None of it's our fault, Maddy."

He looks at me and gives me a small smile, leans forward, and kisses my head. "What I should know in here"—he touches his head—"I can't always feel in here," then his chest.

And I know that's the end of our conversation. Maybe I should push, but I don't. I might not have tried to make Adrian talk, but I pushed my way into his life. It's hard to regret it because regret would mean not knowing him, not loving him, but I regret the pain I caused. I'm trying to learn from that.

"Have you talked to him?" my brother asks.

"No...I still haven't seen him. I don't know where he is." It hurts so badly and every part of me misses him, but I get it too. I lied. Things are so much worse because that little boy was his son.

"Pussy," Maddox mumbles, shaking his head.

"Hey! That's not fair. You don't know everything... Ashton was his son..."

I've never seen my brother's face pale the way it does. Regret flashes across his features, colors his eyes. Regret for not giving Adrian a chance? For hitting him that day? I don't know.

"I miss him." I curl up next to my brother and lay my head on his shoulder. He puts an arm around me and holds me. "I really do love him."

He gives me a small squeeze, offering me his support. "I'm sorry, Laney. Sorry about it all. And...I'm sorry for him too."

We sit there, holding each other. Supporting each other, and I know we're going to be okay.

I walk up to my apartment after begging for my job back and stop dead in my tracks. My heart slams around inside my rib cage as I run to the door as though it might disappear.

Bending over, I pick up the clear plastic container and look at the perfect caramel apple inside, and smile. My eyes dart around as though Adrian is standing there and I managed to miss him. Of course he's not, but he was here and it makes me feel like I could fly.

Because he's okay. That's all I need is for him to be okay.

"Maddox!" I push the front door open. "Did you see him?"

"See who?" He's sitting on the balcony smoking a cigarette.

"Adrian. There was a caramel apple by the door."

"And it was automatically him?" He grins. I can tell he's trying not to laugh.

"Yeah...it was him. How long have you been outside? Did you hear him or anything else out front?"

"Christ, Laney. I just texted you a few minutes ago to see how close to home you were. Don't you think I would have told you if I heard from your boyfriend?"

I roll my eyes at him, knowing he's right, but it doesn't matter. All that does is let me know Adrian's okay.

I look at the container again and that's when I see it. The small piece of paper taped to the bottom. Running to my room, I slam the door behind me. My hands shake as I pull the note off.

My little ghost,
Still haunts my nights,
Walking with stars,
I reach out my hand,
Hold the stars
And hope, one day,
They'll be you.
I'm not ready. I'm trying.

Adrian

Clutching the note to my chest, I cry.

"I'm glad you stayed," Cheyenne tells me as we walk up to the apartment complex. I met her at the college. We had coffee before coming back home.

"I thought about leaving, but I like it here. It's not like Maddox and I really have anything at home. He's been training with this tattoo artist he met. He likes it. I'm hoping it will be something that sticks. I talked to him about going to school, but I don't know if he will. I think it's too hard for him unless he can play ball."

She nods. We've been hanging out quite a bit. I'm thankful she forgave me and thankful to have her for a friend.

"Have you heard from Adrian?" she asks, even though I know she already knows the answer. It's been two weeks since he left the apple and I haven't heard a word from him since. Which is okay. He has a lot to work through and I want him to do it. I'd like nothing more than for us to find our way back to each other. To be able to hold him again, but what's more important is that he finds a way to be okay. And that I make sure I'm okay on my own too.

"No. What about you?"

"Colt's been talking to him. I have a little. It's funny because they talk more now than they did before. I think...I think because they both lost someone they love. Maybe it helps somehow. Anyway, we haven't seen him. He's staying with his sister."

My cheeks hurt my smile is so big. Moisture pools in my eyes. "Good...that's good. I'm glad they're close again. They deserve that."

I open the door and Cheyenne walks into the building.

"I need to go check my mail," Cheyenne says, so I go with her to pick up mine. There's a big manila envelope inside my box and somehow, I know it's from Adrian. I pull the package out, being careful not to rip it, and see his name on the front.

Adrian Westfall.

"It's from him. I have to go," I tell her before I'm taking the stairs two at a time to get to my apartment. Maddox isn't home, but I still go to my room, needing privacy before I open it.

When I do, I see it's a huge stack of paper. Hundreds and hundreds of pages.

FOR ASHTON

My hands shake and my heart stutters and I'm both scared and excited to read it. Honored he would share it with me. Curling up on the bed, I start to read. It's more than Adrian's words on the paper; it's his heart. As though he spilled it onto the pages. It's raw and real and heartbreaking...and beautiful.

It takes me five hours to read it, but I don't stop until I've read every word. Until I know his heart inside and out.

Tears rack my body as I get to the end. Ugly crying, tears that somehow cleanse me too. Did they do the same for him? I wonder.

I hope so. I really, really do.

⁂

It's the end of April. Four months since I met Adrian and two months since I lost him. We're crazy busy at work when Jamie comes up to me and grabs my hand.

"He's here!"

"Who?" I start to ask, but that's when I see Adrian standing by the hostess station.

My heart falls to my feet. He's beautiful. Those dark, intense eyes entrancing me. The first thing I think of is I'm glad he hasn't lost that intensity. Glad it's still a part of him.

"Let me help him," I tell Jamie. My legs are so weak I'm not sure they'll hold me, but they do.

"Hi," I say, trying to fight back a smile. To keep myself from reaching for him and hugging him and telling him I love him.

"Hey." When I don't move or say anything, he quirks a half grin. "Got any tables?"

"Oh my God. Sorry. Yeah." I feel so flustered.

I walk over and seat him in his booth. The one he always sat in when he'd come. I try to hand him a menu, but he shakes his head. "Pancakes," he says, and I smile at him.

I'm busy for the next hour and a half, but he doesn't leave. I don't get to talk to him except for doing my job, but he sits at the table, eats his food, and then waits...

Too many emotions to name war inside me: love and fear leading the attack. I manage to sneak into the back and grab what I bought him the other day.

When I finally have a spare minute, I walk back over to check on him. I don't know what to say or how to act. Why he's here or what he wants.

"Do you need anything else?" I ask.

Adrian shakes his head. "I just really like the pancakes here." For the first time since I sat him, we make eye contact. Warmth spreads through me by looking at him. And then he says, "My son...he used to love pancakes. I used to make them for him. Eating them reminds me of him."

God, I want to touch him so bad it hurts. My hand aches to reach for him, but I don't. I have to let him do this on his own. "I wish I could have met him."

He gives me a small nod. "He would have liked you."

"I...I got you something." I reach into my apron and pull out the book. Adrian takes it, looks at it and then at me.

"*The Count of Monte Cristo.*"

"It's silly. I know you have one—or had. I don't know if you still do, but—"

Then he stands. I want to beg him to stay, but then he reaches out and cups my cheek. "Your ghosts are still there." He rubs a thumb under my eye.

"They're a part of me."

He nods. "Mine are too."

And then he turns from me and he's gone.

It's only three days later when the knock comes on my door. I take my time to get there, because I'm not expecting anyone. My breath catches in my throat as I pull the door open to see Adrian standing there. He's wearing jeans, kind of baggy, and a black shirt that hugs his muscles.

He stands outside and I'm inside and neither of us

moves or speaks and everything inside me is pulling me toward him. That thread between us is tightening and tightening to bring him close to me.

"It's good to see you," I finally say.

"It's good to see you too."

I hold the door open and Adrian comes in. He sits on the couch. Not sure what to do, I sit on the arm of a chair, but then he looks at me and says, "I don't bite," and they're the most incredible words I've ever heard.

I move next to him and smell him and feel the heat coming from him and it reinforces how much I love him.

"The book...Adrian, it was incredible."

He looks at me. "I've never felt anything like it. I had this dream...fuck, it felt so real and Ash was there. I got to see him again and we played and talked and then he asked me to tell him a story. He used to like that. I'd make up stories for him and he'd laugh and ask me to repeat it over and over."

It does something to my heart, hearing him talk about Ashton, about his son like this. He never would have been able to do it before.

"That sounds wonderful," I tell him.

"It was. Even in my dream it was. I told him a story and then"—he closes his eyes and takes a deep breath—"and then he died in my arms. It was like he just fucking went to sleep and I was half drunk, in a shitty hotel and I felt...nothing, so I wrote. With each word, I knew it was what I was supposed to do. I knew it was what Ash would want."

Tears are falling down my face now, a mixture of happiness and sadness.

"I've been with Angel ever since. We're getting to know each other again and we talk about Ash every day and it's so incredible to remember him, to think of him without the guilt trying to take away the good memories. In a way I'll never forgive myself for that day, but...I'm dishonoring his memory by trying to forget."

I cover my mouth with my hand and try to hold back the tears. I don't want to interrupt him. I want to tell him how proud I am of him.

"It's not easy...There are still days I take off just to get away or times I'm still so fucking *angry*, but I'm trying. I'm doing better."

The words are impossible to hold back anymore. "You should be so proud of yourself, Adrian. That's awesome. You're making him proud."

He nods his head. "Yeah...I think I am."

"I will never forgive myself for not being honest with you in the beginning. It was wrong of me and I know that." He's not looking at me, but I need him to. I do the thing he's done so many times to me, hooking my finger under his chin and turning his face. "I need you to know, what I felt, the things I said, I didn't fake any of that. All of it was real and it still is. I love you and I'm so proud of you."

He touches my face again like he did in the diner. "So serious, Little Ghost." He's all intensity and sincerity and the words flood through me.

"I am. I'm not good with words like you are, but I can tell you I love you. You say I haunt you, but it's you who haunts me. You made me happy for the first time in four years. You inspire me and your words are a part of me and you make me feel strong. I never realized it, but I never felt strong before. I let Maddox run my life and tried to save people who didn't want to be saved. I know I can't do that anymore. It's not up to me, and you taught me that."

"I did all that?" One of his eyebrows rises.

"Stop." I'm laughing and crying at the same time.

"Don't cry, Little Ghost."

His words make me cry harder.

"Shhh." And then he's wiping my tears. I'm nuzzling his hand. "I missed you. I wanted to hate you, but I couldn't. I know it wasn't your fault, but it's hard when it's all tied together like that, but then...I read *The Count* again after you gave it to me. I remember reading it and always looking up to Edmond. Even when I was a kid because he beat the odds. He beat his shitty life and prison and everything else. But I realized he didn't have what was important. Edmond ended up alone and I already lost Ash...I don't want to lose you too."

I swear my heart leaps out of my chest. I feel weak and like I'm invincible at the same time. "Adrian—"

"Shhh," he says again. "I have to get this out. I can't promise I'll be perfect. Hell, I know I won't be and I have a whole lot of shit I'm still dealing with, but...I can't get you out of me. Your smile's in my head and your voice in my ear."

I'm crying and smiling and so full of Adrian I'm bursting at the seams.

"You helped me stop bleeding. You made my heart beat when I thought it was gone. All those things you said I do for you? They're nothing compared to what you do for me."

"Adrian—"

"Stop interrupting me." He smiles and I smile. I don't think I'll ever stop doing it again. "You reminded me what it feels like to love. You made me fall in love and, fuck, I don't want to lose that. I don't want to lose you."

Unable to stop myself anymore, I lunge at him. He catches me as he falls against the back of the couch. "Kiss me."

So I do. I kiss him and his taste is a burst of familiarity. His tongue teases my lips and then finds its way inside. He's kissing me and then standing, my legs wrapped around his waist. Adrian walks to my room and I kick the door closed behind me and then we're falling to my bed, our mouths still fused together.

"Let me make love to you, Little Ghost."

"Yes." I arch toward him and he kisses me again. And then all our clothes are gone and he's putting a condom on and this time when we come together, we've stepped out from behind our façades. The masks are gone and we're naked together for the first time.

"I love you," he says.

I look at him. This amazing man who's been through so much. "I love you too."

Epilogue

~Adrian~

My hands are fucking shaking so bad I can hardly stand it.

"You're doing great," Delaney tells me as I park the car.

"I'm losing it," I tell her. "But I'm here. I'm doing it."

She leans over and kisses me. Christ, I still can't believe I'm here. I can't believe I'm with this incredible girl and that I'm about to get out and go see my son for the first time in four years. God, I need it, though. Need to talk to him.

We get out of the car and make our way through the cemetery and over to Ash's tiny grave. I close my eyes, not wanting to see it, but fuck if I don't need to for him. I need to do this for my son and I will, so I open them up and kneel on the ground.

I read his name, Ashton Adrian Westfall.

Loving son and nephew.

"I think I overdid it on the *A*s." I try to laugh, but it doesn't really work.

"It's a perfect name," Delaney replies.

"Yeah...you're right. I think it is."

I study his grave some more. "Hey, Ash. It's...it's me, Daddy."

Laney sniffs and I know she's crying next to me. My eyes are wet, too, one of the tears escaping down my face.

"I miss you. I miss you so much, little man." I reach out and trace the letters of his name. "And I'm sorry. So sorry I didn't do better for you, but it was never because I didn't love you. I'm going to start coming to see you too."

It's more than a tear now. It's like a race to see how many can make it down.

"I won't let you be lonely anymore, okay? We'll come all the time and I'll tell you stories. I'll write a new one for you every time."

My ghost's hand is on my shoulder. She doesn't interrupt, just lets me talk. I tell my son that at twenty-two I'm going to school next year. That I'm going to work on telling more stories and maybe one day other people will read them. I tell him I was wrong when I told him about the Count. That he isn't someone to look up to. That I probably never even should have talked to him about it in the first place.

And I tell him everything I do from now on will be for him. How his auntie fights for him and how I want to do the same.

We're out there for over an hour talking to Ash. To my son.

Each word makes me feel stronger. Better. I know I have a long way to go, but I'll keep fucking going because he never had the chance. I'll go for him.

Finally, I stand up. Delaney's right behind me. "We have to go, little man. I'll be back soon. I love you."

She latches her hand with mine and we walk to the car. We drive the few hours back home, to the apartment she used to share with her brother that I now share with her.

Colt's outside, messing with Chey's car when we get there.

"Fucking piece of shit," he says.

I laugh as I walk over to him. "Don't blame the car because you don't know what you're doing."

"Then shut up and help me." He tosses me a wrench, which I catch.

"I'm going to go upstairs. I'll see you later," Delaney says. She leans forward to my ear and whispers, "You did great today. Don't forget you have to go see Lettie in a couple hours." She doesn't pay me for helping her anymore and she still gives me shit the whole time I'm there, but she also cried when I came back. We've talked about Ash and I found out she lost a daughter.

I nod and kiss my girl before she goes upstairs and then I lean over to look at the engine.

"You went to see Ash?" Colt asks.

"Yeah."

"Yeah."

We're quiet for a minute, screwing around under the hood of Cheyenne's car and then he says, "It gets easier. Going, I mean. It fucking killed me the first time I saw Mom."

"Yeah?" I ask him.

"Yeah," he replies again.

We keep working on the car. He talks about his mom and I talk about Ash. I think about Delaney upstairs. The woman I fucking love so much it's crazy. How she's probably sitting there talking to Colt's girl, whose like a sister to me. And my best friend standing next to me. My sister back home who I talk to every day.

I realize I'm lucky. There's an ache inside me that will never go away. I'll always keep his shirt and always write for him. He'll always be in my heart and in my head, but I also know I'll be just fine, with these people in my life, and for him, I'll be okay.

THE END

Nyrae Dawn's powerful
series continues...

See the next page for a preview of

Masquerade.

CHAPTER ONE

~ Bee ~

It's almost perfect. The only thing missing as I stand in the middle of Masquerade is the constant buzz of a tattoo gun. After the past few years, it's my form of comfort. Like a lullaby that sings me to sleep, massaging the tension out of my muscles. But at the same time, it shoots adrenaline into my veins, bringing me happiness—something that's mine and will always belong to me.

Yes, I need to hurry up and open the doors to my tattoo parlor before I go crazy for that lullaby.

I play the words again in my head: *my tattoo parlor.* They're scary as hell and exhilarating at the same time. I'm not sure many twenty-one-year-olds can say they've already worked in five shops, but none of those places belonged to me. This one will stick. I'll stick. I have to, for a lot of reasons. One of them being that despite the fact that it's my name on all the paperwork for Masquerade, my parents footed the bill.

It doesn't matter that I'm paying them back, only that

they did it. After everything I've put them through—after the way that I struggle so much to love them the way they do me—they did it.

Walking over, I straighten one of the frames filled with tattoos I've done. To the right of it is the one and only workstation here. It's exactly what I need, small without too many places to make a mess. Growing up, my parents—shit...I shake my head, Melody and Rex—had both been artists. They would get lost in their zone and the house would be a mess with supplies, but it didn't matter because they were happy.

Then I went back home and everything was different. They were happy just like Melody and Rex, but not in the same way. They didn't get so deep in their art that they'd forget dinner and then order a pizza, which we would all laugh over later.

No, my real parents were perfect. *Are* perfect, and even after eight years, it's still hard for me to be the person they need me to be instead of the one I was.

But I try. For them, I try.

"Christ," I mumble, not sure why I'm feeling so introspective today. I'm a single girl in a new town. What I need to do it get out and have some fun.

After locking up Masquerade, I climb into my Honda Insight and drive to my house. It doesn't take me much time to get ready. I keep my blond hair down. It's long, hanging past the middle of my back. I put on a black spaghetti-strap tank top with silver studs on it. It shows the couple tattoos I have, the two on each of my shoulders and the other above my breast. Slipping on a pair of black heels, I walk to the bathroom and change out the small diamond stud in my nose and then I'm out the door.

It's not like Brenton is very big, so it doesn't take me much time to find a bar that looks like it could be a good time. It's about 10:00 p.m., so a little early, but all I want to do is have a drink and relax anyway. More than that and I'd have to take a cab.

Music pulses through the speakers when I walk in, and I suddenly feel a tinge of guilt for being here pulling at me. I guess my real dad got lost in the bottle for a while after I was kidnapped. I hate using that word because it makes it sound like they were horrible to me. Anyway, he's okay now. They're *those* kinds of people. They make it through everything together, but I wonder if they'd be disappointed I'm here.

No, I tell myself. *There's nothing wrong with having a beer once in a while.*

It takes a couple minutes to make my way through the crowd and up to the bar. It smells like alcohol and too many bodies, but I try to ignore it. A seat opens up and I take it. Men sit on either side of me, but none of them seem to be paying any attention, which is good. I'm not in the mood to be hit on tonight.

The bartender comes over a few minutes later. He's about my age, hot, but a little pretty for my type. He has blond hair and green eyes that run the length of me, telling me it's going to be him who tries to flirt.

"Hmm, let me guess. Cosmo?" he asks. I shake my head. "Lemon Drop? Mojito?" He keeps tossing drink names at me, but I keep shaking my head.

"You're going to have to give me a clue here. I'm drowning and I'm usually pretty damn good at knowing what a girl wants." He winks at me and I can't help but roll my eyes.

"The only thing you have that I want right now is a Corona with lime."

"Ah, a beer girl. I was way off."

He grabs a bottle, twists the top off, and then hands it to me.

"You're new. I would have noticed you before," he says.

I nod. Again, he's good-looking. Maybe on another night I might be interested, or if I was a different kind of girl. The good kind, but I'm not and I swear he looks like he belongs in a college frat, so I just lean back and take a drink of my beer.

"I'm Trevor," the bartender says.

"Bee," I reply. It's amazing how the name just automatically rolls off my tongue. It's almost like it gave me my new identity at eighteen years old. It was my third one, but this one I actually picked. It's the only one that feels like me. I don't remember what it was like to be the girl I'd been before I was taken, and once I went back home, I wasn't allowed to be the person I thought I was.

"Bee? As in buzz, buzz?" he asks, jerking me out of my thoughts. "Did I tell you how much I like honey?"

Yeah, because I haven't heard that one before. "No, as in the letter *B*. It's short for *bitch*. Want me to demonstrate how accurate the name is?" I finish my tirade with the tiniest of wicked grins.

At that, Trevor smiles and holds up his hands. "I was kidding. Kind of. But seriously, that was hot. I think I'm in love with you."

Before I have the chance to reply, someone yells, "Trev! Stop flirting and get your ass down here. There's work to do."

That's my cue to leave. I toss a five down and he grabs it before I walk away. All I want is a nice, empty corner to hang out in and finish my drink. Or, if I'm being honest, I'm not opposed to meeting someone. That someone just isn't him.

When I spot a small table in the back, I head right for it. I'm surprised no one grabbed it as I sit down and lift the bottle to my lips, downing the whole thing.

I set the bottle down, and for some reason seeing the lime inside transports me back in time. Rex used to make all kinds of bottle art. He'd tell me sometimes the simplest things could be the most beautiful. We'd fill different colored bottles with different shades of objects until we found one that we thought was the most unique, and then he would let me keep it. I put it on the shelf above my bed with all my other favorite things. The things I couldn't take with me when they found me.

My hand squeezes around the bottle and I take a couple deep breaths. What's wrong with me? Why am thinking about them so much tonight? I'm doing better. I have Masquerade. I need to remember things happened the way they were supposed to and go on with my life.

"Decided not to flirt with Trevor anymore?" a male voice says. I look over to see a guy leaning against the wall with his arms crossed in the dark. There are stairs that go up right next to him, and it's almost like he's hiding.

"Is there a problem if I was flirting with him?" I reply.

He has a tribal tattoo around his forearm. It's pretty nice work but I could have done it better.

"Not my business. I don't know why I even said anything." He turns his head and scans the crowd. My first thought is, now this is the kind of guy I'd be in to. He has a trail of dark stubble on his face, a tic in his tight jaw, and black hair. It has a few curls in it. Just enough to make you want to run your fingers through it to see how it feels.

I would put money on him riding a bike. I bet he has more tats than the one I can see. He's gorgeous and trouble and from the scowl on his face, he's probably angry at the world just as much as I'm confused by it.

Too bad he's an asshole.

"You're right. It's not your business, but since that didn't stop you from bringing it up, I'll keep it going for you. Let me guess, I'd probably be a slut or a tease if I was flirting with him. Let's for a minute forget the fact that he not only came on to me, but also that men do that kind of thing all the time. It's okay for them to hook up with someone in a bar but not for a girl to want to, right?"

I dealt with stuff like that all the time when I was in school and I hated it. I wasn't like all the other people who joined activities and smiled in everyone's face, pretending to be perfect but then going wild behind their parents' and teachers' backs. I was who I was then and I am who I am now. At home I didn't fit in, which bothered me, but I didn't care if I fit in anywhere else.

The guy doesn't reply to me but continues to look out into the sea of people.

What's his deal?

I pick up my bottle before remembering it's empty and setting it down again. I keep glancing at the guy, but he's not paying any attention to me. It frustrates me, and the fact that I'm letting it bother me makes me even more annoyed.

Finally, he says, "I don't care who you fuck, or who anyone else does for that matter. Doesn't matter if you're a woman or a man."

There's something in the raspy seriousness of his voice that makes me believe him. It makes me wonder what he does care about, if anything, because by looking at him, I'd say it isn't much.

That makes two of us.

I'm not really sure what makes me do it, but I push to my feet, walk over, and lean against the wall next to him. "Your piece is pretty nice. Could be cleaned up a bit." I point to his tat.

He huffs. "And you're an expert, right?" He makes it sound like it's a ridiculous thought.

I smirk because, of course, that's the first thing people

think. I don't know why. It's not like it's so rare to be a female tattoo artist. We keep standing there. People are dancing all around, drinking and talking. He's wearing an earpiece, so it's pretty obvious he's security.

After a few minutes, he tosses a glance my way. "You've got some nice work too." The words seem to physically pain him to say.

"Thanks."

Most of my work was done by the Professor. He's the old guy who taught me how to tat. I don't really talk about the Professor because he's important to me and I like to keep things to myself. Most people wouldn't get it anyway.

"What's your name?" he asks without looking at me.

"Bee. Yours?"

"Maddox." I recognize what he's doing. It's so much easier to talk to people when you don't have to look at them. Looking brings you closer and sometimes it's too hard to get close. I was like that when I first came home. I'm still like that sometimes.

Standing there, I realize I kind of get this guy. I think he might get me, too, and I don't remember the last time I thought something like that. It's not that I need him or anyone else to understand me, but in this moment, it feels kind of good.

"Maddox!" a guy yells from a few feet away. "You're off early tonight. Go ahead and clock out."

Maddox turns to look at me. My skin sizzles under his stare. His eyes are gray and hot on me. Man, this guy is sexy, and for a second, I consider what it would be like to lose myself in him for a night.

"You here with anyone?" His voice is low.

A good girl would probably tell him she wasn't interested. The kind of girl I maybe should be. The kind my sister is or my mom is, but I don't think it's such a bad thing to let myself have a little fun. If I'm smart...safe, what's the problem?

"No."

I push off the wall so I'm standing right in front of him when he speaks again.

"Do you want to leave with me?"

"We go to a hotel, not a house. And it's just one night."

"Isn't that supposed to be my line?" He smirks. It's the first time I've seen him do anything except scowl.

"I'm all about equal opportunity, remember?"

"Are you drunk?"

"No, just had the one beer."

Maddox gives me a simple nod, then tells me the name of a hotel and says he'll meet me there.

Just to be sure, I walk over to a different bouncer than the first one who talked to him and confirm Maddox works here. You never know what kind of scams guys can come up with and I need to confirm he's legit.

A few minutes later I'm in my car and driving to the hotel. Just one night. It's been crazy and stressful getting everything ready for Masquerade, and I really just want to let go and have a little fun, with someone who's safe because I'll never have to see him again.

About the Author

From a very young age, Nyrae Dawn dreamed of growing up and writing stories. It always felt as if publication were out of her grasp—one of those things that could never happen, so she put her dream on hold.

Nyrae lived a fairy tale of her own when she fell in love and married one of her best friends from high school. In 2004, Nyrae, her husband, and their new baby girl made a move from Oregon to Southern California and that's when everything changed. As a stay-at-home mom for the first time, her passion for writing flared to life again.

She hasn't stopped writing ever since.

Nyrae has a love of character-driven stories and emotional journeys. She feels honored to be able to explore those things on a daily basis and get to call it work.

With two incredible daughters, an awesome husband, and her days spent writing what she loves, Nyrae considers herself the luckiest girl in the world. She still resides in sunny Southern California, where she loves spending time with her family and sneaking away to the bookstore with her laptop.